How I Spent My Summer Vacation

How I Spent My Summer Vacation

How I Spent My Summer Vacation

AN AMANDA PEPPER MYSTERY

Gillian Roberts

BALLANTINE BOOKS · New York

ISBN 0-345-38595-0

Manufactured in the United States of America

For Joy Hockman—
cherished friend,
location scout,
and
co-conspirator

How I Spent My Summer Vacation

How I Spent My Summer Vacation

One

THE school year is months shorter than the calendar's, which makes people think a teacher's job is easy, cushy. Actually, summer vacation is a public safety requirement. Rising temperatures bring the unstable mix of teachers and pupils to a near-lethal boil and necessitate a cool-down period. Otherwise, there'd be no survivors with whom to start future endurance experiments.

Two days into my vacation, I was still on the critical list—battle-scarred and shell-shocked—and afraid the condition might be chronic.

I felt so miserable I knew I needed to do a lot of thinking

3

about my life—lives, professional and personal—and what I was doing wrong with them. The trouble was, whenever I so much as thought about the need to think, my brain developed hives and I was filled with a sense of futility and dread.

"You look horrible," my friend Sasha said. We were taking what I had hoped would be a restorative, old-fashioned Sunday stroll through Ye Olde Colonial Philadelphia. "Why don't you get a real job, with real people?" she asked. "What is the point of growing up if you then revisit adolescence over and over for the rest of your life? Get a job with adults!" Sasha waved her arms for emphasis.

I tried to imagine a worklife with peers. People who saw me as an equal, not as an obstacle to be outwitted. People who weren't always testing me or preparing defenses, excuses, or requests. Partners. Team players.

Power lunches. Networking. Ladder-climbing.

Give me a break.

We reached Head House Square, former meat and produce market, current star of camera-ready Colorful Colonial Philadelphia. A table under a cappuccino sign was available. This wasn't a stroke of luck, but indication that summer weather—even real spring weather—had not yet staggered into Philadelphia. Still, we sat down.

It was chilly for early June, and lounging outside was purely symbolic, but I was on my summer vacation and I was going to behave as such. I shivered, ordered, and looked around. The wide cobbled street in front of us was bisected by the former marketplace. Where Colonial chickens and pigs were once hawked there now were objets d'craft: silver bangles, nouveau-native earrings, tooled leather backpacks, and recidivist tie-dyed garments. Whole cycles of fashions and fads had died and been resuscitated while I tried in vain to convince teenagers to punctuate.

I wondered if someday our current markets—say, 7-Elevens—would be converted into craft-laden tourist destinations, with yet more tie-dyed shirts filling shelves now holding Ding Dongs.

"I'll be fine," I told Sasha, who was urging vocational counseling. "I need to decompress. I guess I just want to be *alone*. Present company and present moment excluded, of course."

The waitress brought us cappuccinos and a plate of biscotti.

"You *vant* to be a *lawn*," Sasha drawled. "Forgotten your Garbo clichés?"

"But I vouldn't *vant* to be a *lawn*. Given my druthers, I'd *vant* to be a *beach*."

"There are those who think you are one already, Mandy. Present company not necessarily excluded."

A beach. The image shimmered in front of me. The ocean. Nothing was more restorative than the primal soup. Saltwater slapping onto sand while seabirds shrieked and circled . . . Even imagining it made me feel better. I saw myself alone, tall dunes behind me, a book on my lap, salt air and solitude rejuvenating me.

"On the other hand," Sasha said, "the plus of your job is the humongous vacation. Tomorrow, I'm back to work, while you—"

"As if ninety percent of your daily life weren't a variation on playtime, while mine—"

"Beach, beach, beach," she said softly.

"Sorry. But the trick is, we're paid too little to enjoy that humongous vacation. I have two weeks," I explained, "before I have to teach summer school."

"I forgot. Too bad. So what are you doing with them?"

I shook my head. "Nothing. Cleaning closets." I wouldn't be teaching summer school if I'd had the funds to do anything else. The seabirds circling my imaginary beach turned into winged dollar signs and fluttered out of reach. What economically advantaged sadist started the myth that the best things in life were free?

"Maybe the fuzz'll take you somewhere for R and R."

"Very funny." C. K. Mackenzie, aforementioned fuzz and one of the issues that made my brain itch, was a part of the problem, not its solution. One of the bits of wisdom I would have appreciated from those rolling waves concerned matters of my rapidly hardening heart. I know it's au courant to love the process and not the goal. And even a more old-fashioned philosopher, Kahlil Gibran, had long ago urged that there be spaces in a man and woman's togetherness. As I recall, the winds of heaven were supposed to dance between them.

But Kahlil never deigned to measure those spaces, and in my case, they sometimes felt larger than an airplane hangar, the better to let the winds of heaven howl. Much as I have enjoyed our spaces and our togetherness, much as I have focused on the process of being with Mackenzie for the past year—when his detecting duties didn't interrupt, disrupt, and postpone that process—I would have also enjoyed the prospect of closure. Smaller spaces.

I don't like dangling threads and unfinished stories. I am comforted knowing that a suspenseful novel will have a resolution. Why should I ask less of my own life?

Except, to really make matters impossible, I didn't know what variety of closure I wanted. Maybe the cavernous spaces between us were my best option—or even my choice. My call. Thinking of that, admitting that, brought back the now-familiar agitated dread.

Three steps away from where we sat, a mother who looked almost as frayed as I felt shouted at a squatty kid in a hat with earflaps. "Stop eating! You'll ruin your dinner!" she shrieked. "I said no more snacks! I said it over and over!"

Whatever the kid snuffled back was obscured by the bus on the corner, which emitted a flatulent sound and matching stench as it pulled away.

I willed myself away to a beach, and allowed myself to hear only the wonderful white noise of the waves. And Sasha.

"Your parents would send you a plane ticket," she said.

"You have to be kidding. Don't I look sufficiently stressed out?" Granted, Boca Raton had a fine Floridian beach—but all the same, time with my parents could not by any stretch of the imagination be equated with a rest. Since I'd turned thirty-one, my mother's horror at my unmarried state had escalated beyond direct speech, as if singleness were the dirtiest or most classified of secrets. She used to worry about my sex life—mostly she worried that I managed to have one. Now, the euphemism for unmarried was *financial security*. She mailed clippings about long-term investments and, much more depressingly, about trophy wives. Nothing subtle about her message. My mission was to snag a doddering millionaire and live securely ever after.

The horrible truth was that every so often—as today, lost in my unattainable beach fantasies and not at all entranced with the teacherly lifestyle of making do—the idea didn't sound half bad. Well, maybe not quarter bad. Although where in my daily rounds I was supposed to meet the tycoon instead of his adolescent great grandson, I didn't know.

"So maybe you don't really want a beach," Sasha said.

"Not enough to put up with my mother's nagging. I'm thinking of installing voice mail to save her breath and long-distance charges. You know, 'Press one to nag about my economic security. Press two to remind me that I haven't yet produced grandchildren.' You're lucky your parents let you lead your own life."

"They're afraid I *will* get married. Again. That I'll be like them." Sasha's parents had been in the divorce avant-garde. Long before it was commonplace, they split, reassembled, remarried, and redivorced unto the point of utter confusion—theirs and everyone who knew them. An inability to choose wisely or maintain relationships seemed a genetic inheritance. Sasha herself had already had two kamikaze hitchings, and her quality control, when it came to men, hadn't improved appreciably since. "Every time I mention a man, they shudder. I told my mother about this fellow I'm going to see tomorrow—" She stopped short. "That's it! Cinderella Pepper, you're looking at your fairy godmother!"

I would have thought fairy godmothers were more petite. Six feet tall, with wild black hair, wearing multicolored layers of gauze and high-topped sneakers, Sasha didn't fit the storybook image, but I listened.

"You have just won yourself an almost all-expenses paid trip to the edge of an authentic, genuine ocean! Sand included free of charge."

"How?"

"I have a seaside shoot complete with room and meals. What's the diff if I share my room with you? All you'll have to spring for is what you eat, and you'd have to do that here, too."

"Are you serious?" A genuine getaway, a beach vacation for free? The seabirds struck up the chorus in my head again.

"What are friends for?"

Sasha might bemoan the lack of a regular salary or a predictable income, but she did get to take her photographs in exotic locales now and then. I thought about shoots on the Mediterranean, or the Caribbean, or even the cold waters off Maine. Anywhere would be splendid. I'd pay for the plane tickets somehow.

The boy in the earflaps had snagged a bag of chips, and his mother, face red and puffed, shouted, "Not more *snacks!* What did I tell you? They're *bad* for you!" She grabbed the bag from the boy and pushed a handful of chips into her own mouth. Talk about mixed messages, no wonder the kid covered his ears. By the time he'd wind up in my classroom in a few years, those leather sound barriers would have become internalized and unremovable. And I'd be expected to teach him something.

Sasha ate the last of the biscotti. I couldn't protest or complain, given that she was offering a vacation in exchange.

An imagined sun warmed my head—but I willingly accepted a bleak beach as well. Deserted and overcast, heavy with clouds or fog—it sounded wonderful. The silence, the waves, the chance to think and breathe deeply . . . bliss. "Thank you," I said. "I gratefully accept."

"Thank the saltwater taffy consortium."

"Saltwater taffy? Where is this job?"

"Where else?"

Atlantic City. Of all the beaches in all the world. My good fairy had arrived with a whole lot of small print. Sand and water, yes, but Atlantic City! Casinos and slums and junk food and all-night lights and noise. More high rollers than breakers. More pigeons than sea gulls. Not the point at all.

"Atlantic City is America's Number One Vacation Destination," Sasha said. "Pure adventure, one hour away. Would you honestly rather clean closets? And by the way, my car's acting weird. I don't need it—I hired an assistant in A.C. and she's renting all the equipment there. So could you drive?"

AND THAT'S WHY on Monday morning, while in search of the soothing touch of nature, I instead wound up parking my Mustang in a labyrinth below several stories of steel, concrete, and glitz.

Sasha and I walked through a lobby done in Eclectic Excess, a potpourri of design history. Greek columns separated Renaissance-style murals beside equatorial waterfalls near an Ozlike yellow-brick walkway. Everything was highlighted with tiny white lights. Our bellman's outfit was Mittel European Operetta. A neo-something marble statue in a toga pointed the way to the registration area. I tried in vain to find a theme, a connecting thread—aside from blatant expensiveness.

Outside, the sky had been tight and sallow, but now we were hermetically sealed in eternal, nuclear day lit by a thousand suns. The eye-tearing indoor season had nothing to do with the existence of the clock or the solar system.

"Why a casino, Sash? Atlantic City has normal hotels. Why'd the saltwater people put you here?"

"I asked them to. I thought I'd be alone, and a place like this is more alive. No matter what hour. I was here once. . . ." We passed the entrance to a cavelike side room called the Hideaway. Sasha dropped her suitcase, said, "Just a sec," and ducked in.

I was close to the casino entrance. I waited for Sasha, listening to the siren sounds of silvery music and money.

"He's still working here," she said when she returned a minute or so later. "The bartender, Frankie. One of the good guys."

Which probably meant she had no interest in him. It's women like Sasha who—unintentionally but just as lethally—make men think they have to be rotten with the rest of us. Nice guys do not finish last with me—unless you're being semantically sloppy and equating *nice* with bland or dull. But Sasha's different. Her dials are set for challenge, which often translates into danger or misery.

9

However, at this point in our long friendship, I was trying not to editorialize about Sasha's fondness for losers. As she was overly fond of pointing out, my own off-again, on-again relationship with the detective was no shining example of brilliant selection.

"I was here before," she now said. "Couple of years ago."

"With Frankie the bartender?"

"No, no. This other guy. Dimples. A genuine louse. Frankie the bartender saved the day, and maybe me—from jail. I didn't think he'd still be here."

"From jail? Why? Or do I want to know?"

"Because Dimples was a little bit of a criminal, and the police thought I was his accomplice." She laughed at the thought. I found it less humorous.

We had reached our destination, the registration desk, decorated in the style of medieval French palaces. I wondered which era, theme, and climatological zone our room would feature. Art Deco Romanesque? Tropical French? Greek Chalet?

It turned out to be Basic Brothel. The room was small, its walls covered with silver foil. The bedspread, drapes, and carpeting were as silvery as fabric can get, shot through with metallic threads. Where there wasn't foil or silver cloth, there were mirrors. Including the ceiling. Cigarettes still sealed in their foil-lined boxes must feel the way I did.

"A money motif, do you think?" Sasha asked.

"I'd prefer the greenbacks room, then."

"The room I had with Dimples was nothing like this. But then, we had an ocean view."

We viewed neither ocean nor bay. Instead, we faced the rooftops and fire escapes of yellow-brick buildings that clashed with our color scheme. I closed the drapes. "I'll take the right-hand drawers, right side of the closet."

Sasha nodded, but before either of us began to unpack, our phone rang and she picked it up. "Sasha *Berg*," she said midway through the conversation. "The photographer. Are you talking to the right person?" And: "The saltwater taffy association isn't going to pay for any—" Then she just listened.

She hung up. "They're moving us to a suite." She sounded bemused. "No extra charge. I thought they only did that for really high rollers."

"It isn't possible that this upgrade is in honor of the guy you were here with, is it? The criminal? That maybe they think you're still involved with him?"

"They didn't comp him a suite then, so why now, when he's dead? And it's not like they don't know. It was in all the papers."

"Tell me the man died of natural causes. Please."

"The man died of natural causes."

I sighed with relief.

"After all," Sasha continued, "it's pretty natural to die when there's a bullet in the back of your skull."

I've often wondered why Sasha's incredible bad luck with men doesn't deter or sour her—or leave her with the slightest trace of post-traumatic shock. She's no dummy or masochist. Maybe it's because she has so much fun until each adventure sours. Maybe she's the world's last great optimist.

"We're not supposed to look a gift horse in the mouth," she now said.

I hoped that neither the horse nor his teeth nor the walls were capped in silver. One ounce more and I'd start mining it.

THE SUITE WAS exquisite, leaving me wondering. Were nickel-and-dime gamblers mirrored-ceiling types, while the major players—a group I wouldn't expect to be particularly elegant—connoisseurs of all that was fine?

The living and bedrooms were decorated with Asian tansu chests, porcelain, jade carvings, Chinese rugs in soft pastels, and cushiony contemporary furniture. Shoji screens covered the windows. A six-paneled gilded screen filled the wall behind two oversized beds.

"A Jacuzzi!" Sasha called from the bathroom. "What a shame to be here with *you*!"

Understated and quiet, the rooms were the antithesis of the world downstairs. Things were definitely looking up. This in itself could be my retreat. I unpacked in record time, like a creature nervously establishing her turf.

Sasha dawdled. She arranged her cameras and equipment. She switched to another pocketbook and slowly decided what she'd need. She emptied half her suitcase onto the bed, then worried over the condition of her travel kit. She decided her nails needed polishing and wondered whether she could include a manicure on her expense account. "Did I tell you I'm going out tonight?" she asked.

I didn't mind. This was a place in which to vacate, to luxuriate. This was a style to which I wanted to become accustomed.

I had a four-day vacation and a choice of three books. *War and Peace*, which has been on every summer reading list of my life, because every autumn has arrived without my having read it. *Gift from the Sea*, one of my all-time favorites. And a threadbare paperback with negative literary value and a title like *Lust and Sleaze*. A student had left it behind when she galloped off to summer vacation. Of course, I was reading it purely as research into adolescent interests. But all the same, it might go well with a Jacuzzi.

"I met this guy three weeks ago, when I was down here. At Trump's, the bar in Trump Plaza. We made a date for when I'd be back on this job. If he remembers, and I hope so. He reminds me of Cary Grant."

In what way, I didn't dare ask. More dimpled chins? An English accent? A face to die for? A gift for comedy—or, more likely, a lot of wives?

"He's elegant. Continental. A gentleman." She examined her hand, first with fingers curled toward her, then held straight, nails up. "But not stuffy, the way that might sound." She stood and tossed the nail file back onto the bed.

She pushed back the shoji screens for a view of a chilly—but inviting-looking—beach and ocean, sighed, and looked likely to stay awhile.

I suddenly found the room and the situation less comforting. It was too peaceful, too deliberately serene, too incomprehensible and overrich a setting for the facts of my life.

What am I doing? I don't belong here. This is wrong.
This Asian palace was no place to figure things out. Which I felt incapable of doing, anyway.

What am I doing? What am I going to do?

The angst itch began between my shoulder blades and rose through my spinal column into my brain. At such times, it's hard to sit still and impossible to endure Sasha's glacially slow progress. "How about I meet you somewhere later?" I asked. "Downstairs. Maybe in that bar we passed? I have to ... I have to move around."

"Going up to the health club?"

"No. The beach, I think. See you." I pulled on a sweater and headed out.

In the living room of the suite there was an odd woodcut. A mythical beast, mostly equine, but rearing on thick bird legs. It had thick-lashed almond eyes that seemed to ask me directly, *Do you have any idea what you're doing?* and its mouth was open wide, revealing not horse teeth, but long and lethal fangs.

I looked at that mouth, those fangs. "Tell me you're not the gift horse," I whispered.

TWO

MAYBE I shouldn't have come at all. This was most definitely not the beachscape I'd had in mind.

For starters, there wasn't a hint of salt and sea in the air. When I was a child, sitting in the backseat of the family car, a unique scent gave advance notice that the separate universe of the ocean was close. A mix of salt, fish, seaweed, and something indefinable, it was my favorite perfume.

Nowadays, from far off, the seashore doesn't smell of anything unless it's massively polluted. I don't know what's happened to that aroma. Either it's been overwhelmed by concrete and competing scents, or my nose has grown old and insensitive, or, according to my most Pollyannaish hypothesis, the childhood fragrance I miss was pollutants that have been removed. Unfortunately, that is also my least plausible theory.

Despite the homogenized smell of the wind, and its chill, and even this early in the season, when only private schools like Philly Prep had disbanded for summer, the boardwalk was well-populated. People eating pretzels, cotton candy, fudge, and saltwater taffy. People wearing floppy hats and bare tattooed potbellies and faded T-shirts advertising last year's action adventure movie. Muumuus over flip-flops, and baggy pants over unlaced high-tops. Instead of an ocean flavor in the air, there was the pungency of peanuts, pizza, and hot dogs. Instead of the rhythmic crashing of waves, there were the pop-pops of an electronic arcade, the solicitations of tarot and palm readers, and the repeated warning "Make way, comin' through" from the Atlantic City coolies—men pushing canopied wicker chairs, oversized porch furniture on wheels. The occupants of the rolling chairs looked mildly embarrassed, but happy to be off their feet.

Nonetheless, there was an ocean a few yards off. I hurried across the boards and down the steps onto the beach, imagining the time when this stretch of marshland belonged to the Lenni Lenape Indians and wild ducks.

If I'd been the first outsider to discover the long, windswept sand-edged marsh, would I too have said, "Hey, this is *great*! Let's build a resort here and spoil it!"

"Ocean, emotion, promotion." Somebody's choice of motto for the city built on hucksterism.

Philadelphia was settled by people looking for a new life, new freedom, greater dignity. Atlantic City was settled by people looking for a buck. History shows.

The marsh was gone, but the beach was still there, slowly eroding, slowly choking on pollutants—but still there. And on this chilly day, I shared it with only one man, who made his stooped way across the horizon with a metal detecting rod. He, too, was still there, a familiar piece of my childhood landscape, the beachcomber searching for lost rings and left-behind coins.

A haze of wind-agitated sand gave the tan ground a gauzy

15

edge. Nonetheless, I pulled off my shoes and socks, rolled up my jeans, and headed for the ocean. The sand stung my ankles and was chilly under my feet, and the surf was pure ice.

On the plus side, the beach was relatively clean. No red-bag medical waste floating down from New York's hospitals, no untreated sewage visibly pouring out of storm drains, and none of the heartrending dead dolphins of a few years back. I took a deep breath and, with some relief, watched minuscule crabs diligently wait for the foamy surf to recede, then pock the wet sand with their burrows. Years ago, along with every other child, I had dug up the tiny crabs by the bucketful, and I was comforted that they had survived all of us, that a beach was still a beach, and, even slightly compromised, still good medicine.

I made my way back to the boardwalk stairs and paused to watch a silhouetted seabird dip and swoop.

Something hissed. Loudly, distinctly. The bird was too far up in the sky, and I couldn't see anything else to account for the sound—no cat, snake, leaky steampipe, or deflating balloon.

The sibilant exhale repeated. The metal-detector man had long since moved on to the next section of beach, and there was no one left except a man in a warm-up suit and a golden retriever in a kerchief, both jogging by the water's edge.

Hsssss.

Was this the fabled singing sand? Another example of poetic hyperbole?

The late-day shadows under and around the boardwalk suddenly shifted and fragmented, one piece moving forward and translating into a figure in layers of sweaters, socks, and skirts. Her hair, uncovered, was pale brown, fuzzy and thin, reminding me of a doll I had once overloved into baldness.

Still crouched, as she must have been under the boardwalk, she looked up at me from dark eyes set in a rumpled face, and, having found her balance, slowly drew herself up straight. *"Steps,"* she hissed. *"My steps.* Below for a while because it's nippy, that's all. I'm still alive, you know, even if money thinks I'm dead." Her voice darkened. "My place. Find your own."

"But—"

16

"One part of the beach as good as another." She waved her hands toward *elsewhere*. She wore one red and one blue glove. "People are slobs. Cans and bottles all over come summer. You'll make a buck anywhere. Wherever you are, they try to round you up, roust you out, every night. Here, too."

"But I . . . I'm not . . . I'm just visiting for a few days. At the casino." I wanted to think it was funny that my worn jeans and threadbare turtleneck had made her decide I was poaching her turf. But I couldn't. She was a face for my worst fears, for, I suspect, almost every underpaid, underinsured single woman's worst fears. To become the bag lady, street person—or, in this case, sand person—alone, homeless, destitute, and perhaps slightly mad. "I didn't mean to intrude."

"You get the winners." She made a throwing motion with both hands. "Pennies from heaven. Losers, too. What the hell, they say. Understand how it feels. Turn their pockets inside out."

"I'm sorry I bothered you." And I turned.

"Got a buck, then?"

At home I carry a bill or coins in my pocket for just this purpose, but I hadn't thought the situation would arise on the beach. "I only brought my room key," I said lamely. "I'll be back."

"Sure," she muttered.

"No, honestly. Will you be—are you always here?" What's a nice former girl like you doing on a desolate beach like this? I wanted to know her story—every street person's story—every step of the way down. If I knew how and why this happened, would I also know ways to keep it from happening to me? Unfortunately, the more stories I heard, the less defined and more easy the slide appeared to be.

She squinted at me intently, and, as if she'd read my mind and worst fears, she said in a matter-of-fact tone, "I was once like you. You don't think so, but I was." She chuckled softly.

Her words had a rehearsed or at least overpracticed sound, and probably were both, and she sounded slightly cracked and probably was. And that should have made her and whatever she had to say less ominous, but it didn't.

17

"Yes!" She flung mismatched hands toward the heavens. "Ruined!" she shouted. Then she dropped her arms and looked at me, her brow burrowed. "Men, you know?"

Just exactly how much like me had she been?

"I watch all day long." She pointed the red-gloved index finger in my direction.

"Me?"

"Everybody. The visitors. Saw The Donald last week. You know who he is? Had a good talk with him about high finance." She cackled again. Her right incisor was missing.

Of course that hadn't happened at all, but nonetheless, I had to ask. "Was he generous?"

"Generous?" She laughed so hard, she collapsed down in the sand. "Not a penny. Said he never carries small bills!" She flopped onto her back and looked up to me, and then in a world-weary voice said, "Rich men are the worst, aren't they?"

I went down the staircase and helped her up, brushing sand off her clothing, which was purely symbolic, given her residence. "Are you all right?" I asked.

"I'm Georgette."

I wondered if that was supposed to be an answer to my question. "And I'm Mandy," I said. "Pleased to meet you."

Suddenly serious, she looked me directly in the eye. "Yes," she said. "I was once like you. I had curtains at my windows, too."

SASHA WAS not yet in the bar, but before I went up to retrieve her and money for the sandwoman, I detoured to the ladies' room to, among other things, wash the grit off my hands.

I couldn't stop thinking about Georgette, which is probably why I almost plowed into a nervous-looking, fussily dressed senior citizen blocking my exit. I hesitated, expecting her to move in one direction or the other, as in the normal order of business. She didn't. "Are you leaving?" I finally asked.

"What?"

"Leaving." I amplified my voice. "The door's behind you. May I use it?" I sounded stupid and she looked fuddled. "Are you all right?"

"All right. Am I all right?" She tilted her head, the better to consider the issue. Her hair was baby-chick yellow, sculpted into curls that didn't budge as she moved. "Don't trouble yourself on my account, dearie. You young people have lives of your own. I'll be fine."

Definitely off kilter and none of my business. I reached around her for the door handle.

"That is," she said, "I *hope* I'll be fine."

I took a deep breath. I had already had my peculiar-old-lady fix for the day. I had people to see, vacations to create. "What do you mean, you *hope?*" I asked, my big mouth once again working independently of my brain.

"If you insist." She folded her arms across her commodious bosom and launched into her spiel with so much gusto, I knew that I was the unfortunate fly this spider lady had been awaiting. "I'm being harassed." She leaned closer and whispered, "Sexually, like that sweet girl with the judge on the TV."

"Anita Hill? What are you talking about?"

"Why? You think she lied?"

"No—I just don't see what any of this has to do with blocking the door. Or with me."

"Honey," she said, "my *boundaries* are being *violated*. Just like they say on Sally Jessy Raphael."

"Sounds painful, but I'm supposed to meet my friend, so—"

"You have a heart of stone or you don't believe me? Which one? You think I'm too old? *He's* too old? You ever hear the expression 'dirty old man'? Or do you think men improve with age, like wine?"

I took a deep breath. "If you have a problem, report it to one of the guards, or the management, or the police."

"Nobody can touch him. He's beyond the law."

"I'm sure that's not so, miss."

"Mrs. Rudy . . ." The last name sounded like *Smirtz*. She wiped her eyes and moved on. "My late husband, may he rest in peace, was a good man. Lala. Call me Lala."

"That's quite an unusual name."

"A family nickname. My grandmother's and aunt's, too.

19

We're all really named Henrietta. Lala is short for lallapa-looza." She leaned closer to me again. "Tommy is beyond the law. Nobody would dare touch him. He nuzzles my neck and says I have heroic bosoms like a Valkyrie. He says my ankles make him weep with pleasure. But me? I'm finished with men since my Rudy passed. Tommy says he loves my spirit, that he's a romantic and he'll never give up. He comes down on the bus with me and goes back with me, too. Tries dirty things as we ride."

"Why don't you flat out tell him to get lost?"

"I'm afraid. He's connected, you know what I mean? I can't enjoy my life. I can't enjoy the casino. What kind of woman does he think I am?"

"Look, I have to leave. My advice is: take a different bus."

She curtly shook her immobile curls. "I'm not made of money, dearie. I'm an old woman, and every nickel—the bus is a charter. We pay eight dollars, they drive us here. A bargain, already, right? But then they give us five dollars for the day and a five-dollar voucher toward the next bus. How could I take another bus?"

"Don't come at all."

"I'm not entitled to a little fun? A little pleasure?"

"Well, that's quite a problem you've got." I hated to be rude to my elders, but I was going to knock her down, if necessary, to get out of here. "Be a modern woman. Risk it. Tell him you're not interested. Bring a lady friend. Bring a different man friend. Get a restraining order against him. Learn self-defense. Use your common sense!"

"Actually." She put her veiny hand on top of mine. Her nails were polished the color of bubble gum. "There *is* something you could do."

"Excuse me?" It is possible that I am actually one of those noisy ghosts who try in vain to be recognized because they don't know that people can't hear or see them. "I'm sorry," ghostly me said. "I can't."

"Such an easy thing."

I shook my head.

"Pretend to know me. Please." She stepped back and looked up at me. "Save me." At five-eight, I was a good seven inches taller, and, I assumed, forty years younger.

"I'm sorry, but—" I'm working on this other case, the lady who lives under the boardwalk, you see. The guilt office has met its daily quota and is closed.

"Five minutes, that's all. It's for a good cause. You'll do it, won't you, darling? Play along with me. In the name of sister-hood!" She raised a clenched fist.

Shameless manipulation. Impersonating a feminist. But what the hell? She really seemed afraid of this man. "Five minutes," I said, and arm in arm, we entered the darkened bar. I scanned for someone dark and broody, visibly *connected*.

Lala delivered me to a frail, freeze-dried male.

This villainous lecher who'd struck terror in Lala's heart pushed back his chair and leaped to attention. In thrall to the calendar rather than outdoor temperatures, he wore a seersucker suit and white shoes. All he lacked was a straw skimmer hat to be a perfect turn-of-the-century dandy. "Lala! Dear heart!" he said as she approached. "I was worried."

"Tommy, I want you to meet the granddaughter of an old, dear friend. . . ." Self-absorbed Lala had never asked my name. She merrily skipped on. "You remember I told you about Sherwin? The man who's infatuated with me? Can you believe that his granddaughter just showed up, and says that Sherwin is searching for me." She spoke at about twice the tempo she'd used in the ladies' room, and things moved so quickly that as angry as I was becoming, when Tommy put out a hand that looked like a pterodactyl's, I shook it.

"I'm Amanda," I said.

"Oh, no," he answered. "*I'm* a-man-da. You're a-girl-da. Sit, sit, sit." He waved at the table he'd been at. We all continued to stand.

"Pleasure to meet you," Tommy said, covering his wretched joke's flat wake. "Any friend of Lala's . . ." His attention returned, adoringly, to Ms. Smirtz. "I don't seem to remember any Sherwin," he said.

"Really?" Her laugh was an incredulous tinkled scale, like

21

spoons on crystal. "He's the one who took me to Rome that time I had an urge for pasta."

I exhaled loudly, angrily. "It's been great, but—"

"I think maybe I won't go back to the city with you tonight, Tommy. Sweetie here says Sherwin's desperate to see me." Lala sighed extravagantly.

"Whatever happened to subtlety?" I muttered. "Or honesty?" They both ignored me.

"Please, Lala!" Tommy said. "Come back with me."

Lala shook her head like a wild young thing, although the glued-together curls refused to toss and she looked like she had a crenelated skull.

"Don't make any rash decisions. Let's talk this through." Tommy interrupted his pleas to wave at a beefy bald man. The man's companion, a creature with straight black hair and a red dress laminated to her flesh, flicked a glance our way. The man did not. "I was just telling Big Julius there about you, Lala," Tommy said.

"That's Big Julius? Isn't he . . . oh, my, I've heard about him. The garbage business, isn't it?" She looked at me and hissed, "See what I mean? *Big Julius!* And what did you tell Big Julius about me?" she asked in her normal voice.

"That I was crazy about you, of course." He elbowed me. "I'm crazy about this lady," he said. Then he looked back at his love object. "Big Julius is a nice man, despite his reputation."

"It's been a treat, but I have to run now," I said.

"She's leaving you stranded, Lala," Tommy said. "All mine again. That means you're not running off with this Sherwin person. I'll wine and dine you and we will ride off into the sunset together at the back of the bus. Look, over there. It's McDog. The one whose business partner blew himself up, or so the official story goes. And over there . . ."

Watching them was mildly fascinating, a game of ego Ping-Pong. Tommy served hyped inside dope on mobsters he pretended to have known, and Lala returned the serve with ever-escalating tales of the imaginary Sherwin's generosity and lust.

"They all love me," Tommy said with some desperation. "Every single one of them. They tell me everything. They call me the Safe Deposit, get it? I keep their secrets. See him?" he said of a respectable gray-haired business type in conversation with the bartender. "He has three days left to pay off his loan or die. He's not lucky at the tables the way I am."

"You didn't seem so lucky today," Lala said.

"Not yet, maybe," Tommy answered. "But I was out of the game for a while, after all."

"He was hit by a roulette ball that jumped," Lala explained.

Tommy rubbed the back of his hand. I could see a dark bruise on the leathery skin. "My luck's changing," he said. "I feel it in my bones—long as you're with me, Lala."

"But Sherwin—"

"See her?" Tommy pointed at a woman with yellow-white big hair. "Sinatra used to be very fond of her. You catch my drift? *Very.* But she is reputed to have killed her husband and eaten the corpse so there was no evidence."

"Sherwin says every woman deserves a—"

"See him?" Tommy said of a redhead who had just entered the cocktail lounge. "Supposedly an antique dealer, but really Jersey's number one hit man."

Lala shuddered with delight.

"Aren't drinks free in the casinos?" I asked. "Why are all these men coming into the bar?"

"A change of scene," Tommy said.

"A little socializing," Lala added. "A little schmoozing."

"A little business," Tommy said, sotto voce.

I thought about the vacation plans I had abandoned. At this point, cleaning closets sounded like keen fun.

"I broke her grandfather's heart when I turned him down," Lala said.

"Turned him down for what?" Tommy asked.

Closets sounded irresistible.

"Turned him down for *marriage*," Lala said. "Despite his money."

Tommy is not one of my responsibilities, I told myself. I do not have to warn him. If he'd reached this age without realizing

23

when a scam was being pulled on him—and a shaggy, preposterous, clichéd scam at that—then he deserved Lala.

Tommy was nearly hyperventilating. "You see that woman? A Mafia princess raised in total seclusion, they were so afraid somebody would take her hostage, but she and Ralph the Scar . . ."

I obediently swiveled once again. It seemed the polite thing to do. And I did a double take. The Mafia princess was none other than Sasha, who now stood resplendently at the bar in peacock silk and high-button boots. Gee, and I'd always thought that her father was simply a much-married orthodontist. What a unique front for his criminous ways. "Good luck to both of you," I said.

"Darling," Lala began. "Don't run away because you're so upset that I might not wind up with Grandpop."

I went to join Sasha, who was in a clump of casino escapees. A few were on stools—including the gray-haired man Tommy said had three days to pay or die. He didn't look particularly worried about it, and in fact seemed tilted toward Sasha, a smile on his face. She smiled back. And that's how it was—a pending date with Mr. Wonderful didn't mean you couldn't meanwhile line up his successors.

I tapped her on the shoulder.

"Where've you been?" she asked. "Frankie," she said to the bartender, "this is my friend Mandy, the one I was talking about." Frankie nodded at me without much interest. "You had a call from your detective," Sasha said.

"Mackenzie? Why?"

"He must have detected you."

Which didn't take much skill. My answering machine message said where I was.

"He's here in River City, too," Sasha said. "You can run but you can't hide." She handed me a hotel postcard with a phone number scrawled on its back.

The elusive cop was here. I shook my head in wonderment. "I thought it was only hype, but it's obviously true. This really *must* be America's most popular vacation destination."

24

Three

 NY objective reevaluation of my relationship with Mackenzie required distance, so I gave up on both objectivity and reevaluation for a while.

Mackenzie mysteriously manages to seem writ in capital letters, despite his easy Southern style. He doesn't strut, he doesn't shout, he doesn't push, and I honestly don't know what it is he does do. It can't all be his smile and drawl, can it? That's some of what I'd meant to work out while I was here.

"I came down because Nicky B. grew up here," he explained. Nicky B. was the prime suspect in a missing and presumed murdered child case. The police were so positive that Mr. B. had done it that they had turned the press on him, but they could find nothing except an abiding and unwholesome strangeness in the man's interests, and that was not enough to make a case or an arrest. "Thought maybe there was somethin' we'd missed, somethin' relevant. Turns out, the house he grew up in at the Inlet's gone. Whole street is pretty much gone. In fact, the entire neighborhood looks like Beirut. Nothing but rubble except for a lone, half-boarded-up house here and there an' people who look like they barely survived the destruction."

I knew, so he definitely knew, that he could have found out about Nicky B.'s former neighborhood by telephone and fax and computer data base. Or even through common knowledge. The Inlet, never prime real estate, had been bulldozed a decade and a half ago in anticipation of a casino-supported renaissance that is due to appear along about the same time as Godot.

When the casino referendum was pending, the promoters' ads showed $100 bills falling from the sky, and when the referendum passed, people danced in the streets. But money has not yet descended from the stratosphere, certainly not in the direction of the Inlet, and anybody who knew anything about the gilt-edged poverty-stricken city knew about the ruins at the end of the boardwalk. That probably even included Mackenzie's good old boys back home in the Louisiana bayou.

"Guess I'm not the best detective in the whole entire universe. Guess I goofed and I'm forced to take an actual day or so off," he drawled. "Thought maybe we could spend it together."

Actual time together, without murderous interruptions. My defenses against the man wobbled precariously.

"Thought we might watch the sunset, find a really good restaurant, maybe gamble a little bit, hear music . . ."

His voice was as soothing, his accent as balmy as I'd hoped the beach would be. I shelved all decisions of what to do about him until some less enjoyable moment in our relationship.

THAT MOMENT CAME—and it wasn't even Mackenzie's fault—via a telephone call to his hotel room at approximately one A.M. I could barely remember where I was, let alone where the telephone might be. Mackenzie reoriented himself more quickly, finding both a lamp switch and the receiver.

I heard a deafening squawk from the other end. Yet another crank or drunk or pervert. "Hang up," I said. "Just hang up. Don't listen. Shouldn't have turned on the light." I replumped my pillow.

"She's right here." Mackenzie handed me the receiver. "Sasha," he said.

"Mandy!" she shouted. "Thank God! I was going crazy! At first, I couldn't remember where you'd be. Couldn't remember—"

Shades of my mother when I stayed out too late on a date. But this was Sasha and this was ridiculous. "What's wrong with you? Stop shouting!"

"—what hotel he'd said he was at, so how was I going to find you and—"

Frankly, I had barely thought she'd notice my absence. "Calm down," I said. "What's the big deal?"

She spluttered through every word I said. "Big deal? Mandy, you don't—"

"Calm—"

"*Don't tell me to calm down!* I've been arrested for murder!"

How do you respond to a statement like that? The replies that charged into my mind seemed clumsy and primitive, not to mention disloyal. Questions such as: who? why you? did you? Instead of asking any of them, I mouthed her words to Mackenzie, who glared at the phone. I held the receiver slightly out, between the two of us, so he also could hear.

I took a deep breath. "Tell me about it," I said.

"I came back to the room an hour or so ago."

"Alone?" You couldn't get into trouble if you came home alone. Wasn't that what Mama always said?

"Yes! If you'd just *listen!* Alone. I thought you might be in there, remember? I wasn't going to bring anybody in. But instead of you, there was a dead man in the bed, in my bed! And blood all over the place. And all over my clothing. That lamp— that gorgeous marble lamp, remember? The police think its base was what killed—oh, God—my clothing—my *slip* covered with blood on the floor!"

Maybe my mind wasn't willing to compute everything she was saying, so it fixated on the slip. I hadn't known she wore such garments. They seemed too prissy and middle class for Sasha, wrong for her loose-flowing style. Whole or half? What color? What fabric? I had to literally shake my head to dislodge the issue of the slip.

"My bra. *My own things!* Scattered around, as if I'd dropped them one by one. You know I didn't. You were there when I left."

"Yes." She left her room neat, Ma.

"The beds had been turned down and all. There was still a chocolate on yours, Mandy!" Snuffling and nose-blowing.

"Listen, calm— I'm sorry, didn't mean to say that, but—"

"There's more. Worse. An open bottle of champagne and two glasses. A bloody washcloth, wet towels, as if I took a shower and washed off. I feel like I'm going crazy, and these cops, they act like it's an open-and-shut case. I don't think I even know the man!"

"It's obviously some horrible mistake." I was on autobabble, putting out noise because I wished she hadn't said *think*. "You mean there's a chance you do—did know him?" I whispered.

"I can't tell. If you'd seen him—he was bloody, crushed—I couldn't even *look*, let alone—" She inhaled and exhaled loudly. When she spoke again, her voice was firmer, more resolute. "I didn't recognize him and I certainly didn't kill him. But they found his card in a pair of my slacks in the closet. With a private phone number penciled on it. How did they find his card there?"

I shook my head and made sympathetic noises. I didn't have any answers. Surely not at 1:09 A.M. after forty-two minutes of sleep. I did have a question, however. "Who is—who was he?"

"Somebody named Jesse Reese, they said."

I looked at Mackenzie. "What happens next?" I whispered.

He was shaking his head and blinking hard, trying to wake up fully. He mumbled a catalogue of procedures, all the while getting out of bed. Preliminary examination. Middle of the night. Probable delays. Arraignment. Bail. He left the room.

Obviously, a lot had to happen, and all of it would take time. "So let me get this straight. They think you came in and murdered this guy? What time?" I heard the shower run in the bathroom.

"Around nine or ten." Sasha's voice was dull, mechanical. "They say I cleaned myself up and left, then came back again around eleven and pretended to be shocked by what I found." She sounded exhausted.

"But you have an alibi, Sasha! Did you tell them?"

"What is it?"

She was really not herself. Her brain had frozen. "Your date Cary Grant!" I tried not to sound impatient.

"Dunstan?"

"If that was his name. You were with him, weren't you?"

Only silence on the line.

Having completed the world's shortest shower, Mackenzie reentered the bedroom during this frustrating exchange. He looked at me quizzically. I looked back at him, but not quizzically. I looked at the man's long and lovely body, wrapped in a towel, and I mourned the minivacation we were now not going to have. Worst of all, I couldn't even blame the ruin of this one on him.

"Not exactly," Sasha finally said. "The evening didn't go all that terrifically. He turned out to be pretty boring."

"Listen, I don't care about your romantic life. I care about your *neck*. He can get you out of this mess."

"Don't bother."

"What is he, another one hiding out from the cops like your dead Dimples? Another big- or small-time hoodlum?"

"No. He's a photographer. Like me. But he wasn't with me the whole time. After dinner, we walked awhile, then we split. I went back to our hotel, and he said he was going back to Trump's."

"When exactly did you separate? How long was he with you?"

"Mandy, was I ever the kind to watch the clock? I don't know. That's the problem. Maybe nine o'clock, maybe later. I walked, then I stopped in the bar and kind of made a date with Frankie the bartender."

"God, Sasha, your frenetic social life is literally killing you!" I hadn't meant to be that loud or sharp, but I must say it felt good to be openly angry about her stupidities and excesses. "Okay, then, did *Frankie* go upstairs with you?"

Mackenzie raised an eyebrow at the name switch.

"I told you," Sasha said. "Nobody did. We were going to meet later on. He was working two shifts."

"Even so, if Dunstan was with you till near nine—and maybe it was actually later—and Frankie a while later, maybe between them we could establish that you were not in the room. Where can I find Dunstan? What's his whole name? Is he in the book?"

Mackenzie was almost dressed, and flashing me looks that said I should do the same.

"I don't know his last name or address," Sasha said, "and don't you dare say a word. You don't know the first name of somebody you've been seeing for a year!"

I held my tongue—an extremely painful activity. I didn't say that it was not the same thing at all. I did hope, however, that it was not the same thing at all.

"When I met him three weeks ago, he was at the next table. We were both with groups of other people. It was all very flirty. A fifties movies thing. No data, just patter. Fun, you know?"

I grudgingly admitted that I did know. It could happen. Last names would have weighted down the bubble.

"I was coming back down for this job," Sasha said, "so we planned to meet again, same place, which is what we did. He either remembered, or he's always there. We ate in the casino, at Ivana's—you'd think he'd have changed that name to Marla's, wouldn't you?"

"Dunstan?"

"Donald."

"Maybe somebody at Ivana's will recognize you."

"Yeah." She sounded doubtful.

"Did he charge the dinner?" How many Dunstans could there be? Last name or not, we'd find his charge slip. And while we're visiting fantasyland, let's add that the charge slip wouldn't be the preprinted form, but one of those vertical printouts that list the time of sale. And, of course, that would turn out to be precisely the same moment as Jesse Reese's time of death. Alibi by Visa.

Sasha was silent while she thought about this, and when she spoke, her voice was dull. "Cash. Said he'd just won a bundle. I think maybe he gambles a lot."

"Did you tell the police?"

"About his bets?"

"No, about—"

"That I was on a sort of date with a man whose last name and address I don't know at about the time when they think this man was murdered? Yes. They weren't too impressed." She sighed, and I could feel more bad news coming. "They have a witness," she said.

"How is that possible? To what?"

"To my going into the room with Jesse Reese and another man, right before it happened."

"Another man? Who?"

"How would I know? I wasn't there! The witness is crazy. None of it's true!"

This seemed a good time to reassure her that help was on the way, in the form of the Pepper-Mackenzie posse, and to more privately cross fingers and hope that was the truth.

I SET OUT with Mackenzie for Sasha's jail, but en route I realized that I had to go to Trump's instead. Mackenzie was not pleased by the idea.

"Even if just for moral support, shouldn't you be with Sasha?" he asked. "Ah'm certainly not a real welcome sight to her." He was *ahm*ing, a sure sign he was agitated, really didn't approve of my detour. Or he just didn't want to be alone with Sasha, his longtime antagonist. But the *ahm*ier he got, the more resolute I became.

"Explain it to her," I said. "I'll be there as soon as I can, but meantime, somebody's done a good job of making Sasha look guilty as hell, and this Dunstan is her only alibi."

31

"True," Mackenzie said. "But even so—"

"He told her he was coming back here after their date. We don't have a last name or an address, so the first hurdle is finding him, and I have a better chance of, um, discovering him than you or the police."

"You playin' bar girl or detective?" he grumbled.

He didn't particularly like my playing either role, so I stayed with my thesis. "You have a much better chance of speeding up the process with the local force than I do," I said. "This is an appropriate division of labor. Find out what they know. About that witness, particularly. About what's going to happen to Sasha."

"Still an' all—"

"What if Dunstan bolts and disappears when he picks up his morning paper and sees his date in a mug shot? I have to find him tonight, before he knows what's going on."

"Maybe he's left. Gone to bed."

"Easy enough to find out. If so, I'll nurse a pot of decaf and wait for you. I'll be safe, indoors, and I'll feel like I at least tried to do something useful."

When he let me out of the car, he leaned over and gave me a brotherly kiss on the forehead. "Can't tell you how much I didn't want this kind of adventure," he said. "Can't begin to."

I took that inarticulate pronouncement to be the best news in a long time on the subject of us.

I TRIED to become Sasha, to add four inches to my height and geometric increments to my self-confidence. Otherwise, I would have had to admit how creepy I felt about sashaying into a bar in the wee hours of the morning. Particularly this bar, with columns that looked sequined and a loud combo playing "Feelings." What else, but "Feelings"? How would Sasha do it? *Why* would Sasha do it?

I tried a round of Intuitively Spot the Dunstan, and failed. Cary Grant's image fell between me and the bar like a glowing scrim. Nobody came close. Why hadn't I asked for a description of her date?

I sat down. The bar was copper-topped with red leather trim. Above it two TV's played, their sound off. On the right screen a game of tennis silently proceeded. The left featured men in togas. *Quo Vadis,* I thought, but it was hard to tell, as they appeared to be lip-synching to the band's inimitable and interminable rendition of "Feelings."

"Help you?" The bartender had bright red hair and an air of competent no-nonsense. I ordered a Virgin Mary. She nodded brusquely. It was too early in my truncated day for alcohol. Anyway, at long last, I was high on life. Or at least high on the small thrill of being awake and in a bar at this hour, an experience completely off my bell-shaped curve. I had inverted time and entered a night world I generally missed.

The bartender put down my spicy tomato concoction. "Delicious," I said after sipping. I wondered what she was doing here, past midnight, what kind of a job this was and how it worked for her life. My speculations must have shown.

She chuckled. "Husband can be home with the kids this way," she said. "Until he finishes grad school. That's what brings me here. How about you?"

"I'm . . . my friend . . . I'm looking for a guy named Dunstan."

She raised her eyebrows. "Wouldn't have expected that," she said, with a quick, sad shake of her head. "He's a fixture around these parts. Stays, off and on, till three or four A.M. most nights." She turned around and busied herself polishing the pour spout of a scotch bottle. Then she turned back. "Look, whether you want it or not, here's some unsolicited advice. In the spirit of sisterhood, right? Forget Dunstan. He's all packaging. There's no future there. Not much of a present, either."

"I'm not planning to be involved with him," I said, but of course, that's female code for just the opposite, which is how the bartender took it. "But what are you trying to say? Is he married?"

She looked amused. "I doubt it, although he says so to stay clear of entanglements. Saw it in an old Cary Grant movie."

"Were you here all evening? Did you see him tonight? Was he with a woman?"

She shrugged. "I didn't come on until midnight, and when I saw him, he was alone. I hope that doesn't encourage you." Then she did a minor double take, and cocked her head to the right. "But speak of the devil."

So there he was, the devil or Cary Grant. Take your pick. He wasn't nearly as handsome as I'd expected, and much shorter than anticipated. Not a midget, but average. Sasha must have towered over him in her high-button boots. She might be accused of homicide, but of heightism, never. I took a deep breath, lifted my glass in a toast, and smiled.

If this didn't work, I was going to be profoundly humiliated and my best friend was going to spend the rest of her life in a dungeon. I sidled off my bar stool. "You must be Dunstan," I murmured.

I felt like a fool. Going on two A.M., running on adrenaline and anxiety and borrowing lines from a B movie. But that was all I could think of except for the infinitely tackier "Hi, stranger."

Dunstan didn't faint with joy at my approach, but neither did he hold up a cross and say *begone*. He waited for more data. I hadn't expected him to be this cautious. "Sasha wanted me to look you up," I said.

He moved his head to the left and looked at me from a side view, eyes narrowed, judgment suspended.

How bad of a date had they had? "Sasha Berg," I said. "You remember her, don't you?"

He laughed, showing teeth that did, indeed, rival Cary's. "You mean do I have short-term memory loss?" he asked. "Remember her after what, a few hours?" He waved me to a booth. "Join me," he said. "But what is this? Some sort of tag team? A relay?"

His accent was semi-Cary, like someone from a mid-Atlantic island, if only there were such a place. But unidentifiable didn't mean uncharming.

In his engaging voice he asked standard opening questions.

The how-long-are-you-down-for and where-are-you-from and what-do-you-do preliminaries.

Then I remembered that I was the one who was supposed to be doing the interviewing. "What about you?" I asked when there was a lull. "Your accent isn't quite English or American."

He laughed. "Doesn't it sound like Trueheart, Wisconsin?"

"Not really."

"Thought I'd pass for a native by now. We moved there when I was fairly young." He smiled with the ease of someone who takes it for granted that his audience is smitten.

And in truth, it wouldn't be difficult to be smit. There was something elegant, continental about him. I suddenly remembered a personals ad I'd seen. I window-shop that section. In case of emergencies. This particular ad promised "great looks and manors, too." I, of course, never found out whether the ad-placer had country mansions or simply bad spelling. But Dunstan had that "great looks and manors, too" attitude.

"I'm a Trueheart boy. 'Trueheart, Trueheart,' " he sang. " 'Through all our days, we who love you sing your praise.' Brilliant lyrics, don't you think?"

"Listen," I said. "I need your help. So does Sasha. Not in any big way, just by establishing that she was with you." I told the incredible story of her arrest, skipping the more tawdry details, such as her bloody slip. "Obviously, somebody's done a very good job of framing her, but they couldn't have known that she was with somebody, out in public. Probably other people saw you both, too. Waiters. The bartender on that shift. Other people in the restaurant. Sasha's kind of . . . she's generally noticeable."

"Murder?" He sounded stuck on that, horrified in a refined sort of way.

I nodded. "Isn't it awful? How about we take a cab to the station and you make your statement and clear this up now?"

He looked at me for a long while before speaking. His eyes were pale brown, almost caramel. For the first time, I noticed how little light there was in them. "I'm afraid you've misunderstood," he said. "I have nothing to tell the police. I barely know your friend." Each word was clipped with precision. Trueheart's English teachers must be great.

"But you were with her. You said so yourself, didn't you? Didn't you just say that to me? That's all I'm asking you to tell the police. You two had a date. You're her *alibi*."

"You misheard. I *saw* her. Right here, at some point in the evening. Briefly, and I can't say when. I remember her. That's all I was agreeing to."

Is that what he'd really said? Meant? Why? Unless Sasha was lying. All the deferred exhaustion flooded me. "You're saying you were not with her tonight?"

"Yes," he answered quite calmly. "That is precisely what I am saying."

"But that isn't true, and it would be *easy* to help her out."

He shrugged, and then he bolted. He stood and walked away double time, out of the bar, across a small open space, and into the casino.

He had left me—and the bill—without a backward glance. Once I realized he had gone AWOL, I leaped up and followed after him, but I couldn't see over the tops of the one-armed bandits. I searched each avenue peopled by solemn folk who pulled levers as if it were an obligation to be completed as quickly as possible. Even when their efforts were rewarded by a cascade of coins, they seemed only dimly interested.

I felt like a lost child. The heavy chandeliers and the gilded mirror ceiling that refracted and reflected the scene below further disoriented me. There was light everywhere, its source nowhere, and obscure music as well, a barely audible up-tempo like a subliminal racing pulse.

"Dunstan?" I called, even though I knew it was both futile and annoying. Everyone's eyes stayed glued on the machines. I ran toward where I thought I'd seen him. "Dunstan?" The craps players nodded, pointed, pushed chips across the table, watched with rapt attention as a woman threw the dice. Not a one of them reacted to my voice. I moved aside to make way for a cocktail waitress in a tiny gold-thread tutu. She handed a man a drink, and he plunked a tip of chips onto her tray.

"Dunstan," I said, no longer bothering to call it out. I just barely controlled the urge to have either a tantrum or a crying fit.

What the devil was going on?

Four

I WENT back to the bar, hoping for inspiration. It never arrived, but Mackenzie did. He looked as weary as I felt. He also looked grim as I told him my bad news and he told me his. Sasha was still being held. She'd be arraigned in the morning, if we were all lucky. And bail would be set if we were luckier still.

"They're reluctant to let a killer awaiting trial loose," he said.

"Sasha? A killer? That's the most ridiculous . . ." I shook my head. "She can't hold a grudge more than five minutes, particularly against a man. That's part of her problem. And this man—she didn't even know him."

I brushed away the memory of her hesitation on that point. "Can I see her?"

"Now? At nearly three A.M.?" He sighed and changed the topic. "I saw the witness. He was there, makin' his statement."

"Who is he?"

"Feeble old guy. Looks caved-in, curled up. But he can see pretty well with his glasses on. Came up to his room to take his pill at nine o'clock, he says. Waitin' for the elevator to go back down when he saw them at the door of the room. Thought some hanky-panky—that's what he called it—was goin' on. Somethin' kinky with one big woman and two men. I'm not sure if he wanted to be the morality Nazi—or the third man in the hanky-pank. Anyway, he ID'd a picture of Jesse Reese. That's who he saw. Then he ID'd Sasha in a lineup, too. Says the other guy had dark hair and was shorter than Sasha, but that's all he remembers. Unfortunately, it was 'the big woman'—actually, he said girl, the 'big girl with all the hair' who caught his eye."

"He probably didn't have his glasses on, or he was confused. Maybe he was watching an entirely different room. Did they think of that?"

"They tried to find other witnesses to corroborate his story. Woke up the couple in the next room. They knew nothing. Hearing aids were off. The woman on the other side was down at the tables all night."

"Or so she says. She picks up two guys and frames—"

He shook his head as if it were heavy. "She's maybe three hundred pounds and short. Not easily mistaken for Sasha or either of those men."

"Who? Who is—was—the dead man?"

"Jesse Reese."

"I know that part, but who *was* he?" I wanted to hear that he was scum and that the world was well rid of him.

"Your basic man-of-the-year type. Had a multimillion-dollar investment firm plus did a lot of teachin', 'specially for senior citizens. Courses in Financial Survival. No charge. His way of paying back society, he said. Called it his *pro bono* work. Safeguardin' little old ladies' purses."

I hated it. He sounded like the hero of a Frank Capra movie, which made the whole situation worse for Sasha. "What was he doing in a casino hotel?" I demanded, as if being in such a room—my room, in fact—constituted guilt.

Mackenzie raised one eyebrow. "He was dyin', although I suspect he had other hopes for the evenin'. He was a familiar face there, a regular. Generally given that very suite, in fact. Wasn't expected last night, however."

"So he's a gambler." I folded my hands. "The mob did it, then. I rest my case."

Mackenzie sighed. "It is really not their style to buy champagne first. Or to sprinkle undies around. This is—forgive me, but this verges on the baroque. It's overorganized crime, almost *cute*, an' that is not the mob's style. Assumin' there's a reason for them to be miffed with him in the first place."

"That's the only thing that makes sense."

"Mandy, I think you'll have to accept the idea that nothin' makes sense to you right now. An' worse, it may *never* make sense. But to the police, it makes sense already, and what makes sense to them is that Sasha killed him."

"Simply because somebody chose her hotel room to break into." *Our* hotel room, a solemn voice in me corrected. Ours. What if Mackenzie hadn't shown up? I had planned on room service, an evening of luxurious solo vacationing. Did the real killer know I was also checked in there? Care? Would I have been a second corpse?

Mackenzie tilted back on his chair. I think men feel compelled to balance chairs on their rear legs just so women can warn them that they'll topple over—and be proved wrong. What macho test is it, anyway? I managed not to say a word and almost to pay attention to what he was saying—although, of course, the whole time, I waited for him to fall over backward.

He had the ability to balance on two chair legs and read my mind at the same time. " 'Course," he said, "th'other most likely suspect would be you, darlin'. You are also tall—"

"Not as tall as—"

"—an' dark-haired."

"Sasha has black hair. Mine's brown, a lot of red and no curls."

"The thing is, you need not worry. You have the perfect alibi. Me. An officer of the law. Who could doubt me? Hope you're properly grateful." He brought his chair back to normal position. "Or, when the time is more appropriate, improperly grateful."

"Everything," I said, "is so obviously a setup. Every bit of what they think is evidence could have been planted and arranged—and in a matter of minutes. His business card in her slacks. The slip and the underwear. The champagne. I mean it adds up to *nothing* when you think about it."

"Had a reputation as a ladies' man. Married, but been there before with various and sundry."

"So he *was* a scumbag."

"What's your point? That it's okay to kill people who are morally deficient?" he asked mildly.

"No, but—"

"If we base character evaluations on whether or not somebody's sexually adventuresome, then your friend Sasha is likely to be put in the same cubbyhole as the late Mr. Reese. An' aside from that failure of the flesh, Jesse Reese was considered a paragon of virtue."

I snorted my disdain, something I wouldn't dream of doing at normal hours when I am more in control.

"A real Mr. Do-good," Mackenzie said.

"Well, I'm sorry. I just don't think somebody who is *infamous* for gambling and whoring around is Mr. Wonderful." Nonetheless, I felt a growing chill inside, something like having a prison bar slipped down my esophagus. Innocent though she was, Sasha was in deep and profound trouble.

"Okay," Mackenzie said, "let's look at a different issue." His tone was obnoxiously patient, almost pedantic. I didn't want reasoning or evidence—I wanted magical solutions. "Aside from havin' a witness *see* her enter, there's the question of how an imposter would get the key. There wasn't any break-in. It's real hard to duplicate those computerized cards, and it's not like the last tenant could pass it on, 'cause they change it every time."

I waved away that objection. "I heard that's not true, that they lie and reuse keys. Besides, I'm sure it's possible to get a duplicate."

"How? Go to the desk and say 'Hi, make me a room key'?"

"Don't be facetious. This is life and death."

"What would you say? 'I'm so busy holding this drugged man—' "

"Drugged? They think somebody drugged the dead man?"

He nodded. "Staggerin', the old man witness said. He didn't drink enough to be drunk." He looked at me and shook his head. "Nobody at the desk got a request for a duplicate."

"Maybe she lost her key, dropped it somewhere, and the killer found it."

"And knew the room number, right?" Mackenzie said. " 'Cause it's never on those keys."

"Well, maybe—"

"Sasha didn't lose her key, Mandy. She used it to let herself into the room, remember?"

I sat in silence, fiddling with the wedge of lime on my Virgin Mary. Was it possible that Sasha had become involved in somebody else's bad dream? That she *was* involved, and the second man, the accomplice, was one of her evening's two men? Dunstan, or even Frankie the good guy?

The red-haired bartender eyed me and my second-shift male companion either enviously or suspiciously.

Mackenzie ordered orange juice.

"This is very strange." My voice sounded hollow, foreign, as if coming in on a poorly engineered sound track. I had the dissociated sensation that this wasn't really happening. Soon, I'd wake up and chuckle over how *real* it had felt. "Every detail makes it stranger," I said. "And there are so many details."

I squeezed the lime over my ice cubes. "She wasn't there!" I bleated, lamely, because how was she going to prove that, or anything? Even I was beginning to find her denial boggy and suspect. I couldn't think my way past the bloody slip or the business card in her slacks, or the witness or the door key. The only possible route around that seemed with Dunstan, who, I hoped, wouldn't turn out to be part of the crime, the second man the witness saw. I stood up. "We have to find that lousy date of hers."

Mackenzie's expression was blank, as if he'd turned off his mind. "Not now, surely," he murmured. "I was plannin' on maybe a little rest. It's nearly tomorrow. My eyes feel corrugated."

"Aren't you the one who always says the first forty-eight hours are the most important?"

"Yes, but ... but ..."

I went over to the bartender. Business was slack, even here, at three-thirty Tuesday morning. The combo played "Sunrise, Sunset," in a whine of violins, but softly. "Hate to bother you again," I said, "but I need Dunstan's last name."

She put down a glass she'd been polishing and looked at me with open disgust. "Why?" she asked. "Your new one's cuter. And he's not a lounge lizard. In fact, I've never seen him in here before. Isn't it time to end the stereotype of women only wanting rats? The Dunstans of this world have had a free ride for too long!" She seemed on the verge of climbing onto the bar and declaiming.

"Halt," I said. "This has nothing to do with me. I agree with you completely, but I'm asking on behalf of a friend."

"Hah! The old *friend* business! You tell your *friend* that I don't want anything to do with Dunstan and neither should she!"

"Do you know his last name?"

"He's just Dunstan. Like Svengali. Or Zippy, in the comics."

"Do you know anybody who knows his last name?"

"He gave me his card. Slick piece of work, just like him. Looks like a camera. Clear plastic in the middle, for the lens. That's where his name and phone number were. But why give it to me, a bartender? Unless I was supposed to pimp for him—pass it along to likely conquests."

"Could I see it?" I knew the answer, but I had to ask anyway. The red spikes of hair looked lethal. "Think I'd keep it? Tossed it right out!"

I sighed. "Can you remember what it said?"

"I'm not procuring for an arrogant lounge lizard with an accent!" For emphasis, she pounded her fist on the copper-topped bar. "I'm not one of those traitors who swoons at the sound of the King's English. I don't care what Princess Di wears. I don't even think they should keep that parasitical royal family!"

"All I want is Dunstan's last name."

"I swear, if my daughter shows tendencies in this self-destructive direction, I will personally take her out and—"

Bartenders were supposed to be listeners, not impassioned orators. Another myth shattered, and I had so few of them left. "Please," I said. "I am not interested in Dunstan, except for his last name. Maybe even where he works. My friend is—"

She shook her head in irritation. "Take responsibility for your life! Stop playing games, hiding behind the cloak of a friend. If women would only own their own lives, if—"

What the hell? It was going to be all over the papers in two hours or so. "My friend's accused of murder."

Amazing what that word will do. "Murder?" she whispered.

"She's only accused," I said. "She didn't do it. She was with Dunstan at the time. I came to find him, to get him to go to the police. Only he heard the word 'murder' and ran away. I never found out his last name. My friend doesn't know it, either."

She wiped the bar top, vigorously. "So who is this Dunstan-loving murderous friend of yours, then?"

"Her name is Sasha Berg. She's a photographer. She doesn't love Dunstan at all and she isn't a murderer. And what I need is *his* name."

She tilted her head back, let her jaw drop and rolled her eyes up in a great show of concentration. Even the spikes of hair seemed to stand on tippytoe, the better to strain for memory. "Dunstan, Dunstan," she murmured. "Dunstan—something-wrong-for-him-last-name. Something wholesome. With an S . . . no, an F . . . F-R . . . Frrr . . . Fllll . . . Nothing's coming."

There were other ways, I reminded myself. Even if nothing pulled up from her data bank, I didn't have to despair. There'd been another bartender on duty earlier who might remember Sasha. There was the restaurant, with waiters, hostesses, and fellow diners. Together, they might be able to put together a good accounting of Sasha's time.

If, of course, anyone had been paying attention. If, of course, the tourists who ate in the restaurant tonight were staying over until such time as we found them or they read a notice in the paper about the crime. If, of course, they hadn't gone home, been too drunk to notice, been on some illicit assignation which they wouldn't want to discuss with the police. If, of course, there were enough of those lucky, available rare types who know what they saw at what hour so that together, we could piece together a patchwork accounting of Sasha's evening.

Which meant we were never going to find nonstop Sasha monitors. Even if every improbable witness contingency worked out, there was always the lapse, the unaccounted-for period while the observers got on with their own lives or simply went to the bathroom. Only Dunstan could establish that Sasha had been far from the murder scene for that long block of time.

The bartender was still making sounds, but more feebly. "Foooo . . . Hold on, it's getting close. I can almost hear it now. Fill . . . Fit . . . Fis . . ." She shook her head. "Hell, I give up."

"Keep going—her life is at stake."

"Faaa . . . Famm . . . Farr . . . Farmer!" She was so loud that Mackenzie popped up from his chair.

"I thought he was a photographer." Cary Grant tending New Jersey chickens and pigs?

"That's his name. Dunstan Farmer."

"And where does he live?"

"Someplace nearby, must be. He's here almost every night, after all. In the casino, then in here for finding women. Doesn't seem to have steady male pals. Or steady female pals, at that."

His skewed social life didn't bother me. I had his name now, and a light-headed giddy conviction that I'd find him and settle this—a hope that was so unfounded, it couldn't have happened

45

except at four A.M. to a woman worn down by a year of teaching, a dubious relationship, serious sleep deprivation, and a best friend accused of murder.

THE POLICE WOULDN'T let me have my clothing. Not even my toothbrush. "Crime scene. They're still working on it," the guard at the door said. And then he questioned me on my whereabouts at the time of the crime and brought in a buddy with the same questions all over again, just in a higher-pitched voice. They bullied me in the name of the law until Mackenzie intervened and I was freed.

But I still couldn't have my toothbrush. From now on, just in case of murder or other emergencies, I'd carry one with me at all times. But right now I couldn't understand why I couldn't have the one inside the suite. What need did the cops have of it or of my dental floss? In fact, what were they still doing there? They were supposed to come in, sprinkle, measure, photograph, dust, speculate, and leave. I knew from personal experience that it wasn't as if they cleaned up the messes they created. But these fellows had a real dog-in-the-manger attitude toward the suite, and particularly toward my innocent belongings.

I was pretty sure my insurance wasn't going to reimburse me for the toiletries, let alone for a wardrobe perk-me-up. This was, perhaps, how bag ladies got their start. All of a sudden, through one agency or another, their worldly goods were gone. It wouldn't matter for what rationale or in what way—a fire, a robbery, a murder in their bedroom. Lost is lost. Gone is gone.

I trudged back to the elevator in the same sweater, rumpled linen slacks, and mildly too-tight loafers that I'd put on, taken off, and put on again since the evening before. I felt dirty, exhausted, miserably unhappy, and a victim of police harassment.

The policeman I'd been leasing for a year yawned extravagantly as he punched the elevator's *down* button. "Told you so," he said. "*Told* you we shouldn't bother to come up here. Told you you wouldn't get your things back yet."

And as I stood there without a toothbrush or a bedroom of my own, with my best friend in jail for murder, my already pathetic vacation gone and my sanity definitely questionable—I looked sideways at C. K. Mackenzie and his I-told-you-so's and decided to skip the heavy-duty thinking I'd planned for this getaway. What was the point? He and I did not have a future. The end was near, the hands of the doomsday clock nanoseconds from midnight.

Told you so.

Five

NEXT morning, I was still suffused by a sense of doom, and putting on my shoes added to it. My best friend was in serious jeopardy, my semilove relationship felt like a wobbly tooth waiting to be yanked, and it was possible that I might wind up with nothing in the world except these shoes.

It was easier agonizing over stuff than over people. What if I never got my belongings back? No matter that I had clothing enough at home and at least enough funds to buy a new toothbrush.

Anything could happen. Anything did. You could be suddenly

48

and unfairly arrested. You could have your possessions impounded. You could have very few possessions to start with because you lived on a private school teacher's pathetic salary.

I knew the stats on women and poverty. I knew the odds. Mostly, I knew self-pity.

My dark mood was not helped by the fact that my butter-soft, elegantly cut loafers were too tight. They'd been on sale, reduced so drastically I refused to acknowledge their poor fit. Besides, I had been with Sasha, to whom the only sin was paying retail. She wasn't guilty of murder, but she was surely guilty of coercive encouragement to buy bargains.

To add to my misery, my freshly washed panty hose hadn't quite dried, so the shoes were pinching toes encased in damp nylon.

At some point the night before, my cream cotton sweater had acquired a bloodred Virgin Mary stain. I borrowed one of Mackenzie's summer sweaters, a maroon crew neck that was too large for me but had the advantage of being all one color. Besides, it hid some of my rumply slacks and made me feel vaguely like Doris Day borrowing Rock Hudson's oversized jammies in some schmaltzy old comedy. Maybe we really were a couple if I wore his clothing.

Mackenzie had treated me to a toothbrush at an all-night pharmacy. The hotel provided a hair blower. I did not yet look like one of the homeless, which provided some comfort.

I really missed my eyeliner, though. I felt naked, exposed, something like a cave creature forced into the light.

I'll say this, the *Atlantic City Press* is quick. I'd gone downstairs to buy a paper, and then I was sorry I had. Jesse Reese's untimely death was headlined in type just slightly smaller than might announce the end of life as we have known it.

It was obvious that Reese had been a respected somebody, and that Sasha was on her way to becoming a notorious somebody. FINANCIAL ADVISOR BLUDGEONED TO DEATH: WOMAN HELD. There was a great deal about the esteemed Mr. Reese, advisor and teacher, protector of what he'd called the "potentially dispossessed." There was mention of the first Mrs. R. and of the present wife, Poppy Summerfield Reese, a former Miss America contestant.

There was also an unfortunate overabundance of information about Sasha Berg. This included, much to my horror, mention that she had once been the companion of a reputed gangland figure, the late Peter "Dimples" Bosco, who had, by coincidence, also been murdered.

"Why don't they just hang her and be done with it?" I said. "Guilty by prior associations and insufficient sexual scruples, is that what they're implying? Why isn't anybody saying it's just a matter of unfortunate room assignment—somebody else's assignment, I might add. Who, in fact, arranged to have us in that room, anyway? Isn't it a tad suspicious?"

Mackenzie half nodded, a gesture that meant "I didn't hear a word you said, but I don't want you to be aware of that." He sat on the edge of the bed, thumbing through the phone directories in the night table.

I concentrated on the newspaper. I had to read almost the entire article before I spotted the name of my hotel. It was interesting how scrupulously its reputation was being protected compared with that of the innocent suspect, the former girlfriend of.

Jesse Reese had slightly receding light hair, gray or pale blond. He was a graciously aging clean-cut man complete with the requisite square jaw and earnest expression. He looked like he exercised and ate sensibly. It was a trust-me-with-your-money face, unfrivolous and well-meaning, perfect for an annual report or prospectus. I resented his features—as if he'd shopped for them deliberately, just to make things worse for Sasha. Then I wondered why I was so angry with a dead stranger, why I was having trouble remembering that he was the victim.

And why did he look somewhat familiar? "Do you know this man?" I asked Mackenzie, hoping for a lead. He put his finger on a column to hold his place in a phone book, peered at the photo, and shook his head before returning to his odd reading.

"You think it's a common face, and that's why I feel as if I've seen it before?" I asked.

He continued to read off names, but shook his head. "Not so common. Head's almost square. Mouth pulls a little to one side. Eyebrows are heavy. Big earlobes."

Now that he mentioned it . . . "I finally know what they mean by trained observer," I said.

He turned his trained eyes in my direction and observed me like a pro. I awaited his pronouncement, hoping it wasn't of the nose-slightly-off-center sort. I wanted muzzy generalizations along the lines of *dazzling*.

"No Dunstan Farmer listed in any of the nearby towns." He leaned over and picked up the phone receiver, punched a few numbers and asked for new listings in each of the small surrounding towns, oblivious to having just shattered another romantic delusion.

Dunstan Farmer was neither a new or old listing anywhere.

"Maybe his phone's under the name of his company, whatever that is. Photo-Quik, Dunstan Farmer, Prop., or what have you."

"I looked. His name isn't visibly attached to any of them." Mackenzie drummed his fingers on the night table. "We'll have to interest the police in findin' him. See if they have somethin' on him, maybe. I have a gut feelin' about the man. Bet he won't be easy to find, and I bet he isn't at that bar tonight. Or tomorrow, or ever again, for that matter."

I didn't accept the bet. The odds were all on Mackenzie's side.

THE ARRAIGNMENT FELT like something out of Kafka. We sat in a small but intimidating courtroom. Sasha, up in front of a dark wood barrier, looked as stained as the mahogany, like a sepia print of herself, a browned-out reproduction of what had formerly been living color. I waved at her, smiled, but she looked too frightened to respond.

The judge listened impassively to a full account of the violence of the crime and its damning circumstances. I wished I knew more about the mechanics of raising bail. Did you have to put something up as collateral? Were there good and bad bail bondsmen? Was there some expertise we lacked that would lead to further complications? Did Mackenzie know about this side of it, or did his interest flag after he'd caught someone? What *did* those trained eyes see when he looked at me?

My reveries came to a sharp end. So did a lot of hope. The judge did not grant bail. Sasha would stay behind bars. She was a real and present menace to society.

I couldn't believe it and neither could the lawyer. "I protest, Your Honor!" he said. "This woman has no prior record, and is innocent of this crime as well."

"File a motion," the judge mumbled.

The lawyer nodded curtly.

They apparently were comfy with the pas de deux of law, the dance of power, but meanwhile, Sasha, wide-eyed with fear, was taken back to jail. I thought I had seen this movie already on the late show, starring Susan Hayward. They were going to fry my friend for a crime she never committed, and worse, everyone was behaving as if this were proof positive that the system worked.

I WAS ALLOWED to see the real and present menace to society— but only after Mackenzie had a series of good-old-boy consultations with his peers on the Atlantic City force, and only for five minutes, they warned me.

It was like watching somebody emotionally drown. Sasha would bob up to the surface, her old, buoyant self, then be pulled under, over and over again. I reassured her that all would be well, but her IQ wasn't sinking, only her spirits, so I stopped making nice or treating her like a child and cut to the chase. We had problems.

"The old man saw somebody who looks like you, or who was pretending to be you," I said. "Somebody who knew how to set you up—somebody who knew you had that room. Who?"

She shrugged. She was being dragged under the waves again. "Didn't find Dunstan, did you?" she asked in a lifeless voice.

"No. You remember anything more about him that might help?"

"Not much, except one stupid thing that probably doesn't mean anything. The night I met him, three weeks ago, before I'd really even spoken to him much, a person—a very drunk Brit—came up and called him Edgar."

"Called Dunstan Edgar?"

She nodded. "Insisted he was Edgar, and in fact, was somebody named Jeannie's husband, too, from some little town in Yorkshire. Said how glad he was that Edgar wasn't dead after all. Always thought Edgar was too good a sailor to fall overboard, like they said. And he really did seem pleased, as if he'd found a long-lost friend. I thought it was funny, everybody did. One of those drunk things that you have to be there for. Except Dunstan just got more and more annoyed, and finally said something like, 'Whoever Edgar is—or was—he's still dead, so get lost.' The Brit finally said he was sorry and backed off. That was all there was to it, completely forgettable, except that Dunstan was unduly pissed for a long while after. I mean, people are always mistaking me for somebody they knew back in high school. That's all it was. Not much, I guess, except maybe to show he has a temper or a poor sense of humor and tolerance. And other than that, all I know about the man is that he drinks vodka, knows how to do the two-step, is an only child and allergic to shrimp."

Okay, then we'd drop back five yards and try again. "About the room," I prompted. "Who knew what room you were in?"

She sighed. "I appreciate your efforts, Mandy, but really, who cares? The police think the case is closed. They aren't interested. Won't do a thing."

"I care. I'll do something. Mackenzie, too. So who knew what room you were in?"

"Frankie," she said in a dull voice. "He's the one who got it for us. Well, really for me. He thought I was alone."

"The bartender?" Was he, then, the second man the witness had seen? I tried to remember whether Frankie was shorter than Sasha, then realized she'd been seated last evening, and he'd been behind the bar. I'd have to check it out myself.

She smiled with a hint of the real Sasha's personality. "Frankie always had the hots for me, way back to Dimples, can you blame him? He knew the suite was vacant, and a guy at the front desk owed him a favor, so he—wait a minute!" She sat up straighter. "Last night, at the bar. He made some kind of joke about the room. Anybody could have heard, at least anybody nearby."

Finally. The field had opened, the possibilities of a setup had become real. "Who was there? What was said? Think. Whatever you remember might help."

She took a deep breath and ticked items off on her fingers. "First of all, this guy in a pin-striped suit. Gray hair, nice-enough looking, must be a high roller because he was usually comped the suite we were in. That's what Frankie's joke was about, that I was in the guy's room, and did anybody object. He made it sound like I was in there with the guy, of course."

"Did anybody object?" I wanted her to say that yes, indeed, somebody had leaped up—his furious six-foot-tall wife with curly black hair and her short but loyal man friend—and had publicly vowed to destroy both Sasha and the man in the suit. I wasn't asking for much, just a clear, speedy, and unambiguous finale to all of this.

But Sasha shook her head. "The suit made some really stupid joke back about what a thrill it was to share it with me, how much I had improved its decor. You know the riff. Very stale stuff."

I tried to think quickly, to get something to hold on to before the matron's stopwatch reached home. "Backtrack, then. Who else was there besides Frankie and the suit?"

"Who knows? A bunch of people. An Indian couple—Hindus. She was in a green and gold sari, and he had eyes to die for."

"Control the libido until you're free again, okay?"

"They were amazing eyes, Mandy. And another great-looking man. I thought he was Harry Belafonte at first. He went off with some girl in a black straw picture hat, like nobody except maybe Princess Di wears when she's off to a garden party. Looked great, though." She squinted her eyes. "I'm going to get a hat like that if—when—I get out of this mess."

"Good, that gives you some motivation."

She rolled her eyes. "And there was a young guy—soft, flabby fellow with acne. Wearing a bowling shirt and a baseball hat. He was with a pregnant girl with straw-colored hair in a ponytail. She had to be his wife, and that was about it, except for a couple of other women."

"What about those women?" Sasha had a genetic eye affliction that made her blind to humans with double-X chromosomes. She didn't fully perceive members of her own sex. Sometimes she noticed their accessories, but seldom their personalities, features, words, or actions. "Think hard. What do you remember?"

She tilted her head. "Okay. There was a flashy one who looked bolted together."

"Like Frankenstein?"

"Not her head. Her clothing. Brads down the side of the slacks and the sleeves. Gold chains, gold rings."

"Gold hair?"

"No, dark. And big. You know the type, all teased up and out. And a loud voice that sounded like it had rivets in it, too."

"Age? Looks?"

Sasha shrugged. "Thirty-something, probably? And okay looks, except for the metalworks."

"And that's it? Nobody else? You said *a couple* of women."

"Oh . . ." she said. She shook her head. "No, okay—there was a drab one in there, too. That's what I remember about her. Drabness."

"Come on, Sasha. That's not at all helpful."

She shrugged. "What's to notice about drabness?"

"How old? How big? No rivets?"

The matron cleared her throat. I interpreted the sound as a warning bell and leaned forward, literally pressing for information.

"Not so young," Sasha said. "Not a kid and not ancient, you know? But she had a great bag."

"Her *pocketbook*?"

"Uh-huh. Blue and purple leather."

"For God's sake, Sasha, isn't there anything more relevant?"

"I noticed because I've been eyeing one like it forever. It's Italian and way too expensive and they never mark it down, not anywhere."

"Okay, then, forget her. Nobody would confuse you with a drab woman, anyway. Can you remember anything or anybody else?"

She shook her head just as the matron tapped her watch with great, pursed-lipped solemnity. I stood up and gave up. "I'll be back tomorrow. Is there anything you need?"

"I need to believe I'll be out of here before tomorrow," Sasha said. "My cousin Herb the lawyer's coming down this afternoon. We aren't telling my parents until we have to, okay?"

I nodded. Her parents were far away, one in Canada and one in Arizona at last check. Maybe, just maybe, they'd never have to know.

Sasha suddenly looked panic-stricken. "Oh, God—it's Tuesday, isn't it?"

I nodded. What was wrong with her?

"What time is it?"

"A little after nine."

"My *shoot*! It's supposed to be now! I hired an assistant and a stylist down here, and the assistant rented everything and she's probably *there*. You have to call her, lie, make up some reason I'm delayed. A day, tell them. Say I'll be in tomorrow and . . ." She lowered her eyelids and shook her head. "I'll pay them for the lost time." She sighed. "There go any profits."

She told me how and where to call, and I agreed.

"Tell them I can't be reached," she said. I agreed to that, too. But I had great reservations, because I suspected that to fill the waiting time, the assistant might have already looked at the front page of the newspaper and figured out what was delaying Sasha.

When I finally did call the assistant, I told her that Sasha had been called away. That part seemed true, although *hauled away* would have been more accurate. I said she'd be gone three days, to give Sasha and the legal system some slack.

And that was that for the jailhouse visit, except that as she was being escorted away, Sasha half turned. "I forgot. The woman in the sari?" she said. "She had on sandals and a gold toe ring. Is that the kind of thing you want?"

If ever an accessory committed a crime, Sasha would be a perfect witness.

I RELAYED the bits and pieces Sasha had offered up to Mackenzie, then told him I wanted to go back to the casino. I wanted my earthly possessions back and that room of my own that Virginia Woolf said all women needed. She had also mentioned a small annuity, which wouldn't be bad, but I doubted that the hotel would provide it.

The situation was stupid, perverse. What was I doing in a lavish Atlantic City hotel now that Sasha was bedding down in a cell? But how could I leave town while she was imprisoned—or afford to stay, once the saltwater taffy people noticed that their photographer was missing in action?

"No problem," Mackenzie said in his off-in-space voice. "Gonna find me that Farmer boy, meantime. It's too easy for them to think she made him up."

"How?" I asked. "Can the police find the addresses of unlisted phones?"

He raised one eyebrow.

"Forgive me for questioning your powers. And thanks," I added grudgingly. "This is really decent of you."

He grinned, quite pleased with himself. "This whole business is an elaborate ruse to get your attention. I had a fear it was wanin' back in the city, so I set all of this up."

I put my arm on his sleeve. The feel of worn-soft broadcloth over worked-hard muscle was tempting. There were better ways to spend the day than what faced both of us, much better ways to perk up the waning attention. Although, of course, I had come here to decide whether or not perking was advisable, and just about decided last night that it was not. "C.K.," I said before I thought it through, "we really do have to talk."

His exhales contained an entire vocabulary that could have been translated into comic book cursing—little stars and question marks and exclamation points whooshing out of him. His accent became acute. Verbal farina. "Ah trust you're referrin' to

57

a need for conversation 'bout Sasha and the business at hand," I thought he said. "Your friend's in deep trouble."

I glared. Obviously my eyes did not speak the volumes that his exhalations did, or he would have been horrified. Instead, he went on figuring out what Sasha needed to get herself out of this mess. I couldn't fault him for that—she was my friend and that was generous of him, particularly since he'd never approved of her.

I faulted him anyway.

THE HOTEL MANAGEMENT WAS not glad to see me. Somehow, they blamed me for what had happened in the suite. Who was I, anyway? Ms. Berg's reservation had been made by her employer. Why was I there? Why did I exist? What was the meaning of life?

If they gave me—the person who shouldn't have been there in the first place—a room, did I honestly think the saltwater people would pay for it?

"Listen," I reminded them, "I've been grossly inconvenienced—and possibly endangered. What if I had been in that room? What kind of security do you have here that lets strangers break into somebody's room?"

They huffed and they puffed. They took every precaution, they insisted. Not their fault, certainly. Never happened before. Spotless reputation.

What were my alternatives? Moving in with Mackenzie, even short-term, didn't seem like a great idea when what I most needed was space and time away from him.

Home sounded lovely, but dangerously disloyal to Sasha. After all, I could have easily been the one to come back to the room first. I could have been the one in jail. Or another one dead.

I finally handed over my credit card as collateral for their least expensive room. If management didn't relent, or Sasha didn't return to snap photos and get a free room, I would check out tomorrow and commute from the city to Sasha's rescue.

I tried not to remember that this was supposed to be my vacation. While the officious desk clerk grappled with finding me a lousy room, I tapped my too-tight loafers, readying myself for the next battle, the repossession of my wardrobe.

"Well, young sweetie! Look, it's Sherwin's granddaughter."

Tommy and Lala seemed characters out of another, more comic, life. "Hi," I said. "But weren't you supposed to go back on that bus yesterday?"

"Well, if you recall, when you left us, we were having a drink and talking about Sherwin," Tommy said. "One thing led to another, I guess, and we never did make our bus."

Lala tittered. There was no other word for the sound that came from between her clenched lips. She batted her heavily mascaraed eyelashes at Tommy, her tormentor, her sexual harasser.

Tommy, dressed in his white shoes and seersucker, shorter than I remembered, bowed at me and grinned. "Tell Granddad that it's too bad, but he lost out. Sweet Lala has honored me by promising to become my life companion." He enunciated with great solemnity.

"His *wife*." Lala eyed me intensely. "I'm marrying Tommy." Did I get it? His sexual advances were going to be legitimized and therefore no longer offensive or unwelcome. She held out her hand on which glimmered a knuckle-sized diamond ring. "Bought it on the boardwalk last night, the impetuous man!" she simpered. "This big softie had a big win, and spent it all on me!" She winked at me.

"Told you my luck was changing," Tommy said.

It would serve her right if the headlight on her ring finger turned out to be as fake as Tommy's organized crime stories or his imaginary rival, Sherwin. This betrothed couple should skip the blood test and have a premarital lie detector test instead.

"Grandpa's heart will be broken," I murmured.

"What a day," Tommy said. "Good news and bad. You heard, didn't you?"

"About you? No, actually, not until you just said."

"No, no. I mean the other news. Jesse Reese. It's all over the papers."

"Oh. Yes, I . . . I heard."

"Remember who told you first," Tommy said.

I must have shown my confusion.

"In the lounge," he said. "I told you he was in deep trouble with you-know-who. Only I was wrong on one point, I admit. I thought he had three days to live. I was two off the mark."

Yesterday. In the bar. That man Tommy had used as one of his stories? I remembered a man in a suit—*the* man in the suit? The one that Sasha had mentioned? It had to be the same person; he was the only man in a business suit I'd seen in the hotel. That must be why the photo in the paper had looked vaguely familiar. Jesse Reese had been in the bar last night. Jesse Reese had been the man who'd joked about what was normally "his" suite. I took a deep breath and exhaled loudly.

I was disproportionately relieved, the doubts and nagging questions I'd had about Sasha now gone. Sasha had not known Jesse Reese, had no prior relationship—but she'd been honest enough to acknowledge a sense that she'd met him, had known him in some way.

And then I was disproportionately upset. What had happened in the bar after I left? Had Sasha really gone out with Dunstan? I remembered Jesse Reese tilting toward her, my sense that low-level flirting was under way.

Had Sasha perhaps switched from Dunstan to Jesse, in which case anything was possible? Had she gone back to the bar to make plans with Frankie—or with Jesse Reese? I hated thinking in these terms, but it would be foolish not to consider the possibility.

The desk clerk rang a bell—as if I had luggage.

"You and Granddad will come to the wedding," Tommy said.

"If he can bear the heartache of the loss," I said. With Sasha in jail and Mackenzie in limbo, it was good to have an imaginary friend as company for the ride upstairs. Just me, Granddad Sherwin, the dead Jesse, and a hundred million questions.

Six

Y new digs were neither gilded nor sophisticated. They were grudgingly designed in serviceable style for those who worried about money and weren't likely to be real gamblers. A no-frills room. No hair dryer or complimentary bathrobe. A small clock-radio, and no premium channels or in-house movies on the TV. In their place, a VCR—bolted down—and a notice that nearby video rental stores would be glad to deliver one's tape of choice.

I pulled the bedspread off one pillow, just to make a personal statement. Otherwise, I had nothing to unpack, nothing to mark the place mine, and no sense of what to do next.

I had detoured to the scene of the crime en route to this room. The men hanging around the place were unaware of how crucial, how central, a woman's makeup is to her mental health. They insisted on continuing to hoard every bit of it, including my hairbrush. Either they were doing make-overs on one another or they were as sluggish and inept as I suspected.

Or maybe they'd cut an overnight deal for yet another instant crime-of-the-week movie and were already using the room as a set. I wondered who was playing Sasha. Cher had the right spirit, but was too short. Sigourney Weaver was the right size, but insufficiently wacky. . . .

There had to be something more profitable to do with my time than casting the film of my friend's worst moments. I thought about Dunstan—or was it Edgar—and I checked the clock. It was early morning in Trueheart, Wisconsin, and most public schools, unlike their private cousins, were still in session.

After several conversations with robots who knew phone numbers, I reached an actual human being, who identified herself, rather merrily, as "School office, Jean speaking."

I was immediately suspicious. Not only did she not sound computerized, she also did not sound angry, grudging, or particularly wary. My experience with the guardians of attendance records and supply cabinets had not prepared me for civility. Maybe it was true what they said about the Midwest's friendliness.

The unexpected cordiality made me stumble and stammer. "This is—I'm— This is so embarrassing!" I squealed. "I'm with Photos R Us here in New York. We're a clearinghouse, you know, and—"

"*Just one moment!* With whom am I speaking?" So much for geographical differences. All school secretaries are sisters under the skin. They don't burn out the way teachers do; they calcify.

"My name?" I decided to tell the truth. "Mandy Pep—" But why tell the truth about that when I was lying about the rest of the call? "—salt." I never claimed to have much imagination.

"Mandy Pepsalt?"

"Right. So this man sent us photographs of Trueheart. Absolutely *brilliant*, and we want to hire him and use them for syndication, you know? Except—this is the humiliating part. Someone who shall remain nameless spilled her coffee all over the cover page, and the man had written in ink, and his address just floated off in a mess of coffee. We are *beside* ourselves here."

"I'm quite busy, Miss Pepsalt, and I can't really follow why you're calling me from New York."

"Because he's one of your graduates. Grew up out there. His pictures are a photo essay called 'Hometown,' and I'm hoping against hope that you keep up-to-date alumni records and that you'll know how we can contact him. Unfortunately, I can't tell you what year he graduated because the, ah—"

"*Coffee?*" Her tone was disdainful. She would never spill her coffee on an important document. She would never ingest anything spillable around an important document.

Dunstan had looked in his forties. "I think I see a six in that blur," I said. "So he graduated mid- to late sixties, I suspect. I must assure you this has never, *ever* happened before. I don't want you thinking we are anything less than meticulous in our care for our clients' portfolios."

"Miss Pepsalt! This is a small high school. I'm the entire clerical staff. If students contact me, fine. If they come in and visit me, fine. But this isn't like a college that has a regular alumni news. If you knew his exact year—"

"Oh, if I had only taken proper precautions with my coffee! There! Now you know who the clumsy culprit is. Can't you help me?"

"—and if that class had a reunion lately, the chairman of the event might have traced the man. That's who does that kind of thing, calling parents and last known addresses and asking other people for information. I certainly can't. I'm too busy with the current crop of students to bother with somebody who was here a quarter of a century ago!"

Now she sounded like a school secretary. It simply took longer to get up to speed in the Midwest.

"I know the ones who come say hello," she said, "bring in their children and, a few times now, their grandchildren. But the others, no, so if that's all you—"

"It sounds as if you've been there awhile. Perhaps you'd remember this man."

"Only if he was exceptional. Good or bad. If I had to order engraved awards or trophies for him—or put him on the detention roster a lot of times. Otherwise, the hairdos change, the music gets worse, but all the same, they blur, Miss Pepsalt."

"Does the name Dunstan Farmer strike a chord?"

She gasped. The chord had been struck. Would it be trophies or detentions she recalled?

"So you do remember him? The boy who moved there from England when he was young?"

"Is this a prank call? Because I don't find it funny at all."

"I'm sorry. I don't understand."

"Of course I remember Dunstan Farmer. Everybody in these parts would. We knew his parents, too, since they were born. They didn't move here from any foreign country. They've lived here forever, for generations, except for when the family moved South and the tragedy happened. Atlanta, or Mobile—one of those places. They came back after. And stayed." She sighed, twice. "Broke the town's heart, how bad we felt for them."

"How . . . what happened?" I whispered.

"Broke his neck in one of those freak accidents during a practice scrimmage down in Atlanta—or Mobile. I never can remember. He was a junior in high school. He was a good young man and it was a hard loss when he died. Family never got over it, either. Whoever you met, whoever sent you those photographs, was most certainly not our Dunstan Farmer."

When I hung up, I was dizzy, light-headed. The man who'd borrowed the identity of a dead teenager could be anybody—Edgar from Yorkshire, that married man who'd made himself seem dead. Or he could be a murderer. And where did Sasha fit into all this?

I felt as if I were in that Poe story where the walls contract and crush their inhabitant. Something dreadful had happened and was continuing to happen, and I wanted desperately to do something about it, but I had no idea what that something could be. In lieu of action, I accepted motion.

I left my room and walked down the hall toward the elevator bank, pondering the past twenty-four hours spent in the Twilight Zone. Nothing whatsoever made sense, yet it had all happened, starting with the mysterious motives, methods, and identities of the people who'd used Sasha's and my room as their killing ground. And how the devil had they gotten in?

And then I stopped in my tracks. At the other side of the elevator bay, a chambermaid's cart piled high with towels and cleaning apparatus propped open a door. The most ordinary of hotel sights—but now it looked like one of the puzzle pieces.

I tested my hypothesis by rushing through the open door. "Oh!" I said to the startled woman making up the bed. "I'm interrupting, sorry! I had wanted to use my bathroom, take a shower, but I'll come back later."

"No, no. Is fine." She waved me toward the bathroom. "Has clean towels already."

I went into the bathroom, closed the door, ran the taps and flushed. I went back into the room, sat down, picked up a book on the desk, flipped through it, then smiled at the chambermaid, who was nearly finished. "I'll come back later," I said. "No problem. Thanks for making the room look so great."

And that was how it could be done. Nobody had needed a key to our room. Chambermaids couldn't be expected to know the ever-changing guest faces. So anyone could enter, look as if she belonged, and wait out the maid. And then later, after propping the door to make sure it didn't lock, reenter along with an accomplice and a future victim.

And the entry technique was possible twice every day. The same open-door policy held in the evenings, when towels were replaced and bedspreads removed. Sasha had mentioned that throughout the carnage, my bed had remained pristine, turned down, a chocolate on its pillow.

A good thing to know if I ever wanted to murder or even simply ambush somebody. A bad thing to know if I ever again wanted to feel entirely comfortable or safe when entering a hotel room.

It was only after I was downstairs and out on the boardwalk

that I inventoried what I'd seen at the site of my room experiment. A pair of men's shoes near the bed. A technothriller as leisure reading. A man's leather toiletry kit in the bathroom. Not a sign of a female inhabitant. I tried to imagine what the chambermaid had made of my intrusion.

I walked briskly past a woman standing by her storefront fortune-telling parlor under a sign reading KNOW THE FUTURE. I might have been tempted—the future was certainly something for which I needed a clue—but she was talking on a cellular phone. It seemed to me that people with extra powers should not need to rely on Ma Bell in order to find something out. I walked on.

I paused at the wide-open front of a raucous arcade. I could see a Skee-ball game that I remembered from years past, although that was the only manual, nonelectronic game in sight, almost a fossil. The aisles were packed with loud machines. A talking tic-tac-toe was nearest to me. This, then, was casino prep school, or the really poor man's casino, where a quarter would buy a chance. More likely, this was where the people who had my room and a losing streak came to get rid of their spare change.

I wandered inside and saw that if you took chance after chance and won, you were eligible for the world's sorriest collection of prizes. A life-sized moose head made of polyester plush. Almost life-sized plastic figures of the Brady Bunch. Garishly painted plaster carousel horses.

I was on my way out when I saw a machine that promised to tell my romantic future. It wasn't quite as valuable as finding out who the real killer was, but neither could I pass it by.

I put in my four quarters and punched in my name and birthdate. And was almost immediately stymied, because next I had to enter Mackenzie's name. Feeling vaguely ashamed, I pushed a C and a K. Let the machine figure out how to pronounce it.

After a lot of whirring and flashing, a computer printout emerged. I took it onto the sunny boardwalk and read it en route. It wasn't a real mood lifter. *You're a dreamy-eyed idealist,* it said under ROMANCE. *You become enslaved by negative situations.*

Mackenzie, on the other hand, seemed straightforward and to be envied. *It's sheer romance,* it said. *You love love.*

What did a machine know, anyway? *You love school, or the learning process in general,* it said for me. Okay, so it guessed well now and then. *You are a workhorse,* it said of Mackenzie. *You can drive souls past their point of sanity.* I cut to the quick and looked at our overall compatibility. It appeared that I needed distance, while Mackenzie needed partnership. Ridiculous.

I tossed the printout in the next wastepaper basket I passed and focused on my fellow board-strollers, but that didn't provide relief. The look of the place had certainly changed since its glory days. My mother sometimes reminisces about the times she paraded her new spring suits and hats on the boards. Today, white gloves and a flowered bonnet—except on the stunning woman Sasha had seen with the almost–Harry Belafonte—would be hooted off the place, and an elegant suit would be a shocker.

When my mother talks about long-ago stays at the shore, the place sounds regal. Hail Britannia and all that. Her hotels had names like Marlborough, Blenheim, and Claridge. Now, in the cause of progress, or all-Americanism, it was de-anglicized. Bally, Caesar's, and Trump this and that. A potpourri of nowhere.

But that train of thought chugged into the station called Dunstan, the de-anglicized man. The thought of Dunstan still made me nervous, and nerves made me hungry. Besides, it was close to lunchtime, and breakfast had been a shared bagel en route to the arraignment.

However, the boardwalk had never been an epicurean haven, and now it was a junk-food smorgasbord. Peanuts, saltwater taffy, pizza, hamburgers, assorted candies, and my secret favorite, a garlicky hot dog dipped in cornmeal batter and fried—just in case its innate fat content wasn't sufficiently astronomical.

I zipped over to the yellow and green stand. "A lemonade and a . . . a Dip Stick," I said in the voice of a spy passing on information.

"Miss Pepper!"

A Philly Prep student. Eric Stotsle. He of the amazing Adam's apple. He'd been in my homeroom, but not my class yet, and had seemed one of those ordinary people with a mildly annoying tic—his was an unblinking stare—who never receive attention until they take down an entire village from its bell tower. "He was a good kid," neighbors and classmates tell the press. "Never would have suspected this. Stared a lot, sure, but otherwise . . ."

You just didn't notice Eric Stotsle, except for that bobbing apparatus in his throat. But Eric Stotsle noticed you.

I looked plaintively heavenward, but saw, instead of a compassionate deity, the inflated Dip Stix lemon. I therefore asked a plastic citrus fruit whether this, too, was necessary. I already had a murder and a jailed friend. Did I also need to be observed by a Philly Prep student? The lemon did not choose to answer. Never ask a sign for a sign.

"What are *you* doing here?" Eric stood, mouth slightly open, a lemonade cup in his hand.

"You mean at a Dip Stix stand?" Wasn't a teacher allowed to clog her veins?

"I mean in Atlantic City!"

Ah, yes. He, too, had the common student delusion that when school wasn't in sessions, teachers were deflated and stored in trunks along with the basketballs. "Vacationing." I took the lemonade out of his hand. "And you? Aren't you a little young to have this kind of job?"

"Look, I—don't say anything, all right? It's legal. Really."

He had fudged some form somewhere, I was sure. But given that the purpose was to get himself an honest job, not to deal crack or run guns, who was I to squawk?

It was Eric who squawked, actually. "Hey," he said, flicking his wrist dismissively. "Get lost. Do I have to tell you again?"

"Excuse me?"

"Not you, Miss Pepper!" Various portions of his face flushed. He looked down and to his side. "You, out! I'm gonna get in trouble! You can't stay here."

"I could pour lemonade," the voice said. "Put in ice."

"You can't even reach the spout. Besides, you're too young to work." Eric heard his own words and looked at me guiltily, then back down again. *Really illegal* for you to work, understand, man?"

A door in the counter swung open and a small child—I estimated five or six—walked out. Like Eric, he wore a baseball cap backward and attempted a serious swagger as he made his way to a three-legged stool, high enough to give him difficulty perching on it. "Then do you have like leftovers?"

Urchin was the only word for him, with all its Dickensian overtones. "Are you lost?" I asked softly.

He stared at me as if I were one of the deinstitutionalized his mother had warned him about, then seemed to decide I wasn't dangerous. "I know where I am," he said.

"Your mom waiting for you?"

He shrugged.

I turned and tried to see if I could spot his mother, but I couldn't find a woman watching the boardwalk stand.

"You sure you don't have food?" the little boy asked Eric. "Something that didn't come out looking too good?"

"Ask your mother for money, like I told you," Eric said.

"I can't," the boy said. "I'm not allowed in."

Barred from his home? What was going on here? It was lunchtime, and the child was hungry. "Here." I handed him the sizzling hot dog Eric had given me. A cardiologist of the future would thank me for this. I ordered a second one, so my future cardiologist could also pay his mortgage. "What's your name?"

He took an enormous bite and answered unintelligibly, muffled by corn-battered hot dog.

"Lucky," Eric translated. "That's his name, he says. You really shouldn't encourage him."

Encourage him to do what? Eat? "Let me take you home to your mom," I said. That was a definite action I could perform. It wouldn't help Sasha's mess or my pending romantic incompatibility, but I'd be doing *something*.

Lucky shook his head and chewed away. "Plin." He sounded like somebody talking through flannel.

Eric translated. "She's playing. He's not allowed."

He wasn't making sense. I imagined Lucky's mother turning a jump rope, covering her eyes for hide and seek, tossing a ball.

"Have to be twenty-one," Eric said, "to get in."

"She's in the casino?"

The little boy nodded and finished off his hot dog. "I'm dyin' of thirst," he said.

I wondered how long he'd been on his own while his mother gambled. I wondered if she'd understand if I tracked her down and gave her whatever piece of my mind I could spare. I wondered if she'd remember her kid if I reported her to Family Services.

Oh, God, but I didn't want to have further doings with the police just now. I handed Lucky a lemonade.

"She said she'd only be a while," Lucky said.

"He was here last night, too," Eric said. "I made him go back inside the casino. It was like *dark*."

The hot dog smelled delicious, but suddenly my stomach didn't feel up to it. I offered it to the boy, but he declared himself full, so I held it like a small pennant. "Come on, Lucky." It felt indescribably sad calling him that, and even sadder that he was so willing to go with me, to trust me, to be taken care of. "Let's find your mom."

I wished I had never come to this city.

Seven

"HEY!" It was the homeless woman who lived under
the boardwalk. Georgette. She raised her fingers in
an almost military salute. "Who you got there?"
She lounged on a bench by the stairs that led to the beach, her
thin hair ruffling in the breeze. She wore a knee-length denim
skirt with a ragged hemline over a long plaid skirt that touched
the tops of her orange socks. A small and rumpled stack of
newspapers was next to her, but she wasn't reading them. I was
glad of that, because the topmost page featured the portrait of
Jesse Reese.

There was no escaping the murder. There was no trying not to think about it.

Georgette was reading a thick paperback that looked bloated, as if it had done time in a tub.

"This is Lucky," I said. The little boy stared at her gravely.

"Yours?"

"Borrowing him for a while." I could see the faded but still legible title of her book. *War and Peace.* Her thumb held her place far into its depths. She followed the track of my eyes. "Saw this goin' out to sea one day."

So that's what other people did with their overly ambitious biodegradable summer reading lists.

"Nearly done now," she said. "It's good, except those Russians have so many names it hurts the eyes. So hello, Lucky. Makes sense I'd meet you today. This is a lucky one for me, all right." She leaned closer to the little boy. "I've been at war, but now I'm at peace," she said in a stage whisper. "Get it?"

Lucky shook his head.

"Don't have to." She flashed her gap-toothed smile. Then almost immediately, her expression darkened. "I had my own kid, once." She looked up at the clear blue sky, blinking hard.

I watched her mood dip and wobble and was reminded of Sasha earlier today. I knew what had hit Sasha and sent her reeling, and I hoped it was short-term, and that she'd regain her equilibrium soon. I wondered what had slammed into Georgette with such hurricane force that it had permanently destabilized her emotions.

She regained composure and sniffed deeply. "Good air here, ozone, they call it. Nice people, too." She nodded in the direction of the hotels. "The chambermaids over there, they let me wash up in the rooms. Before they make it over for the next people. Who does it hurt? Nobody did that for me anywhere else. Better money than Philly, too. People are on vacation, in good moods, they share."

Speaking of which. "Want this?" I asked. She accepted the hot dog for which I still had no appetite.

I retrieved Lucky from using the boardwalk railing as a tightrope. "Dangerous," I said softly.

"'Ahhh . . ." He sneered at my old lady timidity and shook me away with five-year-old daredevil disgust.

"Worked after Kurt was gone," Georgette said when she'd finished eating. "But then we were robbed." Her voice had no emotion. "And I got sick. Since then, money thinks I'm dead."

I needed to know how a woman who read *War and Peace* had come to this.

"Sister . . . my sister, she . . ." Georgette twisted the denim skirt fabric with both hands. Lucky fidgeted, darted forward then back, nearly tripping half a dozen slow walkers. I looked across the boardwalk at a store that said PEANUTS on a hand-lettered sign. I missed their fresh-roasted smell along with Mr. Peanut, a seven foot legume who used to nod and greet strollers, but he'd fallen victim to newer advertising concepts, or to his flashier kin at Disneyland. A sophisticate like Lucky might have sneered, anyway.

"Over there, you see the store that sells peanuts? Here, look, I'll show you." I lifted Lucky and my lower back twinged, or perhaps that is too mild a word. What I felt was more like the muscular equivalent of a warning gong. I put Lucky down, took a deep breath, convinced myself that my back no longer hurt as much, pulled out my wallet and gave him a bill. "Buy nuts for the pigeons." I wondered if his mother had ever ventured out into the fresh air and shared such a moment with him. "And come right back." He scampered off, again heedless of approaching pedestrians or rolling chairs. I sat down next to Georgette, so that I could watch Lucky's whereabouts. Near to her, the salt air took on a hint of recently ingested alcohol.

Georgette snuffled. "My sister should have lived." She nodded, almost rhythmically, as if the motion were also a part of her fixed story.

I nodded, too. Why not? Meanwhile, my mind had become a multiplex theater. On one screen, I monitored Lucky. On the next, Georgette told her fragmented tale. And in the main theater, Sasha's saga endlessly replayed, word by word, except when interrupted by short features about Dunstan and Jesse Reese.

"If she'd lived, this would be her lucky day, too."

"Why is that?" I murmured. "Because it's so beautiful?" I tried to calculate exactly how long it would take a peanut seller to notice and serve a small boy whose head was counter height, exactly how long before I checked up on him.

"What does weather have to do with it? Today is lucky because our enemy perished!"

"Good." Lucky reemerged with a small paper bag. A dollar was at least worth peanuts. Center screen I once again watched the scene with Sasha in the bar last night. It seemed central, pivotal, but I couldn't yet see it clearly enough.

Georgette sighed. It was a contented sound. "I wrote President Reagan about it, and he listened. Took time, but look." She picked up the stack of newspapers to make room for Lucky. He gave each of us a nut.

I replayed the scene in my head again, and suddenly saw the other eyes that were watching. Frankie. The bartender. I really had to talk to him.

Georgette snapped apart her shell. "Look what that President Reagan did for me—even when he's retired." She tossed the peanuts to a nearby bird. Within seconds his extended flock received an extrasensory nut alert. Lucky giggled and tossed peanuts to a chorus of ruffled grabbing sounds.

"You see?" Georgette's hands didn't seem to belong to her. They were gnarled and arthritic, the hands of a very old woman. One slightly twisted index finger pointed at the uppermost newspaper, the one featuring the recently perished Jesse Reese. Her ragged nail tapped his nose. "You see?"

I could see the dead man's photograph and her finger, but not her point. Because, of course, even disregarding the theory that the ex-President had executed Jesse Reese on Georgette's behalf, the woman was missing a few connector wires and had been drinking. The picture must be serving as a generic enemy. I could even understand it if she considered the entire world her enemy.

In any case, her need to share her story seemed abruptly over. We fed pigeons in silence, and when the bag was empty, I gave Georgette a few dollars and made my way into the hotel to find Lucky's mother and talk to the bartender.

Two real things to do. I was on a streak.

"WHERE WERE YOU supposed to wait?" I asked Lucky.

"On the stairs." He pointed to the carpeted flight that led to a balcony lounge. "But it's boring, except when you slide down the rail."

The brass rail was periodically ornamented with spiky protuberances, and at one point it rose a good thirty feet above the lobby.

I expected to find a terrified woman racing up and down the staircase, calling his name, or perhaps the police, or the hotel staff or a posse engaged in an all-points search. But no one was looking for him.

Of course, he wasn't allowed inside the casino. If he were, there would, presumably, have been no problem in the first place. I wasn't eager to leave him unattended again. I corralled a security guard. "Is there any way to page somebody in there?" I asked.

"Well . . ." He looked reluctant to tell me, then he noticed my companion. "Hey, Lucky boy," he said. "Found yourself a friend, did you?" He winked at me. He was in his sixties, with florid good looks, a snow-white crew cut, and a trustworthy, experienced sense about him. "Hope you won't take this as an insult, ma'am, because it's meant as a compliment—he always finds attractive friends."

"Always? His mother has left him before?"

"It's not my habit to keep tabs on them," he said. "But she's a not unfamiliar face."

"But—he's just a baby!"

"I am not!" Lucky insisted. "I'm five and a half!"

"I didn't mean it that way," I said. "He was out on the boardwalk, panhandling. That's neglect. That's abuse!"

"It's just that nobody likes to report them—"

"Them? Who? Lucky and his mother?"

He shook his head. "Them," he said very gently. "The ones who leave the kids. His mother, she's at least here mostly in the daytime. It's the ones left all night long, tired and hungry, that are the real problem. Or the little ones still in their carriages. They're left out here for hours, with all that goes on in this world." He shook his head wearily. "I try to keep an eye on our own casino kids, but it's not right."

Casino kids. There was even a term for it. I was furious.

"Just between us, we need child care here," the guard said. "They have health clubs for the grown-ups, so why not a place to park kids?" He waved away his words. "Ah, but they say there's no problem, so they aren't likely to fix it, now, are they?"

I was itching to fix it single-handedly, to create the episode that made them admit there was a problem, to haul Lucky's mother out of the casino by her follicles and make her an example for all the fools who gambled their children's welfare along with their money.

The guard read my face. "Listen," he said in his soothing voice. "I'll find her, and I'll keep an eye on Lucky meantime. You've been a good Samaritan, but he's safe now, and if it's all the same, I'm nearing retirement and I'd like the management to stay fond of me, know what I mean? She intends no harm, you have to understand."

I climbed off my high steed and became a mere mortal again. I pictured the boy's mother, probably very young, already semidefeated, raising him without help, coming here when possible for entertainment, escape from her routine, hoping to make a quick killing, to be a winner, to find the round of luck that could make a difference. Look what she called her baby boy. "You'll try to make her understand what could happen to him?" I asked.

He nodded. "I've got five grandkids myself," he said softly. "I'll give it my best. And I'll explain about having to report it next time, except that might make her switch casinos, not habits."

I hugged Lucky, suggested that next time he bring along books and crayons and something electronic for entertainment. Maybe if he made enough little-boy mess and noise, and I made some very real grown-up noise, our combined impact would stun the management into noticing that they had both children and a problem on their hands.

I checked the desk for messages, but Mackenzie had obviously not yet located Dunstan Farmer, a situation I found both frustrating and oddly satisfying. I left a message as to my whereabouts and set off for Frankie.

There were very few patrons in the bar. My back hurt and my head was dizzy with competing problems. I wanted wine along with information, but I hadn't eaten all day and was afraid of making alcohol my midday meal. I sat down at the curved teak bar and ordered a glass of mineral water. "I'm Amanda Pepper," I said, to jog his memory.

"Hey, no problem." I found that response distinctly confusing. "I'm permitted to serve alcohol to strangers," he added. Obviously, I had not made much of an impression on him.

He didn't ask for my ID, either. I have not, alas, been carded in the past three years, since two days after my twenty-eighth birthday, not that I'm counting.

"I'm Sasha Berg's friend. I met you last night."

He sucked in his breath and nodded. "Big mess, all right," he said. "I can't believe it, just can't believe it. You're the roomie, okay. But where were you? I mean when it . . . it happened in your room."

"Out. On a date. All night." I felt a recidivist flash of embarrassed fear, as if Frankie might phone my mother. "Mandy didn't come home *all night*," he'd tattle.

He did some more deep breathing. "You know, she came in here yesterday to say hello when you were checking in, and I thought maybe I'd impress her. Always had a soft spot for Sasha. So I called on a favor and got her that suite. Didn't know you were along, by the way. Then Reese shows up dead in that very room. Some way to impress a girl, right? She was going to meet me here when my shift ended. Finally going to get the girl, like in a movie, only my luck . . ." He shook his head and sighed.

"Do you remember what time she came in here last night?"

He shrugged. "Tenish? I dunno. I been stuck with two shifts, covering for a sick pal, like today again, and it gets blurry." He was tall, with wide shoulders, around Sasha's height, but quite slender. He didn't fit the witness's description of a small man—unless the man was referring to girth, not height, but even so, and despite his candid style, I couldn't bring myself to trust him completely. Frankie was still in the best position to have set Sasha up.

"If we can get her out, maybe you can still get the girl," I said.

"You know her date? This Dunstan Farmer?"

"Never heard of him."

"How about Jesse Reese?"

Frankie shrugged. He was probably a good and classic bartender, best at responding quietly to others' stories, but not too good at telling his own. This was the time for the other night's—impossible to believe it was only last night's—aggressive and verbal bartender, but life doesn't work out that way. "Knew him like I'd know you if you came here on a regular basis and talked a little."

"Is—Was—he a drinker?"

Frankie shook his head. "Not particularly, although last night he seemed tanked by the time he left. Probably would have flagged him if he'd asked for more. Started celebrating somewhere else, I guess."

Not tanked. Drugged, Mackenzie had said. Very possibly and logically in here. By Frankie? Was his wide-eyed speculation all an act? "What time was that?" I asked, inwardly begging him not to say *with Sasha* or *when Sasha left*.

Frankie shook his head again. "Like I say, it blurs, but it wasn't till . . . he stayed awhile. He wasn't gambling last night, just stopping by."

Odd. The paper said he lived in Haddonfield, almost all the way back to Philly. Why would a gambler come down here, if not to play?

"Maybe he left around the same time that Sasha left for her date," Frankie finally said. "Or a little after? I can't remember."

One more unanswered prayer. Or maybe Frankie was trying to frame Sasha. I surely wasn't suddenly accepting Sasha's judgment as to whether a man was or wasn't someone to have faith in. "Do you know if he's in debt?" I asked. "In trouble?"

Frankie laughed. "You mean was like the Godfather after him?" He laughed again. "The man was clean. Gambled a lot, but he had the money. Always paid up. I got the feeling he'd never mess with his image, you know? They called him Professor Money. He taught in the junior colleges and retirement centers and he was even going to have his own show on TV."

"What do you mean?"

Frankie put his finger up, signaling me to wait while he poured a draft for a young man whose belly testified to a precocious and continuing affection for the brew. And then he was back. "An infomercial. He'd be selling his business, but it'd look like a seminar on investing. A first seminar—there were also going to be tapes to buy. He's—He *was*—pretty good at what he did, I hear. And successful. Costs a lot to produce those things, don't you think, and it came from his own pockets. And he was ready to roll. Already taped the whole first show."

"I wish I could see it."

"Won't air now," Frankie said. "Besides, it'd be boring. Or maybe that's just my point of view. Financial management is not my strong point." He laughed softly, a little bitterly.

"But it'd give me a handle on the man."

Frankie shrugged. "Like I said, the man was doing fine. Only trouble he was likely to get into would be with his wife, because half the time he's up in that suite with somebody else. As a matter of fact, his wife used to be one of those somebody else's, and she can't forget how she got her current position, so she's always looking over her shoulder to see who's gaining on her, especially since the accident."

I must have looked puzzled, because he offered further explanation. "Car crash a year or so after they married. Something doesn't work in one of her hips anymore. Uses a cane and has to drive a special car. Damn shame. She was a gymnast when she ran for Miss America." He wiped at the counter. "But the thing is, this one time, he was here on business, he said. No hanky-pank. Not even gambling."

The good news was that there was a perpetually jealous wife as suspect. The bad news was that she was lame.

"And she didn't seem angry last night, anyway. She smiled at some dumb joke I made about Sasha sleeping in Jesse's room."

"She was here?"

Frankie nodded.

"What's she look like?" I asked.

He shrugged. "You know," he said. This, then, was the definition of a not-trained observer. "Nice-looking."

Which one had been Mrs. Jesse Reese? Not the sari, not the pregnant ponytail, so if I remembered correctly, that didn't leave a wide field, and as she'd once been a pageant contestant, she wasn't the drab one, I'd bet. "Does she wear a lot of metal on her clothing?"

His eyebrows rose. "So you've seen her. Sure. Mrs. R. designs the stuff. Once, she's sitting in here and I comment on the brass trim, and she says, 'Frankie, this is not trim. This is a fashion statement.' "

Good. The wife, the often deceived wife, had been here last night and had known who was occupying the suite. And she had big, teased dark hair, Sasha had said. "She's tall, isn't she?" I asked, allowing myself a flare of hope.

Frankie shook his head. "You're thinking of somebody else, then, maybe. Mrs. R.'s an itty-bitty one."

A small, lame woman. We were back to zero. "Who else was here?" I asked. "Who else heard the joke about the suite?"

"Anybody who was around, I guess." Frankie worked at an imaginary stain on the bar top and I drummed my fingers. Finally, he looked up with an expression that suggested that he was tired of the conversation and of me. "There were people all over the place. I don't pay much notice. They're faces and orders."

People were haircuts and bad music to the secretary in Wisconsin, faces and orders to Frankie. I couldn't decide whether I'd stumbled on a great unifying truth or a trivial sadness.

"Was anybody else here, aside from his wife, who knew Jesse Reese?"

"How'd I know something like that?" Frankie asked, with some justification. "He had his briefcase. I guess he was doing business down here, so whoever that was with might have been around."

"Do you have any idea with whom?" Why did I ask?

He shook his head.

"Do you remember anybody else? How about a woman in a sari?"

"Probably. There often is, even though they're not drinkers, you know."

"Somebody pregnant with a ponytail?"

Frankie shrugged. "Why would I remember? And what are you trying to say? That somebody who heard my joke about the room framed Sasha?" He sounded nervous, overly incredulous, like a bad actor. "That doesn't make any sense." He wasn't doing a convincing job of making the idea preposterous.

Neither of us mentioned that there was one person who didn't have to overhear a thing in order to know about the room because he'd arranged for the switch.

"Who'd have done such a thing?" Frankie asked.

"Somebody who wanted to get away with murder, that's who." I left him a generous tip, to stay on his good side.

Eight

I CHECKED the desk. Half an hour ago Mackenzie had called in a message that he'd be back "soon." Exactly how long from now constituted soon? An advanced degree in semantics would come in handy around that man.

Explication would also be helpful with Frankie the bartender. I mentally poked through everything he'd said, and came up with precious little. The papers had already made clear Reese's solid financial status and prestige, but they hadn't mentioned the angry wife. Or the pending TV show—could it be relevant? Or the business he had in Atlantic City. What had it been?

The paper had said that Jesse Reese's office was in Cherry

Hill, New Jersey, about an hour away, just across the bridge from Philly. What better place than a man's home away from home to dig for information about appointments, angry wives, and pending TV shows? I knew I was throwing out a net over nothingness, but maybe something would come up. Something that would get Sasha out of prison before sundown.

I wished I were wearing more businesslike garb than Mackenzie's oversized maroon sweater over linen slacks which were even more intensely wrinkled after the hour-long drive to Cherry Hill. And my convertible-whipped hair was the most rumpled of all. I smoothed myself down, futilely, and hoped my creased aura made me look authentically a member of the working press. Whether I could behave like one was another question. I had only old movies and the six o'clock news upon which to base my performance, but I felt in need of an alias here. I didn't want anybody associated with Jesse Reese to know that I was associated with his accused murderer.

I was surprised by the modesty of the investment counselor's offices. I always thought the handling of money required vaulting spaces and the hush of expensive carpeting, but Jesse Reese's reception area looked a lot like a dentist's waiting room. Three chairs covered in a blurred orange and brown stripe sat on colorless flat carpeting across from a desk occupied by a middle-aged woman in taupe hair and suit. A small name plaque said NORMA EVANS.

"Yes?" She stood up. She was about my size, but managed to make me feel unequal, intimidated. "Can I help you?"

"Hildy Johnson here," I said, hand outstretched. Would she recognize the reporter in *His Girl Friday*? It was the only journalistic name my mind summoned. "Hilda," I added. "Glad to meet you, Ms. Evans."

She looked at my hand as if it were a puzzling offering. "What is it you want, Ms. Johnson?" She sat back down, but did not invite me to do the same.

"Well, a good interview, of course. Or did you mean that metaphysically?"

83

She blinked, her mouth set in a tight, straight line. "I'm afraid I don't do interviews."

"I meant Mr. Reese. I'm his three-thirty appointment." I looked down at her desk, pointing my index finger, pretending to be aiming for a date book, pretending to believe that Hildy Johnson would be written on it.

Miss Evans, who, after all, had just lost an employer and probably a job, looked at my pointed finger as if it were a gun, and seemed ready to call the cops. "If this is a joke," she said, her bottom lip just this side of a tremble, "it's in poor taste."

It was in poor taste, and I knew it, but Sasha's being in jail was in worse taste. "A *joke*?" I said. "I sent him tear sheets and my résumé, and drove all the way from McKeesport. I specialize in geriatric issues, for *Modern Maturity* and *Senior* and oh, geez, you wouldn't believe how many publications there are for our older citizens. I'm calling my story 'More Gold for Your Golden Years,' and I have an editor really excited about it."

She looked so unhappy and uncomfortable, I felt like the predatory press, the people who jam microphones into the faces of the newly bereaved and demand to know whether they are really, really upset or not.

Norma Evans seemed unable to compose herself. She aligned the edges of papers, tapping them this way and that, her full attention on the job. As soon as they were uncovered, I tried to read the top one, a list of names or words and numbers, but it was upside down and she kept the papers in motion. Finally, she lifted the stack and slid it somewhere out of sight, and only then did she look up at me. She cleared her throat. "I'm sorry, Miss— Jackson, was it? I'm not quite myself today."

"Um . . ." Was it Jackson? What was it? "Johnson!" I finally said, rather too urgently.

"Johnson, yes. I've been with Mr. Reese for seventeen years." She paused, closed her eyes and took a deep breath. "He always praised my command of details. I never forgot things. I took care of every aspect of his personal and professional life and work, and certainly of his calendar, and I don't remember any . . . But in any case, there's been a tragedy, you see. Mr. Reese . . ." This time she groped for a handkerchief, but her suit skirt had no pockets. I pushed the box of tissues that was on the side of her desk in front of her, and she nodded, took one and dabbed at the corners of her eyes. "Mr. Reese died last night," she whispered.

"*Died?*" I sat down in the chair next to her desk. "Ohmigod! That's *horrible*. I didn't even know he was sick. It must have been so *sudden*."

"It was."

"Heart attacks are scary," I whispered. "I did an article on ten warning signs that your heart might—"

She sniffed loudly and put the tissue to her nose, shaking her head all the while. "It's worse than that. He was murdered. Killed by a young woman, a, um, brand-new acquaintance. Such a good man." She glanced at me. "But human. That little . . . weakness for women. Still, it's terrible. Terrible. I'm sorry about your story," Norma Evans said, "but of course, as you can see . . ."

"I'm sorry for you. You seem to have been quite fond of Mr. Reese."

"Seventeen years," she murmured. "Longer than either of his marriages, he always said. You know they call a man's secretary his office wife, don't you? Not, of course, to imply that we had anything except a professional relationship, but when you take care of every detail of a man's life for all those years . . ."

"Then who—what should I—what's to become of all this—are you running the office now?"

"The office is closing. Is already closed."

"You mean for the day?"

"I mean forever. Without Mr. Reese . . ." She shook her head. "If he still had a partner, maybe, but on his own, who's to replace him? But I'm sure you can find another counselor to interview."

"But Mr. Reese's focus on senior citizens was the whole point, and how many financial advisors specialize in that? Especially to the kind of small investors he cared about. Could you recommend somebody else?" It was hard to whine, seem sympathetic, and simultaneously snoop. "That former partner you just mentioned, maybe?"

"Ray Palford?" She looked doubtful, troubled. "I wouldn't bother. I don't even know if he still handles the elderly. As you said, not many people are interested in the ordinary retiree, the modest portfolio. Mr. Reese was a rarity. Besides, Ray Palford moved his office all the way down to Margate. I don't think it would be worth your while." She waved off the suggestion, but I definitely did not. Margate was a hop, a jitney ride, or a brisk boardwalk trot away from my hotel. What a happy geographic relocation.

Margate was also a close enough home base from which to zip down and murder someone in Atlantic City. "Was the partnership dissolved recently?" I asked. "Because maybe Mr. Palford would remember—"

"Three years ago."

Not exactly the kind of new and painful rupture that could lead to murder. I was disappointed. The image of a tall ex-partner in a wig had a lot of appeal.

"I'm sorry I can't be more helpful."

"Looks like I'm back at Go," I said. "Could I bother you for my tear sheets?"

She was going to have neck problems if she didn't stop punctuating her sentences with head shakes. "I'm sorry, but I don't understand what sheets you're talking about. I'm sure I would have noticed if something of yours came in, and we wouldn't have torn it, anyway. Now if you'll excuse me, as you can see, I'm packing things up and there's so much to do. . . ."

I wanted to see the inner office, to get to know Jesse Reese by his artifacts, if through no other way. "Tear sheets are pages from magazines with my stories on them," I said. "I know it's crass to ask for them when you have so many more important things on your mind, but I don't really have all that many—I sent him originals, not copies, and if I have to start all over again . . ."

"There are no magazine pages in the office. I would have noticed."

"There must be! He *thanked* me for them. *Complimented* me on them—and said he'd return them."

She had a sturdy middle-aged body, but the suit enclosing it behaved as if there was nothing inside it at all. There wasn't a wrinkle anywhere, not even at the lap or inner arms. Some other time I'd love to ask her the secret of her imperviousness. "Please," I said, really into my role as professional pest, "maybe you're not recognizing them. *Senior's* on newsprint. It doesn't look like a magazine." My parents always picked it up at the deli. It was a free paper.

Miss Evans raked her fingers through her gray-brown hair. "If I let you peek in his office, do you promise not to touch anything? We have to get things ready for the estate and the clients."

"We? Are there other employees here?"

"A figure of speech. I'm so used to referring to us as . . ." This produced another round of head-shaking and nose-blowing.

"Normally, I wouldn't intrude," I said, "but free-lancing's so hard, and a good set of tear sheets is pretty valuable."

The phone rang just as she touched the doorknob to his office. "The machine will pick up," she said. "The message says everything anybody needs to know. I wouldn't get a single thing done if I answered every call. Besides, I can hear the caller, in case of an emergency."

I was glad I hadn't phoned ahead. I would have been told that the office was closed, which was the message I now heard beginning, in Norma Evans's patient but tired-sounding voice. She didn't say what had happened, but you could tell by her melancholy timbre that something dire had occurred.

Jesse Reese's office was a larger, slightly more opulent space. Still, there was something slick and surface about it, a sense that the woods were veneers, the velvet sofa a rental item, the liquors in the cabinet inferior brands poured into expensive bottles.

It was obvious that most of Reese's business must have been carried on elsewhere, at those junior colleges and retirement homes Frankie had mentioned, with elderly people reluctant to travel.

There were few personal touches, although some things had

either already been put in cartons or were never unpacked. Two boxes, flaps open, sat near the bookcase. The books on the shelves looked fake, or chosen for their binding colors, the furnishings safe and predictable. The only individualized items hung on the wall behind his desk; a plaque from the Chamber of Commerce, a framed photograph of Mr. Reese and a hearty-looking man, and a soft-edged portrait of a woman, painted, apparently, by a brush full of marzipan. "His wife?" I murmured. "Yes."

The portrait must have been commissioned in Mrs. Reese's pregrommet phase. She was wearing something translucent and dreamy.

Half Norma Evans's attention was still in the outer office, listening to a droning male voice on the answering machine. I could make out his inflection—questioning—but not the words.

"Poor Mrs. Reese. She must be devastated," I murmured. Jesse Reese's desk was bare except for a clock and a narrow dish in which lay a pen, so I looked back at the wall, at the photograph of Reese in this very room, at this very desk below a wall that then held only the saccharine portrait of his wife. He was half out of his chair, en route to a handshake, one hand extended, the other flat on the desk, giving him balance. His little finger touched a photograph of a woman in a swimsuit and high heels. Miss Wannabe America. A smiling man who looked like a gone-to-seed athlete offered up the Cherry Hill Citizen of the Year plaque that now hung on the wall next to this picture.

Those tear sheets in which I had come almost to believe were, not surprisingly, nowhere to be found. "I don't know what I'm going to do," I said in my Hildy whine.

She shook her head. "Sorry. I can't imagine what became of them."

"Did his wife take her photograph?" I asked. "The one on the desk in this photo?"

Miss Evans looked startled, checking me, then the desk, then the photo on the wall, then me again. "No," she said. Miss Evans wasn't in a mood to chatter.

The phone rang again, and again was followed by the patient, tired sounds of Norma Evans explaining the changed status of the office. It was a very changed status and a very long message.

"Maybe my tear sheets are inside one of the cabinets," I suggested.

"I'm sorry, but those cabinets are false fronts," she said in her near whisper. "They contain stereo equipment and a TV. There are no tear sheets here, Miss Johnson."

In the outer office a querulous voice spoke—shouted, actually. *"Norma,"* it said, "don't give *me* that crap about being closed. I know you're there, so . . ."

The voice sounded mixed in a cement truck.

Norma Evans bolted and raced from the office, diving for her desk. She got to the receiver with amazing, middle-age-defying speed. For a second longer I heard the voice utter expletives, but then Miss Evans pressed a button and the sound stopped. "I'm *here,*" she said. "Somebody was—is—in the office and I'm *busy.*"

I couldn't hear anything more, except for excited squawks from the caller. I crossed the room and looked into those two cartons.

Videotapes. Prerecorded. "An Afternoon with Jesse Reese," it was. "Seminars on Savings." My pocketbook was too small, but I shoved a tape under the baggy excess of Mackenzie's sweater, my heart racing. Then, taking a deep breath, I went out to the reception area where Norma Evans was still on the phone. As I walked in, I faced the back of the woman's desk, and I saw that the papers she'd been straightening so obsessively had been shoved, corners helter-skelter, into a large violet and navy bag, not into a desk drawer. Norma Evans, receiver still to her ear, followed the arc of my eyes and looked ashamed. I'd caught her being less than efficient. Downright slovenly, in fact.

When she hung up, I thought it was time for Hildy Johnson to be concerned about something besides her own prematurely terminated story. "The people who had accounts with Mr. Reese, what happens to them?" I asked.

"But surely," she said, "since you won't be interviewing—"

"I was thinking that if we're protecting financial futures, we have to know what happens when your financial counselor dies." Well, actually, it wasn't John Q. Public as much as I who needed to know if there was any percentage in killing off your financial advisor. "Is it possible to get a list of his customers? Or do you call them clients?"

"I'm sorry," she said once again. "That's privileged information, not something I could share with you. But I can assure you that Mr. Reese's clients are being duly notified." She took a moment to compose herself. "It will be up to each of them to determine how and with whom to manage their funds from now on."

"Given"—I gestured at the unoccupied office—"what's happened, I'm thinking of a whole different spin for the article. 'The Death of Professor Money.' That's what they called him, wasn't it?"

"That sounds ghoulish," she whispered, her hands to her chest.

I agreed, but there were still things I wanted to know. How did real journalists ferret out information, aside from those who arrived with big bucks as bribes? "It wouldn't be," I assured her. "I promise you that. It would be . . . moving. A *tribute* to him. You said . . . it . . . happened in Atlantic City. Was he there to see a client? Maybe that's my angle."

She looked startled again. She had a very small repertoire of visible emotions—timidity, unsettledness, shock, sorriness.

"Oh, maybe you're worried about that . . . that woman. I wouldn't mention any of that in print. I promise. That's just between the two of us."

"And the entire world. There will be a trial, of course, and it's already in all the papers."

"I meant, was he on business before then? Could I interview his last client? Follow her through what she does now, something like that?"

She shook her head. "The fact is, I don't know who his appointment was with last night." She looked as if that failure burned inside her with an angry flame. "It wasn't on his calendar. Just the way you weren't."

"So, then, you can't help me?" I forgot myself—Hildy Johnson forgot herself—and gesticulated, thereby almost dislodging the pilfered tape. I gasped and clutched my side, holding the tape in place.

Miss Evans blanched. Her eyes widened. A tiny spot of rust appeared on each cheek. She shook her head. "Are you all right?" she asked.

I nodded. "Just . . . disappointed," I stammered.

I knew what was coming next.

"I'm sorry," she said.

Me, too.

I GOT into the car a bit shakily. It must take a while to get used to stealing, lying about who you are, and preying on and pestering the newly bereaved. I was really tired, and the recent tension had upped my back pain a few notches.

I thought longingly of my house, my bathtub, my bed, and my cat, but I didn't feel brave enough to visit the last of these love objects, Macavity.

Leaving home without Macavity is more dangerous than without an American Express card because of the unique attention he receives at Old Mrs. Russell's Cat Camp.

Nancy Russell, a lovely dealer in tribal jewelry, is my friend and neighbor who lives, when not shopping in obscure slivers of the world, with her mother, who is deaf, dictatorial, and convinced that most people and all "strange" animals are verminous disease carriers. Except for Macavity, who's been granted special exemption from disgustingness. When I leave town, he goes to Old Mrs. Russell's Cat Camp, where he does not exactly pine for me.

Old Mrs. Russell poaches him fresh salmon and bluefish fillets. She lights a fire on even the muggiest days and has a special Macavity pillow that she places in front of the flames. She tells him stories of delectable mice and exotic alleys, and makes sure that a dozen new catnip-laden play toys are on hand per visit. She provides a constant on-demand lap and petting hand and a special litter pan that's got a little house built around it.

And then, to my and her daughter's amazement, one day Old

Mrs. Russell produced—proudly—her secret weapon, a vibrator with which she massages old Macavity's stomach. "A nonsexual massage, you understand," she said in her prim and haughty voice as I stood gape-mouthed. "But quite satisfying, as you can see."

Neither I nor her daughter dared cross the haughtiness barrier to ask where and how the elderly woman had procured her instrument of delight.

But the bottom line is that a cat's loyalty—make that *my* cat's loyalty—is not the stuff of heroic ballads. Cats are pragmatists, not romantics. They know a good thing when they find it, and are not big on altruism. Macavity doesn't speculate about whether he can go home again—he just knows he doesn't want to.

So if I did visit, he'd ignore me, hoping I'd go away, and I wasn't sure I could handle the additional stress right now.

I mentally wished my kitty a gloriously hedonistic holiday, looked up at the sky, which had turned thick, ominous, and lifeless, and reluctantly put the convertible top up, pointed the car east, and heard the first smack of rain as I pulled away. A summer storm without a summer. Or perhaps the half day of blue skies this morning had been it. I hoped I had enjoyed it sufficiently.

Nine

SOON obviously didn't mean quite this soon, even though nearly three hours had passed since I first read Mackenzie's message. Well, it was commuter time now, so I gave him further slack on getting back from wherever he'd gone in his search for Dunstan.

I wanted to believe he was taking his time because in the interim he'd found, arrested, and booked Dunstan Farmer.

I pushed Jesse Reese's tape into the VCR and looked for the *play* button. And then I laughed out loud. All alone, laughing at nothing like a crazy person, but all the same it struck me as nearly hysterial that here I was, on the world's most pathetic vacation, doing exactly what I had left home to avoid: sitting alone, watching a tape, and waiting for Mackenzie.

The musical introduction to Jesse Reese's seminar sounded prefab, as if someone had pushed the soothingly-nondescript-background-tune button on a computer.

But the man himself was definitely not nondescript. Properly lit and photographed, he was better-looking than his portrait in the paper had suggested. His voice was deep, soothing and convincing. A man to be trusted with your life's earnings.

After a short introduction the screen was filled with a shifting montage of senior citizens enjoying what he called, in his voice-over, the dividend years. There were golfers and sailors and mall-walkers and grandchildren-cuddlers and travelers and gardeners and ballroom dancers and hammock swingers. The images almost made me want to fast-forward the next thirty or forty years of my life and get to this plane of pure pleasure.

Then Reese's voice faded and we heard from the seniors themselves. "My whole life I dreamed of getting a college degree, and at age seventy-six, I . . ." "I always loved dollhouses, and now, with the time to collect and design them, I . . ."

I, of course, was Jesse Reese's nightmare. A pension plan that wouldn't kick in for years, and then only feebly. No savings. No safety net. Where would I be when I was their ages? On a soup line along with Frankie the bartender and other merry souls who thought financial planning was a boring topic? In a rocker at the Indigent Old Teachers' Home? Or—worst of all, the nightmare—under the boardwalk along with Georgette?

Jesse Reese infomercialized me into slavish attention. How could I save myself before it was too late?

He sat, elegantly tailored, in a living room that had an edge of forced fakery, like a homey talk-show set. Two women and a man faced him, smiling nervously. One of the women looked like Norma Evans might if she invested in makeup and time.

Everybody's awkwardness was endearing. They were marvelous actors who imitated nervous amateurs brilliantly.

"I've been a homemaker all my life," a blond marshmallow

puff said. "When my husband died, I realized I didn't know the first thing about how to take care of myself financially."

"My investment goals are pretty simple," the man said. "I want to be able to stay independent. Don't want to rely on the kids or anybody else, ever. Don't want anybody's handouts, but I don't have enough money to interest one of those professional money managers, so what do I do?"

"I've worked all my life," the second woman said. I squinted at her. She was handsome, in a large-boned, strong way. Clearly defined, and not all muzzy, the way Norma Evans had been. Her eyes were lined and lashes mascaraed, her lips were a bright crimson, her cheeks rosy. I was certain, almost, that she was, indeed, Jesse Reese's secretary, testifying for her boss, being the serious ant contrast to the chubby blond homemaker's grasshopper. "I couldn't save much until recently." She sounded like somebody who hadn't quite fully memorized her script. "For a long time, I had a lot of family expenses because of illness and things like that. So now I'm really concerned about protecting myself."

And to each, Jesse Reese extended sympathetic sounds, a pat on the hand, a smile, and then advice. He stood and made lists on an easel that happened to be part of his living room decor. He explained, he charted, he offered suggestions. And through it all, like a subliminal message, was the clear idea that if you wanted more guidance than a thirty-minute tape could provide, and no matter how large or small your net worth, Jesse Reese, a man who cared, a man with years of experience, would be more than happy to become your personal financial advisor.

"You convinced me, Jess," I said. Talking to one's TV is one of the ten warning signs of Needing to Get a Life. There was a message in all this, and it wasn't about investments.

The rooms here had doorbells. Mine made an unpleasant noise between a honk and a howl. I wonder what designer having a bad day decided that all the irritants of home should be built into the hotel's wiring. The bell sounded again, like an agitated goose.

And here we were, together again at day's end, Ma working over a hot TV and Pa bringing news of the larger world.

"Find him?" I asked when he'd settled into the second upholstered chair.

"Him?" He pointed at the television.

"No," I said. "That's Jesse Reese. We know where he is."

Mackenzie looked at the screen. "What's that you're watching, the news?"

"A tape," I said. "An infomercial that was going to run, probably on a local cable channel. Seminar number one for senior citizens on what to do to protect their futures. I don't think it's soon to be a major motion picture."

"Where'd you get it?"

I stopped the tape. "I'll tell if you don't lecture me on ethics. In fact, I'll tell you everything about today if I can be spared the voice of the law."

"Stole it, didn't you?" He sighed, then smiled. "That wasn't a lecture, so tell me about your day."

I did, as much as I could remember in one gulp. He already knew whatever Sasha had said this morning, so I began with the business with the chambermaid, awaited applause, which I found rather stingily meted out, then grudgingly continued with Frankie's additions and the details of my expedition to Cherry Hill.

"I just wish I could have found out why he was in Atlantic City, if not to gamble," I said. "The fact that Norma Evans wouldn't say means it must be important. She's shielding him."

"Maybe she didn't say simply because she didn't know."

"You're kidding. The woman made it very clear—was very proud of the fact—that she organized every detail of his life and had done so for seventeen years."

"Maybe this one time he had no intention of lettin' her know, and she couldn't admit it. The woman's embarrassed."

"But she was there. She didn't say so, but Sasha mentioned somebody with a blue and purple leather pocketbook, and there was one like it under Norma Evans's desk."

"Don't women change purses?" Mackenzie asked with real curiosity.

"She isn't exactly a fashion plate. The bag, to tell the truth, was a lot spiffier than the rest of her. I bet it was a gift from Reese. For Secretary's Day or something."

"But don't hundreds of women own the same bag?"

Of course they did.

"Did you ask her where she was that night? Her whereabouts?"

I shook my head. "I was supposed to be writing about investments for seniors. Interrogation didn't exactly fit the role. Sorry."

"Well . . . good job, anyway," Mackenzie said. Rather grudging, just because it would have been illogical to ask the question he had in mind. I wondered if Mackenzie's competitive streak was as erratic and ineradicable as mine, and whether it bothered him that I'd detected something on my own.

I moved the topic slightly off the mined ground. "What happens when an investment advisor dies?" I asked, somewhat rhetorically, because there wasn't a business-oriented brain between us. "Who takes care of the money that's invested?"

Mackenzie slowly unwrapped one of several peppermint candies in a small glass bowl. "Probably just give it back and the folks have to choose somebody new." He didn't seem particularly worried about Jesse Reese's clients.

"Do you think one of his investors could have had it in for him?"

His voice was muffled around the candy, which bulged in his cheek and compounded his accent. Slowly, I deciphered each word. "Anything's possible," he said, "though I thought his clients tended toward senior citizenship. Could they overpower him? Bash him with that heavy lamp?"

There was that. "A surrogate?" I asked halfheartedly.

"I did find out some about Dunstan," he said when the candy was down to talking size. "At least where he lives. Lived. His place was locked up and his next-door neighbor told me he'd gone away for an indefinite period. Left early this mornin'. So I didn't find out much. He lived out a piece in one of those standard-issue condos. Fake Tudor half-timbering on a three-year-old cinder-block building, for whatever that says 'bout his character, taste, or means." He slouched in his chair, long legs straight out into the room.

I couldn't believe it, but I had forgotten to tell Mackenzie about my phone call to Wisconsin. "Well, I found out more than that. I found out that Dunstan Farmer died in some big city in the South when he was in high school." I thoroughly enjoyed the blue flash of interest that ignited Mackenzie's pale eyes. Gotcha. I know that my competitive attitude is unworthy of me and unhealthy for any relationship I might have, but it feels good not to squelch it all the time. Besides, if *that*'s what terminates C.K. and me, if we can ever whittle our problems down to one such issue, I'll be happy to work on it. And very surprised.

"The dead Dunstan wasn't foreign-born, was he?" Mackenzie asked.

I shook my head. "Dunstan Farmer's family goes way back in Wisconsin, where he, too, was born, although they moved to the South when he was in high school."

Mackenzie sat up straighter and rewarded me with a companionable grin. "Good goin'," he said, not at all grudgingly.

Brilliant going, I told myself.

"That's what I figured myself," he said, even more slowly than was normal.

"How?" I said. "Why?"

He shrugged. "Why not? Had lots of time to think today. Couldn't find his place—he's moved three times recently. That ride was incredibly boring. How come they call this the Garden State?"

Only God—or the advertising agency that had invented the slogan—knew. And the garden's culmination, America's number one vacation destination, was no more picturesque than the roads that led here. Driving back from Cherry Hill, I'd again been struck by the depressing decay behind the boardwalk. Atlantic City was a one-dimensional backlot facade, the only place

I know where the expression "The buck stops here" is literal and visual. The place where the bucks stop is one block back from the boardwalk and as clearly marked as a high-tide line.

But that was beside the point. Dunstan was the point. Mackenzie's ability to have known my great revelation in advance was the point. The itchy flare of that competitive annoyance was yet another point.

"You know," he said, "I should have mentioned somethin' this mornin'. Maybe could have saved us both time."

"Mentioned something like what?" It didn't matter what Mackenzie would specifically say. The thing was, he'd been ahead of me all the time. I was no more than a dogsbody. The dummy Watson bringing home tidbits to Holmes. "Something like what?" I repeated, trying not to snivel. I hate not knowing things.

He stood up, making the room look even smaller, the ceiling even lower. He's not gigantic, although he is tall, but wherever he is, in some secret alchemy I have yet to figure out, he dominates the space. He can stand unobtrusively, his colors pastel—blue eyes, salt and pepper hair, unflashy clothing—slouching mildly, and he will nonetheless still be the focal point of the room, its chief architectural adornment. Besides, this particular room didn't have much space for pacing, but moving his long legs seems to crank his brain, so I let him pick his way in a half loop around the bed, then back. And again. "You told me this mornin' and it makes sense, long as we assume Sasha's tellin' the truth," he said. "An' why shouldn't we?"

That was kind of him. There were actually lots of reasons why we possibly shouldn't, given that she was charged with murder.

"An' anyway, I'd already been wonderin' what would have kept Dunstan from simply admittin' he was with her, except bein' afraid of the law. An' why would he be afraid, this photographer who's unknown to the local police, unknown far as we could check to anybody much, certainly not *wanted*? Why would he refuse to just plain say he was with Sasha?"

I twiddled with the cellophane wrapper of another peppermint. I could nearly hear him processing his thoughts, the squeak of ideas moving through neural pathways, each grabbing the next connector, whispering "Pass it on."

"I considered that maybe Dunstan was part of the witness protection program," he said, "afraid of havin' his picture in the papers. But hell, he's a photographer. Out at public functions all the time, an' the kind of functions where distant relatives and complete unknowns are likely to show. Weddings, bar mitzvahs, anniversary parties in the number one vacation destination of the entire country just doesn't seem a way to hide. Besides, he's obviously foreign-born, some English-speakin' country, so if he needed protection, why wouldn't we send him back home, wherever that is, but out of the USA, and safe?"

Mackenzie was remarkably calm about the idea of somebody's being an imposter. Was the world, then, full of Dunstans, people trying to be invisible? The landscape suddenly became one of those hidden pictures of flowers and butterflies that turn out to be people upside down and in fetal positions. How many convicts and escapees can you find in this drawing? I didn't like the idea one bit.

"So I figured his fear prob'ly wasn't based on what he'd done, but on what he *hadn't* done." Mackenzie stopped next to the night table and held up a hand, like a professor. "Or maybe," he added, "it was based on both. What he had and hadn't done." Then, having dramatized his cryptic point, he started pacing again, but at a speedier, corner-cutting tempo that didn't work. He bumped into the edge of the bed in his excitement, then bent to rub his shin. "So," he said, his voice muffled, "it seemed a matter of finding out what country and what he was running from and why he didn't become a citizen the normal way, with a green card, etcetera. Then you told me about that drunk who called Dunstan 'Egbert.' "

"Edgar." At least he'd slipped up somewhere, even if it was on an irrelevancy.

"So he ran away from Yorkshire and his wife, faked a drowning, and became Dunstan Farmer." Mackenzie straightened up, probably so that I could see how innocent, how truly superior, how devoid of smugness he managed to be.

"It's hard to think of Dunstan as an illegal alien," I muttered.

"Not quite the stereotype, is he? He's countin' on that. So do a lot of other Brits. Right color skin, an' even though he has an accent, it's our accent of choice, the one we've decided shows breedin' and class."

Mackenzie was a tad oversensitive on the subject of accents, but I shelved that issue for another time.

"What he's done is a good way of establishin' a whole new identity," Mackenzie said. "Take the name of a dead person who'd be near your age and whose birth record is in one part of the country and death certificate in another. The records aren't consolidated anywhere, an' anybody can get anybody's birth certificate. Then you're off and runnin'. You get a new Social Security number based on the certificate, ditto a driver's license. Get a passport with that piece of photo ID, and so forth. Build a person from scratch, each new piece of ID leadin' to more. Show the driver's license and get a charge at a department store. Show that and get a credit card. And so forth."

I forgave him for figuring out the essential points without my help. I even admired him for it. I didn't feel the need to tell him that, however. Instead, I simply said, "You can make yourself up, then. Make yourself over."

Mackenzie nodded. "And you can unmake a whole life that you didn't like. Egbert—"

"Edgar."

"Edgar of Yorkshire was uninvented, and I'll bet Dunstan Farmer is currently evaporating and somebody new is startin' even as we speak. We are never going to find the man. At least not in time for Sasha."

His words made me feel imprisoned along with my friend. I had to establish my own freedom, at least. "Let's get out of here," I said. "Let's take a walk."

Mackenzie, rubbing his injured shin again, agreed.

THE RAIN that had hit me in Cherry Hill had not made it all the way to the ocean. The afternoon was cloudy, but dry. Georgette was no longer anywhere in sight, which I mentioned to Mackenzie.

"She's homeless, not immobilized," he said. "We tend to look at those people as if they're less than human, a different species. Don' patronize her or infantilize her."

"Is it my imagination, or have you mutated into a pompous, pontifical, pretentious, self-important, bombastic bore?"

"It's your imagination," he said.

The boardwalk was not exactly the fix I needed. After two blocks I felt terminally bombarded by blinking lights, blasts of music and electronic sound, the mixed aromas of grease and plastic, and the people. Nothing connected or made a whole. Not on the boards, not in real life. "Let's go on the beach," I said. "I love it when the shadows start getting long."

Holding our shoes in our hands, we walked down to the surf line where tiny stalk-legged birds rushed for crabs each time a wave receded, then backtracked as a new wave came in. Talk about a lousy way to make a living.

Finally there was time to tell Mackenzie about the little boy, Lucky. I felt a residual flare of anger at the child's mother and at the hotel management. "I think it's criminal," I said.

"So does the law," Mackenzie said. "Leaving a kid unattended is neglect or abuse, and there are laws against it. And, in fact, it's also a crime to not report it when you've seen it."

"So why aren't all those parents being hauled off to prison? Because it's bad for business?"

"Maybe because the witnesses are troubled by the same issues that must be troubling you, or else why haven't you reported Lucky's mother to the police yet?" he asked in that infuriatingly noncombative tone of his.

"Because it seemed . . . because I don't want anything more to do with the local police right now?"

He turned toward me and raised one eyebrow.

"Okay, because I want a chance to warn her first. It isn't going to make Lucky's life better if his mother's in jail. That should be a last step."

Mackenzie nodded. "You could work on the business end of

it, alleviate the problem by makin' a stink with the casinos for child care centers."

I hadn't even made a small peep, let alone the squawk I'd promised myself. I felt the full weight of my crimes of omission.

"But you're right to hold off on an all-out effort in that direction till after Sasha's out of jail."

He was a kind, face-saving man, I decided. And then I thought about how many times a day I revised my opinion and description of him. I wondered what that meant.

Mackenzie told me that he'd spoken to Sasha again. The imminent arrival of her cousin the lawyer had elevated her spirits. "She says this is all a crock," he relayed, "and that she didn't do it, and that all she's letting herself worry about is whether the saltwater taffy people won't mind a short delay."

We talked more about the case. "I still can't figure out who in that bar did do it, though," I said. "None of them fit the witness's description."

"Except Sasha." Mackenzie spoke softly, watching me all the while.

"What?" I asked with a smile.

"You really, truly believe the killer was in that lounge?"

I nodded. "At least one of them. There were two, remember? Killers. Plural."

He brushed my small point away. "In the lounge, already festerin' about how to get rid of Jesse Reese—for reasons we cannot even begin to speculate on now, correct?"

I nodded twice for that one.

"An' this killer person, he says, 'How convenient. Just as soon as I finish this martini, here, I'll frame that big black-haired woman.'"

"Well," I said. "Well . . . yes."

He shook his head and said nothing, which is one of the single most annoying actions a person can make. Back and forth, back and forth, despairing of my logic, of my intelligence.

"Mandy." He finally spoke, thereby avoiding death by mischance at my hands by a fraction of a silent second. "Mandy." He made my name sound heavy, something he must bear. "That is just too ... Sure, there could be a little coincidence in this world, and if you consider bad timin' a form of coincidence, then there's sure a lot of it in crime. But still, somebody who wants to kill Reese happens to be there, in the same cocktail lounge? What is he doin', trailin' him? And Reese wouldn't notice or react?"

"Yes. He was there, drugging him, too. Starting his plan. The bar was *full* of people who knew Reese. Frankie. His wife. A woman with rings on her toes." He was decent enough to refrain from once again pointing out that none of the aforementioned fit the witness's description. Only Sasha did.

I kept pushing my theory, ignoring its holes. "Even Lala's boyfriend Tommy pointed him out and knew who he was. Maybe Reese didn't know that the other person wanted to do him in, but that's not relevant. Why are you acting like this is all silly?"

Mackenzie shook his head again. "We don't *require* fancy theories like that—"

"*Requahr!* We don' *requahr*?"

He sighed rather histrionically. "That sure wasn't a professional assassin that did Reese in. It was somebody madder than hell at him. Right then. Doesn't require old secrets or a long history, either. A minute of fury, that's all it took." His voice dropped until it was barely audible above the soft hum of the sea. "Enough anger and a key to that room, that's all it took."

"Not a key—I *told* you." But that hadn't been his point. I lowered my voice. "You're not a hundred percent sure that it wasn't Sasha, are you? You've been really nice about this, and I thought you—but you aren't sure, are you?"

He didn't answer right away. "I'm a hundred percent sure I don't *want* it to be Sasha," he finally said.

"But what?"

"But nothin' else—nobody else—makes a bit of sense."

"*Sense!* How could it make sense to bludgeon a man you didn't even know? How could it make sense to think that my friend since childhood, that Sasha Berg could ever, *ever*—"

He was shaking his head back and forth again. I shut my eyes and resumed ranting blindly until I ran out of steam.

"The *witness*—" Mackenzie began.

I found a further supply of steam. "The so-called witness saw *two* people. A woman and a man. If you're so eager to lynch Sasha, tell me who the man was."

Return to head shaking. I was causing him either palsy or massive despair, and worse, it was giving me a bitter pleasure. He had to atone for his lack of faith, for his policeman-deep love of evidence. "That second-man business doesn't help Sasha's case, y'know." His voice was soft and menacing, as if a silencer had been put on it. "Or Dunstan's, either. Bein' party to a murder is a mighty good reason all by itself to not want to be found."

That's about when I stopped talking to him and started wondering how deep a hole I'd have to dig to bury a body Mackenzie's size in the sand and keep it hidden through the time, tides, and tourists of the summer season ahead.

Ten

"**M**AYBE," Mackenzie said as we walked back across the soft sand, "we need a little perspective."

Our silences had grown incrementally along with the lengthening shadows of afternoon. "Everybody needs perspective on everything." I admit I was snappish. I also admit I didn't care. "What else is new?"

"Maybe we need a little distance, a little time apart."

I didn't know what to say to that. It's scary when men over-use adjectives, as in a *little* distance, a *little* perspective, a *little* time apart. Besides, Mackenzie and I already had our full measure of distance, only not in well-placed or meaningful spaces.

That was part of the problem. Plus, *I* was supposed to be the one saying sentences like that. When I decided to say them.

"Ahm not much use here. The police are real competent, an' Ahm an outsider."

He sounded serene, devoid of emotions, but according to the *ahm*-slurs-per-second test, he was either upset or pissed with me. Sometimes, it's affection that's on the upswing, but I was pretty sure this was not one of those times.

We meandered toward the boardwalk. It looked chilly and dark in the recesses under it, but Georgette wasn't underneath. She was, however, crossing the sand toward us along with a shaggy, bearded man. Both were swathed in layers of shirts and socks, and both carried lumpy bundles.

"So now that you can get your things back," Mackenzie said, apropos of nothing.

It took me a second to grasp his meaning. "My things? The things up in the, ah, suite? They'll let me have them now?"

He nodded.

I felt a new surge of irritation. Why hadn't he told me sooner? My *feet* hurt. I wanted my other shoes.

"Hey! Where's the kid?" Georgette's voice was loud and hearty.

I could sense Mackenzie's muscles tense at the ready, so I spoke quickly. "Hi, Georgette, this is Mackenzie."

She nodded. "Didn't think anybody grew up that fast."

"Lucky's with his mother, or at least with the security guard."

She pointed one half-gloved finger at me. "He'll be out again before the sun's down. I see him and lots others all the time. I always watch. I see everything. And this here is Blinks."

He was aptly named. It was a twitch or an old injury or a tic, but his eyes moved up and down double time.

"Been hunting." Georgette lifted her bundle as proof. "Tuesday pickings are best, you know."

"Wednesday's trash day." Blinks was either ill or had a naturally hoarse voice. "Won't be much for the next few days." His unkempt beard and bleary eyes made him look old, but he was really only worn, the lines on his face unnatural, like scribbles defacing a photo. His hardscrabble life didn't allow people to live long enough to be as old as he looked like he was.

Georgette's age was equally unreadable. The etchings on her forehead and below her eyes were like scars, the result of external, not internal, processes. Her lips were chapped, she was missing teeth, and her wispy brown hair belonged on a person twice the age I was sure she must be.

She smiled now, cradling a bundle that was larger and more bulgy than her companion's, but less expertly tied. "Didn't I say this was my lucky day?" she asked with a low chuckle. The high heel of a shoe poked out of one of the bundle's openings, although I couldn't imagine her tottering on spikes across the sand. In another gap in the fabric, I glimpsed something metallic, and in still another break, a brown and hairy swatch I didn't want to think about. I just hoped it had never been alive. I could see, too, the edge of a bright red book. Not her *War and Peace*, then, but another paperback chucked by a tourist. Georgette was a literate pack rat.

"Didn't I say?" she repeated, looking right at me.

"You did, indeed." Seeing her clutching other people's trash and beaming her gap-toothed smile produced a dull ache at my center. What made a day lucky for her except that it hadn't rained or snowed and no one had hurt her?

Oh, yes, the zapping of her enemies, she'd said. Well, whatever her imagination seized upon as a source of joy, whatever provided her with a sense of justice, was fine with me. The woman had precious little to hang on to in her life.

"I thought Mr. Hoover would get him," she told Mackenzie.

"Who's that?" he asked mildly.

"J. Edgar. Our FBI in action."

"Yes, but I meant—who was the person he was going to get?"

"That no-good Reese."

"Jesse Reese?" His deceptively mild voice was a dead giveaway that he was suddenly and intensely interested.

Wisps of her fine hair floated as she nodded. "Hoover didn't care. President Reagan wrote me back, though. Thanked me for my interest. Presidential seal on the paper and everything."

Mackenzie's interest level flagged. Georgette's combo platter of Ronald Reagan and the long-dead J. Edgar was a bit much for credibility. "So ... you knew Jesse Reese," he said with minimal interest.

Georgette nodded. "Not like I know *you*. Not to *hang out* with, friendly like. But I knew him. So did my sister. He gave talks. Took money. I know lots of people. Everybody on the beach and on the boards. Everybody. Like The Donald, you know?"

My turn to nod.

"And Prince Charles? People think he's stuffy, but he's a very good singer. Lots of pep, poor, blind thing. Wouldn't think he was royalty."

"You mean Ray Charles, maybe?" I asked.

She waved the question away and peered at Mackenzie. "This your husband?"

I shook my head. I didn't look at my nonhusband because I didn't want to know how he had greeted this suggestion.

"Husbands don't last," Georgette said. "My Kurt died." She seemed still surprised by the loss. "Went like that." She tried to snap her fingers, but the cut-off gloves got in the way.

The Ancient Mariness was at it again, schlepping out her story at the slightest—or no—provocation. I remembered Kurt's name from this afternoon's portion, and now I knew he'd been her husband. She'd been married. She'd had a sister, a home with curtains on her windows, and a child. She'd had more ties and more stability, at least at one point, than I'd yet managed to obtain. And she'd wound up on the beach.

"No money then," she said. "No job. No more house." Her eyes misted up, then over. "Money thought I was dead."

Mackenzie's interest reignited. "Heap o' stir and no bisquits," he said.

"Hey!" Georgette smiled with delighted recognition.

Blinks and I stood watching. It was hard, though, with his incessant eye movements, to know whether he was as confused by the exchange as I was.

"Enjoyin' poor health," Mackenzie went on. "Life is short and full of blisters. Money thinks I'm dead."

"How'd you know that?" Georgette asked.

"Had an uncle sang it all the time," Mackenzie said. "Kind of the family theme song, to tell the truth."

"He's okay," Georgette said to me.

Blinks, still clutching his hobo pack, winged out an elbow and pushed at her. "Hurry up," he said. "You gab too much. Everybody we meet. Makes me crazy. Miss dinner you keep talking."

I thought she might slug him, but instead she smiled almost coquettishly. *"Men,"* she said, but she turned and followed him up the stairs and onto the boardwalk.

" 'Home is the place where, when you have to go there, they have to take you in,' " Mackenzie murmured after they were gone. "Do you think Frost was talking about a rescue mission?" We slowly walked toward the boardwalk. "What a life. Particularly in the shadow of those casinos. You know they give away seventy mil a year in complimentary food and drink and rooms like yours?" He appeared lost in his own dark thoughts. " 'And homeless near a thousand homes I stood / And near a thousand tables pined and wanted food.' "

"Who said that one?" It was embarrassing that a cop knew more poetry—or at least could quote more—than an English teacher, but that's how it was.

"Wordsworth, a hundred years ago. How did he know how it was going to be?"

"Sometimes," I said, "I think about the poorhouse scenes in Dickens, and how righteously superior to those times I used to feel. Now, I'm not sure. Maybe they were kinder back then. A poorhouse has to be better than no house at all, no place on earth that has to take you in."

"Or my grandma," Mackenzie said. "She used to talk about how her house was marked with a chalk that told hobos—a nicer word than *homeless,* don't you think?—she'd feed them. Somehow, back then, they were thought of as unlucky victims of the system. Now, we blame the victims instead. I know some of them made bad choices and crash-landed on the streets, but still . . ."

My urge, as always, was to do something about it, but this one was beyond even my most ambitious imagination. We walked along, kicking sand, sighing, lost in our separate thoughts. But by the top of the steps Mackenzie began talking again, and not about contemporary social problems. Georgette and Blinks had not been forgotten, but put in a mental pending file, to be retrieved only in proper sequence. Meanwhile, like a needle lifted from, then put back on the same track of a still-whirring record, to use an archaic image, he was right back where he'd been when we were interrupted.

"So you can get your things," he said, "then pack up. I have my car, too, a real shame, but if you want, we could both use mine, then come down on the train later this week or whenever, and both use yours and—"

"Wait a minute." I stopped just in front of the hotel doors and nearly caused a domino effect of falling pedestrians. But once inside, I'd have to be more polite to Mackenzie than I thought he warranted. Out of doors, almost anything goes.

"Can't wait a whole lot of minutes," he said. "I'm really tired from last night, and I'm due in early tomorrow. You know I'm here—officially—to check Nicky B.'s old haunts. How long can I pretend to inspect a city block that no longer exists?"

"But that has nothing to do with me. I'm not leaving. Not tonight, anyway."

He looked flabbergasted. "Why not? You can't be havin' a good time." People shoved their way around him, clearing their throats, trying to make him aware that he was blocking the door. He finally noticed and moved to the side, and I shifted over as well. "Your roomie's in jail, it's too cold for the beach, and you don't gamble," he said. "Why not?"

His argument contained several salient points, but it nonetheless missed the relevant one, which was Sasha. "I can't walk away and leave her here to rot!"

He rolled his eyes, seeking the compassion of the patron saint of those who deal with nincompoops. "You watch too many old movies. Sasha's not likely to rot. That jail's not even damp. Besides, her lawyer cousin's goin' to spring her."

"How do I know that? And won't she still need some kind of help, or attention? And even if the lawyer gets her bail, which isn't a for sure, will they let her leave the state? Go back to Philadelphia?"

"Depends," Mackenzie said. "Long as there's no threat she'd run, they probably will."

"But you don't know for sure and you don't really care." It was literally painful to say the words. "Not enough. Not about anything, except crime." Somewhere in the last twenty-four hours I had been pushed over my emotional boundary lines, into the swamp of sloppy sentiment. I was not only ready to cry about Mackenzie's callousness, I wanted to, I ached to do so. "You aren't really committed to—to *anything*!" A small and rational part of me knew that was unfair as well as untrue, but it *felt* right. And I was sick of facts. Facts didn't make sense. "*Nobody's* committed to anything!" I lamented. "The whole world's—"

"For Pete's sake!" he said.

A kid of about thirteen, in uniform—baseball hat turned backward, baggy droopy pants, cloaked expression—stopped about three feet from us and watched, warily. I couldn't decide if he wanted to prevent violence or witness it firsthand. I gave the kid my best teacherly scowl, meant to pierce and draw blood.

The kid shrugged a shoulder, said, "It's your funeral, lady," and meandered off.

"That's what I mean!" I said. "If he really thought something bad was going to happen, he should have stayed!"

"After you made it clear he should leave? Give him a break. Give ever'body a break."

I could hear the exhaustion in his voice, and that should have slowed me down, but it didn't. I don't know if anything could have. Accumulated frustration pressed at my back like the Furies. I felt the pressure of the long teaching year and my mother's reality-based nagging about my lack of financial security and my own ambivalence about my lack of emotional security, and—

and—and— "Nobody cares *enough*. Not Reese, as far as his wedding vows, not Lucky's mother. And Dunstan's not even committed to being himself!" Everything I said felt urgent, as if I were carrying the single message that could save the planet. Paulette Revere waving her lantern and shouting, "Commit! Commit!" I couldn't have said to what he or I was supposed to commit—that was part of the problem—but I also couldn't bear for Mackenzie to be part of the great indifferent, to be like everybody else.

"I'm impressed, or depressed," he said, "by the scum and cads you've encountered, but it's nonetheless time I headed home."

"And what about Lala?"

"That a person or a pastime?"

"The woman who told me a man was harassing her, so I'd make him jealous and get him to propose marriage to her. How's that for integrity?"

"Have you switched tirades? I thought you were doin' commitment, not integrity."

I heard him through an internal yapping chorus, each voice cataloguing offenses against my person. "I thought you were *committed* to helping Sasha!" He surely wasn't committed to *me*—and I still didn't know if I wanted him to be, but I knew I wanted him to want that—but I couldn't, wouldn't, say that. Yet. Talking—yelling—about Sasha and Mackenzie's relationship was much, much easier. "So now you want to shrug it off, return to business as usual, not try to prevent a horrible miscarriage of—"

"Whoah!" He took a step back and looked at me with a profoundly sorrowful expression. "Mandy," he said, his voice low, "what's this really about?" His eyes narrowed, upped their intensity. "Tell me this isn't that talk you've been sayin' we should have."

"Well, of course I wouldn't—this isn't the time or—"

"You sure?"

I stopped. The blithering emotional surge drained and I was riding on empty. "I don't know," I said, softly and honestly.

"This is an awesomely dumb time and place for it." He was almost whispering. We were retreating, voices first.

"I came here—to Atlantic City—in the first place, mostly to figure out—to think through—"

He took both my hands. "An' I didn't really come here to find out about Nicky B. But . . . stuff happens. Your friend got herself in big trouble."

"Framed. Got herself framed."

"An' you're rattled."

"Of course I am! I'm sane, I'm human. But under the rattles, I still have questions."

"Such is the nature of existence," he said. "It generates business for philosophers, theologians, and comedians."

Such was the nature of our current existence that two things were true: one, that wasn't at all the answer I'd wanted, and two, he didn't know that. I looked at him and felt wistful, a galloping case of the might-have-beens, and for what blighted outcome, I couldn't even say.

A bad blend, my granny would have cautioned me. Two people trying to have street smarts above love, or whatever it was we'd have if we relaxed long enough to define it. Dummies, she'd have called us. But it was easier for Granny, who married her first love at sixteen with the optimism that only a person with zero experience can possibly have.

"A man died in your hotel room, Sasha's in jail, you've been meetin' slippery characters, an' you're probably hungry," Mackenzie said. "Look, it's gotten dark. So here's the plan."

I shook my head, refusing him the right to organize my thoughts or behavior, but he ignored me.

"I'm goin' back to my hotel. Give us tahm to . . . think."

He meant to calm down. He meant me.

"I'll get my bag—I checked out earlier and left it in storage—"

So his leave-taking had been a fait accompli hours ago, not subject to discussion, and I could have skipped my Elegy on a Theme of Noncommitment.

"—then I'll pick you up and we'll go to dinner and, although Ah have never found it an aid to digestion—" He swallowed and took a deep breath while I translated his words, which were drenched and runny with emotion. There wasn't a consonant or hard end to one of them. He cleared his throat. "—we'll Talk. Like you mean. With a capital T."

I don't remember agreeing, but I must have, because I remember watching him walk down the boardwalk—his hotel was many blocks up and a few over—lit by the bulbs of the stores along his route, his salt and pepper curls jostling, and for one sudden burst, neon-pink.

And I remember thinking that for all my insistence, we really could skip the capital-T talk. It would only be a stopgap gesture. We were a wrong combination, a forced match. I was incredibly fond of him, but I couldn't handle the way he could segment his life, his attention, and his emotions. I couldn't handle some of what kept him sane—a rational detachment, an objectivity in the face of horror. His work had changed and hardened him, I thought. He was used to ugliness and violence, and charming though he was, he'd curled up inside himself and taken to hiding, and at this stage in my life, I couldn't handle it.

I couldn't cope with his job—his real life—and its intrusions and messiness. I couldn't deal with the uncertainty it produced.

They say a man's job is a tough mistress, but Mackenzie's was worse than another woman would be. It was his other self, a doppelgänger. And all for the sake of goodness and right, which made the struggle between us impossible.

Of course, he thought I created artificial barriers and hair splits. He thought this was all my problem, easily remedied by an attitude adjustment on my part.

We were both bullheaded and stubborn, unlikely to give up beloved convictions, so what was the point of discussing and analyzing and trying to effect change?

Look, I've read too many books not to recognize when a story is winding down, when logically, the next words have to be: The End.

Eleven

OR a nanosecond my emotional tank registered empty, but that vacuum, being abhorred by nature, was immediately replaced by a depression that barreled in with the force of a typhoon. I could barely drag myself through the enormous front doors of the hotel.

If I'd been asked to design the atmosphere I least desired, it would have been the one I was now in, the bustling, bemarbled commercial palace's. The building was much fancier than its mostly elderly tenants dressed in the nondescript pastel knits and cottons that are supposed to camouflage middle- and post-middle-aged indignities, but instead advertise that they're there.

There's a comic who claims that the average age of Atlantic City's visitors is dead. It always gets a big laugh.

And among the average-aged gamblers was Lala, straight ahead and waving to catch my attention. I refused to let it be caught. This was the worst possible time to hear her version of the war between the sexes. I simply couldn't.

My only available escape route was the casino, into which I hustled, sure that I could make a quick detour and lose her in its blinking, dazzling interior.

And I did. Until, that is, I decided to get on with my life and reemerge, and there she was again. I turned and reentered the casino's inner recesses.

I watched a determined, jaw-set elderly man pull the handle of a machine edged in blue light. The machine twinkled a message: COLUMBUS TOOK CHANCES, TOO!

Columbus was a better gambler. He found a new world. The man I was watching lost a dollar, stared blankly, put more coins in and pulled again. GOOD LUCK, the machine responded with a flirty twinkle of lights.

I walked down the row. The opulent, almost hysterically exuberant surroundings were in depressing contrast to the players, most of whom looked as if they needed those quarters and nickels—an elderly and frail woman on a walker—a thin man in threadworn work clothes and floppy hat, a young woman who could be Lucky's mother. Their faces and movements had the grim resignation of people working on a factory line.

I moved to the craps table, where there was a little more life but even less sense. I had assumed that I could comprehend anything Nathan Detroit understood. Yet another wrong assumption. I tried to decipher the many meanings stenciled on the table, the source of the muted excitement of the people gathered around, but quickly gave it up. It would take too long to understand. Besides, I felt a certain urgency about getting my belongings from upstairs quickly, before they locked up for the night. But as I turned, there was Lala again. The woman was really good at dogging a person. She could have bailed herself out financially by becoming a P.I. instead of Tommy's wife.

I slipped out of her line of sight and found myself having another unasked-for reality check outside the baccarat salon. Somebody had told me that baccarat was the one card game that required absolutely no skill, and in fact couldn't utilize it, because it was based on pure chance. Which left it with only style, precious little of which was evident. The table, separated from the rest of the casino by a maroon velvet rope, was surrounded by Asian men in windbreakers. The *shoe* that held the cards was red plastic.

Baccarat. I yearned for tuxedos, Grace Kelly, Monte Carlo, the splash of the Mediterranean on the rocky coast outside, balconies and palaces, designer gowns, and croupiers with sexy accents and knowledge of old world evil.

"You all right, hon?" The accent was domestic, the voice metallic, and my clean escape a flop. Lala peered at me from beneath aquafrosted eyelids. "I've been calling and calling," she said. "You were a million miles away. I'm out of breath from trying to catch you."

I wondered if there were equally annoying people in Monte Carlo, and whether it would be my fate to attract them there as well.

She put her hand on my forearm. Her engagement ring sparkled. "I wanted to explain," she said. "About, well, you know."

"No need."

"You're young; you can't possibly understand."

I wondered why people always insist on telling you that you're not going to understand something they are going to insist upon telling you anyway.

"About how it is to be an older woman, alone and without money," she continued. "You know how many of the poor people in this country are women?"

"How many?"

Her mouth opened and closed a few times. Then she pursed her lips and spoke. "A *lot*, that's how many. Maybe *most.* Women just like *me.*"

I moved in the direction of the lobby.

"I never worked," she said, hustling to keep up with me. "My husband wouldn't hear of it." She sounded as if she were hyperventilating, in some medical danger.

I slowed my pace, accepting my fate and not willing to be responsible for hers.

"I had no idea we were in debt, or that he didn't have enough insurance until after he died."

What was it I did that made people decide it was always story hour? "I'm sorry," I said, "but I have something I really have to do upstairs. Excuse me." That was true, but another truth was that I didn't want to hear about how easy it was to become frighteningly poor. I wanted to reclaim my possessions and pretend they were protection from becoming old and without resources.

"But I got a job then." She trotted behind me, as if my words had been no more than white sound. "I had to. Didn't have a cent. I worked in a discount luggage store. Three years, and then I was a recession cutback. My rent went up. My son's wife left him and their boy and he needed help, and money for help." Her voice dropped to dirge level. "A woman alone . . ."

Oh, goody. You could really try hard and things could still get worse. Things *would* get worse. First aid for the insufficiently depressed.

"He liked me," Lala said. "Tommy. But I could not get him to go one step further, to get off the stick, you understand?"

It's an interesting expression: *get off the stick*. Doesn't make any sense when you think about it, unless it meant get unstuck. But yes, I definitely understood what she meant.

"So I thought," she said, "if I made Tommy a little bit scared, less sure of himself . . . It always worked in the old movies."

We had reached the elevators. "Do you love him?" I asked.

Once again Lala put her hand on my arm. "Even in the dictionary, love means a lot of things, darling. But having nothing only means trouble."

I got onto the elevator. By the third floor I couldn't hear even her echo. By the top floor I had almost convinced myself that I had nothing in common with Lala, and that there were no similar sticks to get off of between C. K. Mackenzie and Tommy.

A drowsy security guard sat outside the suite. "Can't come in here, ma'am," he said. "This here area is not open to the public."

I told him my name and purpose. He checked a clipboard and looked disappointed that I had passed muster. "Thought you were another gaper. People act like this is a set for *Unsolved Mysteries.*" His scowl made him look like a pink-skinned bulldog as he heaved himself out of his chair with a great sigh and turned the knob of the suite.

"Thanks." I stepped in. I expected many things, but not a curvacious bit of a woman dressed entirely in black—hat, gloves, shoes, stockings, slacks—except for the flashes of brass on every one of the above garments and the yellow-gold hair cascading over her shoulders. Even her cane had a brass head and rivets all the way down its shaft.

Rivets, I thought. The bolted Mrs. Reese. Jesse's widow. But something was wrong.

The widow Reese stood near the door in the suite's foyer, pursing her red-gold mouth, tilting her head and listening intently to a stocky patrolman in uniform. He interrupted himself and looked me over.

"She's the one," the hall monitor said.

"Oh, yeah?" He looked disgusted.

"The last to know," the woman in black said in a gravelly voice. She pressed one gloved hand to her ample bosom. "Like they always say. Isn't that so, Holly?"

A loud, commiserating *tsk* came from a blaze of hot color across the entryway, and then a slow "he was—such a—son of"—words rolling out in a deep female voice—"a bitch."

The widow sniffled into a black lacy handkerchief. I knew what was wrong. She'd bleached her hair overnight. From raven to brass. What a weird expression of grief. Or was it suspicious?

The patrolman looked at me with contempt. "What do you want?"

"My clothing and things."

"You?" The widow practically shouted it. "You're the one he was shacked up here with?"

I shook my head. "I'm here for my toothbrush and—"

"They let you *free?*" Her voice sounded stone-washed and bruised.

The deep voice of the other woman, the pink one, joined in. "You have some nerve showing your face. Don't you have any respect?"

"Listen, I'm not—this isn't—" I glared at the policeman.

"My poor sister. Bad enough that son of a bitch humiliates her with his bimbos!" I wondered how she'd define herself, bandaged as she was in hot-pink spandex that barely coexisted with her carotene hair. "But to have his playmate—his *murderer—*"

I was almost flattered at being called a bimbo. I felt haggard and shabby in my oversized borrowed sweater and yesterday's slacks, my too-tight loafers and my post-Mackenzie, post-Sasha, post-Georgette, post-Lala, post-Lucky funk.

"This here's the *other* one was staying here," the policeman said. "Needs her toothbrush and things."

"What did you have planned for up here? Something really kinky with both you girls?" the hot-pink woman demanded. Her ensemble was also outlined in rivets. The bolted look was a fashion development I didn't mind having missed.

"Didnja hear what he said? She isn't the one who was here," the widow told her sister. "I didn't mean to infer. Imply. Suggest. I'm rattled, you know?" She put out her gloved hand. "I'm Poppy Reese," she said solemnly. "That's my sister Holly."

I wondered if they had other botanically named siblings, if there were boy-children with plant names as well.

Then she turned to the patrolman. "We spent a lot of time here together, you know. It brings back too many . . ." She dabbed at her eyes, although there was no moisture for her black lace hanky to catch.

"Sorry, ma'am. We thought maybe you'd see something out of place, or wrong. You know."

"My sister's upset," the woman in pink said. She lounged against the silk-covered wall and tapped one hot-pink shoe. "Her

121

husband—her lying, cheating, no-good husband who'd already wasted half *their* money—was killed yesterday, in case you forgot. Her whole entire world has just collapsed."

"We're out of here," Poppy Reese said.

The law nodded. "You'll be home, then? In Haddonfield?"

Poppy shook her head. "My *sister's* house. Holly Booker, up at the end of the boardwalk, in Ventnor. I gave you the address already."

"Why should my sister be in her big house all alone? It's too far away and too full of memories, am I right, Poppy?"

Poppy's nod was woe itself.

"This way, we can walk the boards, come in here for a massage, a little workout. It'll be good for her. Physical activity, a little pampering—it's always good for a person."

"She works here," Poppy said. "In the spa."

Holly worked here. And what was her relationship with the deceased? Could Jesse have happened to be around the bar because he was seeing Sis on the sly?

"Besides," Holly said, "we haven't seen each other for a while. Ever since her car went into the shop, like a year ago, she can't get here, and that no-good husband of hers, you'd think he'd bring her? I picked her up this morning. I said, 'You're staying with me.' "

"It's been in the shop two weeks," Poppy corrected her. "Not a year. I drive a special car," she said to the policeman. "Because of my . . ." She looked momentarily sad for real.

"Besides," Holly said again, "she has her businesses to look after. Especially now that—"

"Business?" the cop asked.

Wait, I thought. Wait. This was all wrong. Poppy was in Atlantic City last night. Why didn't she want her sister to know? Also, if she couldn't drive herself, then with whom had she come, if not her husband? The suspicion that she'd been spying on Jesse, perhaps because of her sister, grew.

I'd have to talk with Mackenzie about this—but when? We were supposed to for once and finally talk about *us*, and who knew what would happen after that?

"Businesses," Holly said. "My sister's very talented. You're looking at the next Liz Claiborne, so help me."

Holly wasn't behaving like my idea of a woman who'd been cheating with her sister's husband. Or someone whose lover had just been offed. Or maybe she was. Maybe she was being overly solicitous, overly obvious about her solicitousness.

Holly patted her sister's shoulder and winked at the cop, like a mother pushing her child forward for praise. Make the kid feel better, she seemed to be saying. "The store has three lines—Glitz for Gals, Studz—with a z—for Guys, Twinklz—with another z—for Tots. Three entire lines. Rivets are her personal fashion statement. You heard it first here."

"I'm sorry." The patrolman looked apologetic. "I don't know a whole lot about fashion, so . . ."

"Well," Holly said, "it isn't exactly open yet." She sounded a little testy, as if we were demeaning her sister by quibbling over inessentials—real store or figment, who cared?

"And now, look what happened. Talk about a setback," the widow said. I found it an interesting way to categorize—or dismiss—her husband's death. "You never know, do you?"

Poppy took a deep breath. "Still, life must go on." And then, followed by her pink sibling, she left.

The patrolman stared at her afterimage. "Did you know she was Miss Nebraska or Kansas—someplace like that—awhile back?" he asked me. "They're usually a lot taller. A real shame about her being lame now and all." He kept staring at the space she'd vacated until her lingering spell finally broke. Then he nodded me in the general direction of the bedroom.

Once again, and probably for the last time, I admired the elegant serenity of the Eastern Suite. Only its name troubled me. East for me would be England. A room filled with Hepplewhite would be an Eastern Suite. Why had we adopted England's egocentric and geographically backward labels, as if we were still their colony?

"Don't touch anything except what you have to," the cop said. I wondered why, at this point, it mattered. Everything must have been long since dusted, sprayed, photographed, documented, or removed. I decided he'd said it out of sheer spite. He wanted to make everything hard for me because he didn't like me as much as he'd liked the widow Poppy. But then, I'd never been Miss Anything except Pepper.

At the bedroom door I gasped and put both my hands up to my mouth. Perhaps I'd unconsciously assumed that once everything was measured and noted, the room would be freshened up by a special postmortem chambermaid, but the room looked as if the murder were happening now, but for the absence of the victim.

One of the two beds was pulled apart, the bedding dangling onto the floor, pulled half off the mattress, but that wasn't it.

It was the red-brown splat on the sheeting, the gory spread, the rusty mattress pad. *It* was where blood had arced and dripped in splatters across the once beautiful screen behind the bed, and onto the wall beyond it.

"Dear God." I turned my head away, nauseous and on the verge of tears.

The detective said nothing, but I felt his eyes on my skin, studying me, as if my every word and action were important evidence.

I ducked my head, averted my eyes, and pulled my suitcase out of the closet.

"Make sure you only take your own things," he said. "Let me know if you notice anything out of the ordinary—you don't have to check the pockets or anything."

Because they already had. The idea made me even sicker. Had I left anything peculiar, unethical, or unworthy in my pockets? Was this like having an accident with ripped underwear?

Oh, God, my underwear. Surely they'd been through that, too, so it was *exactly* like that! I hoped nobody told my mother.

"But anything out of the ordinary," he repeated.

Such as what? A ten-million-dollar check from Publishers Clearing House stapled to the hem of my green blouse? A komodo dragon on my blazer lapel? My jeans' legs sewn together? What could possibly be out of the ordinary about my pathetic wardrobe, given that disarray and poor maintenance was the norm, and that they'd already examined every fiber of it, anyway?

I folded each piece carefully, wanting to impress the officer with my wholesome packing expertise. "Couldn't somebody from the hotel do this?" I finally asked. "Bring a rack and hang everything up?"

He nodded. "Except you'd still have to say which is yours and which is hers, you know. This is just as efficient."

Not for me. The process seemed voyeuristic and creepy. I tucked the sandals I'd optimistically packed for the beach into the edge of the suitcase, scooped up my underwear without checking it for imperfections or fingerprints, and retrieved my tennis shoes, remembering bitterly the peaceful solitary walks I'd also fantasized. "Is it all right if I change shoes?" I asked the detective. "These loafers are . . . my feet have been hurting since last night."

I wanted him to smile, to ease up, but he didn't oblige me. He shook his head, somehow conveying that I was yet another Cinderella wannabe, squeezing my feet into tiny sizes. Or was that my own crabbed conscience speaking? In any case, the man said my footwear didn't make any difference to him.

I didn't think I should muss the good bed, certainly didn't want to go near the gory bed and didn't want to ask Officer Smiles's permission to sit on any other surface, so I accomplished the great shoe switch on the floor. The back throb I'd felt earlier with Lucky upped its voltage. I switched positions along with shoes and convinced myself that I did not have anything as trite and boring as a back problem. What I did have were blisters on both my heels and, when I stood up, a very sharp and extremely painful pressure on a toe.

"You done, then?" the policeman asked.

"No. Sorry." I sat back down. "A pebble," I said by way of explanation as I pulled the shoe off and shook it. He yawned and turned away.

A former pebble, I should have said. Once upon a time, when it lodged itself in the belly of an oyster. Now, a pearl earring with a sharp post that had been drilling through my toe. I shook

125

the shoe some more, to see if the clasp was in there as well, but it was not.

I bent over the earring on the carpet, afraid to touch it. Surely it had prints on it. I didn't know good pearls from paste, but this one had a nice sheen and a quietly elegant setting that suggested it had not been a K mart special.

I stood up straight and rubbed my back. I didn't own anything like that earring, and Sasha wouldn't. It was too understated, too unobtrusive. With her wild curly mane, she felt there was no point to earrings unless they were humungous enough to swing free and shine.

"Excuse me," I told the cop, whose back was to me as he stared out the window. I was glad he didn't seem literate enough to read my mind and find me thinking of the expression pearls before swine.

"Yeah?" he asked, back still to me.

"I did."

He turned my way slowly, reluctantly. "You did what?"

"Find something out of the ordinary in my clothes."

126

Twelve

YOU'D think he'd be excited—a genuine, honest-to-God clue to the presence, in this room, of another woman besides Sasha. But his attitude suggested that I was fixating on a bit of flotsam simply to add to his workload and give him grief.

He lumbered over with all deliberate sloth, grunted as he bent and reached for the pearl with thick fingers.

"Wait!" I said. "I mean, of course you know what you're doing, but isn't it possible that—don't you think an earring might—probably would—have fingerprints on it? I mean, given how you'd—how I'd—put one in, you'd almost have to get your

127

prints on it, wouldn't you? Do you think you—do you think we should touch it that way?" It was necessary to overstate the case because he failed to react normally. He hunched over the earring, watching it with the blank goggle eyes of a guppy.

I was proud of my tact and reserve. I had refrained from using the word *stupid* or any of its synonyms, which was better than he deserved. But virtue was rewarded because the patrolman slowly unbent and gave me a hooded, disdainful look, as if all on his own he'd decided against pawing the earring with his bare hands. "It's not like I don't know about prints," he said.

It was no mystery why, at nearly retirement age, he was still precariously balanced on a very low rung of the police ladder.

"But have it your way," he said in a standard-issue dismissive male tone that makes my viscera churn. He picked the earring up in a piece of tissue, looked at it and made a small *pfffut* exhalation. "Not much," he said. "What do you people see in pearls, anyway?"

"Us people?"

"Yeah. You people. Women. What do you see in pearls?"

"Normally, nothing. Right now, *evidence.*"

"Not really. Lots of people use this room. Atlantic City's real popular, you know. Number one tourist destination in the U.S."

I wondered how many times a day that statistic was dragged out.

"You know," he continued, "some of the help nowadays, well, they're not necessarily the most perfect cleaners in the world. I could tell you stories—"

"I'll bet you could. But as I'm sure you realize, that particular earring couldn't have been left here by a previous tenant. No matter how sloppy the chambermaid was. Don't you agree?" I was really afraid that out of spite toward me, or life, or bad cleaning-women, the oaf was going to discount and thereby ruin this chance to prove Sasha's innocence. "I mean," I said in such a simpering tone I nearly made myself nauseous, "one need not be female to know that does not compute, isn't that so?"

"Well," he said with a shrug, "I guess I . . . what was that again about computers?" His face grew ruddy, as if slowly building up pressure.

"What I mean is, even if a person doesn't *wear* earrings, he can understand that a little leftover pearl earring cannot jump into a shoe. It's funny even to think of such a thing."

"Not so silly if you think about it a little longer, miss. If you think about it *logically*, you'll realize that if, say, it gets itself stepped on the right way and ricochets . . ."

I cut to the chase and did not react to his emphasized *logically* and its sexist undertones. "Have you ever noticed that if the back of an earring comes off—as in a struggle of some kind—then the front part's unmoored and it can fly through the air like a little missile when the woman shakes her head. Want me to show you how?" I reached for my own earring.

He didn't want to see, which was lucky, since I was wearing a hoop that was all one piece, and I couldn't have demonstrated a thing. "Somebody wearing that earring was in this room last night," I said. "Somebody who is not my friend Sasha."

"Yeah? How can you prove this doesn't belong to your friend? Or even"—an actual idea had just now crept into his head—"it could belong to *you!*" His voice dripped with suspicion—of what, I couldn't have said.

Did the dimwit think I would have mentioned the earring if it belonged to one of us, or that I would have shown the thing to him if it were in any way self-incriminating? He should have been suspicious about whether I was planting false evidence to implicate somebody else. But I saw no need to direct his thinking or to instruct him. I was on vacation, after all.

"Maybe you brought it from Philly," he said.

"You mean accidentally? The way ships carry rats, or produce carries insects?"

"You probably packed it. It's pretty small, you know."

"I don't own pearl earrings." I had to grit my teeth to keep my temper. "So it wouldn't have been around my house, falling into my shoes. Besides, I wore those shoes yesterday. Here. I drove down here in them and kept on wearing them when I

129

went on the beach. I didn't change my shoes until I was going out later on. There wasn't any earring inside of them. I would have felt it."

"Okay, fine. We're wasting time. I'll take care of it. You packed?"

I ran into the bathroom for my toiletries, which were in appalling disarray all over the counter.

"Looks like they scuffled in here, too," the patrolman said.

It wasn't a question, so I said nothing, just tossed shampoo and eyeliner into my travel pack. I was relieved that I'd screwed the top back on the toothpaste before I left last evening, and ashamed of myself for thinking about such an inanity.

He stood at the bathroom door, arms crossed over his chest, waiting for me to finish.

"Okay, that's it." I rushed back to the bedroom and tossed the last of my belongings into the suitcase. I was beyond caring what he thought of my packing expertise or how I handled toothpaste tubes. "I'm out of here, okay?"

He shook his head. I had to walk through the living room with him, slowly checking whether any other possessions of mine were in evidence. I retrieved my untouched books, hoping he'd noticed *War and Peace* or *Gift from the Sea* and not the sex and shopping tome, and solemnly assured him that there was now not a trace of me left in there because I hadn't had the time to further litter the premises.

"You know," he said, "the eyewitness . . . what he saw was a tall dark-haired woman. You think much about that? Because you know, you're not exactly short yourself, are you? What do you have to say about that?"

All I said was goodbye.

I COULDN'T REMEMBER whether Mackenzie had mentioned when he'd be back. Since the scheduled program for the evening was breaking up, perhaps I'd blocked the time frame specifics. I tried reading *War and Peace*, but like Georgette, I had trouble concentrating on their various names. I wondered if life were more interesting when everybody called you something different the way they did in old Russia. I wondered if that tradition had persisted right through Perestroika.

I wondered, too, whether Mackenzie, had he been born Russian, would have actual names, and lots of them—or would he simply be known by ever-shifting initials? C.K. for one social situation, T.K. for another, and so forth, à la russe.

I wondered where Mackenzie was.

Although I was staying in Atlantic City for only one more day, I completely unpacked, stacking undies tidily, making sure my toiletries were arranged with military precision. Nothing encourages good housekeeping as effectively as having your most personal objects pawed through by officials.

I waited for Mackenzie some more. I was no longer certain that the man was ever going to show up, although a silent disappearance was not his style.

"I was stood up for my break-up," I sang, plucking at an imaginary guitar. "Stood up 'fore my break-up. Breakin' up is harder to do if there's no one to break up with you." The next Nashville sensation. Words and life by Mandy Pepper.

Just as I got to wondering whether I could stand a life of eternal touring and whether female stars had groupies, the phone rang.

The man sounded anxious and official. "Miss Pepper?" he asked solemnly.

"Yes?"

"I'm calling from the Atlantic City Medical Center to notify you that we've admitted Mr. Mackenzie."

"*Mister* Mackenzie?" I pictured someone foreign, a gentleman in a bowler hat, a spy on *Masterpiece Theatre*.

Medical Center, he'd said. My pulse escalated and words popped up and down like frightening flashcards. Hospital. Injury. Accident. Emergency. Dead? "But how could he be in the hospital? He isn't even working!" I said.

"Am I speaking to the right person? Is this Amanda Pepper?"

"I . . . ah, *yes*."

"Because your name was in his wallet as someone to call in case of an emergency. The message on your answering machine in Philadelphia said you could be reached at—"

"He has my name in his wallet?" I was surprised at how profoundly that affected me. I had my mother's and sister's names in those slots, but Mackenzie had mine. I would never have dreamed. Besides, while I fixated on that, I avoided letting the word "emergency" fully register.

"—this hotel, so I—"

"Please," I finally dared. "What . . . what happened?" Everything slowed down—my breathing, time, the speed of light, and the course of my words, floating listlessly as dandelion fluff. Slowly—more slowly, please—toward the receiver, into the phone wires, down, through—everything slow except my brain, which was snapping and connecting double time and in no particular direction, so that between my question and his reply there was an epoch filled with theories and refutations.

First theory. Mackenzie's heart broke. Literally. Heartbroken suitor—with my name in his wallet—requiring hospitalization. Extremely romantic. A reunion at bedside, complete with violin background.

Second theory. Mackenzie was dead.

The man from the hospital cleared his throat, hiding in my time warp, afraid to break the news. They must rotate the chore, take turns, punish employees by forcing them to make these calls.

Food poisoning. Something he bought en route to the hotel. Some sleazy off-boardwalk stall food. My mother was right. You couldn't trust those food vendors.

I knew it wasn't that. Okay, then. What happened was: he gagged on the idea of our Talk with a capital T. Had to go to the hospital to have a Heimlich maneuver to get his heart out of his throat.

Appendicitis.

Jackpot. I'd found the acceptable emergency. I could imagine them wheeling him into surgery, no time to phone and cancel our last date.

"There was an accident, ma'am," the man said with excessive politeness and patience. "He's in surgery now."

It took me a moment to remember what *accident* and *surgery* meant. "A collision?" Why hadn't I thought of that? Of all the possibilities, the most logical, a car smash hadn't even crossed my— He had walked back to his hotel, so this must have happened later, while he was driving to see me, and—

"A gun, ma'am."

"A *gun*? He hit a gun?" An incredibly dumb response, but trust me, as soon as I'd heard this stranger say "Medical Center," I'd burned off half my IQ, and whatever was left was busy trying hard to not hear, not know, not get it.

"A gun hit *him*, ma'am," he said gravely, precisely, kindly, as if he weren't talking to an idiot. "Or rather, a bullet from a gun."

"You mean . . . you mean . . ." I knew what he meant. He'd been as clear and coherent as a person could be. But I couldn't believe it or accept it until I heard the actual words, one after the other, in an orderly, definitive sentence.

So he provided that sentence. "Yes'm," he said softly and gently. "I'm sorry, but your friend, Mr. Mackenzie, has been shot."

Thirteen

"**Y**OU'LL do anything, Mackenzie, won't you? You'll even get yourself shot to get out of a capital-T talk."

He didn't seem to be registering what was in front of him, i.e., me. He blinked, proving that he was at least partially alive. Otherwise, no matter what the nurse had said, I'm not sure I'd have believed it. His skin was a close match for the gray sprinkles in his curly hair, his features expressionless, his body inert.

And then he blinked again, did a double take as comprehension flooded his eyes into such neon-bright intensity, I was surprised the bandages on his head didn't catch any of their blue light. For once, I knew precisely what it was to be a sight for sore eyes, and I knew how good it felt, too.

"Welcome back." I was proud of my composure and lack of sentimentality. Here I was in a hospital room, the perfect setting for a schmaltz-intensive scene, and I was having none of it. I spoke in an upbeat bedside voice. "Do you know you're in a hospital with a Frank Sinatra wing? And that you're a stone's throw away from Bally's Grand and Caesar's Palace?"

"Hey," he whispered. He looked like a fair-skinned Sikh in his gauze turban. "You're here. You're really here."

And that was it for stoicism and ironic detachment. I burst into tears. Flying Chagall characters did a freefall through the room, their violin bows going a mile a minute. So much for aplomb.

Hours had gone by. Hours that took days to pass. Hours during his surgery and post op, during which I grappled with *War and Peace* until I realized that I had read a sentence about Prince Nikolay Andreivitch Bolkonsky's need for a regular schedule for seventeen minutes straight. Or perhaps it was seventeen hours straight. After that, I switched to a *Vegetarian Times* magazine that was sitting on a nearby table. After a few more decades, I retained only a headache and an impression that the rigid Prince Bolkonsky had eaten, at a set and specific moment each day, Easy Tofu Whip. And that the wait had been interminable.

The kindly woman whose function was, at least metaphorically, to hold relatives' and friends' hands, told me as much as she could find out about the shooting. It appeared that Mackenzie had attempted to stop an ordinary, garden-variety mugging. The woman's purse and person were saved and the would-be thief arrested, but C.K.'s right leg had been taken hostage. As a result, he was going to go through the rest of his life setting off metal detectors at airports, given the number of pins now holding a significant portion of his skeleton together. He had also fallen sideways from the force of the blast and done a minor number on his skull, which obviously wasn't nearly as thick as I'd assumed.

I couldn't stop blubbering. I wanted to be angry with him.

135

Who did Mackenzie think he was, Superman saving Metropolis? But it was too much of a stretch, because I knew if I were being robbed by a street thug, I'd want a Mackenzie of my own. That particular thought sent me into further spasms.

"For our hero." In walked a pair of feet topped by a gigantic vase of red roses. "From Mrs. Weinstein and her children and grandchildren." The nurse put the bouquet on his nightstand. The vase occupied so much space, there was no longer room enough for a pill bottle.

"So embarrassin'." Mackenzie spoke dreamily, as if the anesthesia hadn't completely worn off. "Didn't see the gun until . . . Feel like a fool. Wait till they hear about it. What was wrong with me? Where *was* I?"

I appropriated one of his tissues and blew my nose. "You know," I said, "they just stitched you up, so self-laceration seems pretty ungrateful." My voice wobbled and I sniffled some more.

"Huh?" He was still lost in the fog zone.

"Stop beating yourself up." I sat down beside the bed, blew my nose again and took three deep breaths. "You saved that woman. You're a hero, and not only to Mrs. Weinstein."

"Shoulda seen her. Littlest lady I ever saw. Like in a fairy tale. Four-foot-something. Square little body. Old. And poor-lookin'. Old coat, old kerchief on her head. What kind of kid sees that and—" He winced and gasped. He had attempted to shake his head for emphasis.

He wasn't as thoroughly hardened as I sometimes made myself believe he was. He was still amazed and disgusted by what people did to one another. However, he was going to have to hold off on the body language for a while.

"You're a really good human being." I barely got the words out before I was sucked into another emotional wind tunnel.

He waited through my siege of snuffling, either through gallantry or druggy oblivion, I wouldn't know. "So," he finally said, very softly, "here I am. Captive audience. Don' want you thinkin' I forgot our capital-T talk. Shoot. Or is that a poor choice of expressions today?"

"Now? You want to talk *now*?"

"Don' ever want to have that kind of talk, so why not?"

"Did they check for brain injuries, C.K.?"

He grinned. "Lots of time for once. It's a good bet I'm not goin' to rush off for a sudden emergency."

"Is this a play for sympathy? You, wounded and lying there, looking like—"

"No?" he asked.

I shook my head.

"Good, then. Ah gave it my best shot. Why *do* we have so many gun images in our speech, do you think? Anyway, give me points for tryin'." He smiled crookedly and put out his hand. I took it in both of mine. "Feel like a fool, though. A laughing stock. A cop who didn't see a kid's gun. Barely saw the kid—or Mrs. Weinstein. I was lost in my head, a million miles away."

"I understand. It was that kind of time. I was thinking, too." We were having that capital-T talk after all.

"Walkin' back, it dawned on me that I hadn't been payin' real attention. Just goin' along the same old way, in the same old patterns."

"I'm also responsible," I murmured, meeting him halfway. They say compromise is the basis of good relationships, after all. "I didn't make myself clear enough." I squeezed his hand— gently—to show how touched I was with this new Mackenzie. Why had I thought he was one-track, unable to change? "When they called me and said you were hurt—" I hesitated, then decided to be completely honest, the way he was being. "I—"

"So there I was," he said, continuing his monologue, "walkin', tryin' to figure my way out of my rut, to really *listen*, I mean really *hear*, and—"

"—realized how much you mattered to me even if there are problems," I said. "Tonight's been a hard lesson in how much I care about—"

"—even if she's cracked—"

"She?" The word reverberated in my brain. *She? She?*

"Mandy? You okay?"

I shook my head, nodded, felt my chin dangle, my cheeks burn with humiliation. What had we been talking about? Not a tender, if cryptic, lovers' reconciliation, that was for sure. Mackenzie had been off in hyperspace, talking about somebody else—a female somebody else.

"Say somethin'. You sick? What is it?"

I wasn't uttering another word until I had some sense of the topic. Instead, in a mean-spirited urge for revenge, I turned his hand palm up. At least I'd find out one of his secrets—his first name.

The plastic hospital wristband said only, *Mackenzie, C. K.* It didn't say *Gotcha!* but it might as well have.

"Livin' on the beach doesn't mean she doesn't know somethin'." Mackenzie continued on in his parallel dimension. "She did mention Jesse Reese by name, after all."

"Georgette?" It emerged a squeak.

He made a throaty noise of assent. "Georgette. I was tryin' to remember her name an' exactly what she said when Mrs. Weinstein and the kid came out of nowhere."

"Georgette?" There it was. And there Mackenzie was, still and always putting murder first. Except . . . my name had been in his wallet. I knew that now, and he knew that I knew it, too.

I gave up. There was simply too much feeling—good and bad, loving and infuriated, pro and con—to be ignored at this stage. We had flubbed breaking up. Done it wrong, thwarted our mutual escapes, thanks to fate in the squatty shape of Mrs. Weinstein.

"So do you think she knows somethin'? Could Reese maybe have robbed old women the way she said?"

I shrugged. "Perhaps you've forgotten that she also said Prince Charles was a good singer and had a lot of pep."

"He may."

"She said he was blind." I realized I was trying to discount Georgette, because Mackenzie had been thinking about her when he should have been thinking about me.

"Why Reese?" Mackenzie said in a slightly dreamy voice. His mind was fighting through the drugs and making it halfway. "She said J. Edgar Hoover, Prince Charles—"

"She meant Ray Charles."

"Donald Trump, George Bush, an' Jesse Reese. That's like one of those lists on a test—which one doesn't belong."

I wouldn't think he could have carried the woman's monologue through a trauma, but I seem to consistently underrate him.

"Hate things that don' make sense," he said softly. "Makes me mad to be stuck here, not knowin'." He closed his eyes, breathed deeply. "An' I . . . I think I need a little . . ."

"Sleep? Bedpan? Food? Quiet?"

He inhaled sharply. "Oh, boy," he said in an exhale.

"Painkiller?"

He tried to nod, winced again and grunted. It was almost a relief to know he really, truly wasn't Superman.

I rang for the nurse and kissed him very lightly on the forehead. "So this is how it feels to know exactly where you are," I said. "And where you'll be. I thought it'd be more fun than this. See you tomorrow. Heal."

I was at the door when he said, in an almost inaudible murmur, "Tonight made me realize how much I care, too."

I was going to have to really get it that no matter how slow and out of it he might seem, even when drugged, Mackenzie heard and remembered. His brain had parallel tracks, and he could monitor them all, and make you think he was daydreaming the whole time. I was going to have to stop underestimating the man.

Although, of course, he hadn't said just what it was he so much cared about. Or even who. Or even whom.

THE NEXT DAY DAWNED sunny and calm, very close to beach weather. Good thing I had no hopes of enjoying it, or I'd have been more upset when I swung my feet off the bed and my lower back clenched like a fist.

Hysterical ailment, I told myself. Jealous of the attention Mackenzie is getting. Garden-variety back pain, the first herald of middle age.

I walked around like a crone, trying, perhaps, to look like Mrs. Weinstein so that Mackenzie would come rescue me, too.

Then I forced myself to stand straight. Later I would arrange for a massage in the health club. Until then I didn't want to think about it.

The *USA Today* shoved under my door didn't mention anything as mundane as a local murder. But downstairs the Atlantic City newspaper on the rack outside the coffee shop still featured the story. NO FURTHER CLUES IN BRUTAL SLAYING, the headline said. SUSPECT IN CUSTODY. And then it rehashed Sasha's long-ago association with the dead mobster. I read on with incredulous amazement.

"It's not that much of a surprise. Sasha Berg always played with fire," former high school classmate and current A.C. resident Candace Winter, was quoted as saying.

Candace Winter? My former high school classmate as well, then, but the name . . . Then I realized who it had to be. Smarmy Candy Conroy, whose boyfriend had dropped her because of an infatuation with Sasha, who, for once, had done nothing to provoke trouble. Candy had screamed, "I'll never forgive you for this!" at Sasha—and at me, too, for remaining Sasha's friend. Who could have dreamed that she meant it?

But, incredibly, thirteen years later, Candy, married, settled down, was still angry enough to call the papers and have her revenge. People were perpetually amazing.

I took the paper to a table and settled in, marveling at Candy's ability to hate. For one happily crazed moment I decided that Candy Conroy Winter had murdered Jesse Reese and framed Sasha as final payment for the shame of losing Elliot "Rocky" Feinstock.

I'd thought that having breakfast in the coffee shop would be quicker than room service, and I expected it to be a quiet and meditative kickoff to the day's work. I was wrong on both counts because I hadn't factored in yet another encounter with Lala.

The woman was certainly making the most of her fiancé's largesse. She'd come to Atlantic City as a day-tripper, yet she never left, and furthermore, each time I'd seen her, she'd been in different ensembles.

This morning's was nautical. Her sailor collar was trimmed in gold braid, as were the cuffs of her slacks. She looked like an admiral in the AARP's navy.

"May I?" she asked even as she pulled out the chair across from me. I guess I could have said no, grabbed the chair, held her under the arms to stop her from sitting, but that required too much energy. "I had no idea Tommy was such a slugabed!" She shook her head, but the lacquer kept her buttercup curls immobile. "He'd like to sleep till noon and be up all night. What am I going to do?"

What she was going to do was have serious marital problems. Or perhaps no problems at all, because they'd never see each other.

"It's like I was telling my cousin Belle," Lala said. "Who, by the way, is down here. Arrived last night. You'll just love her, sweetheart. I told her all about you—well not exactly about how we met, if you know what I mean. But I was saying to her that I'm a morning person. And Belle said—oh look, there she is now. Would you mind awfully if she joined us? She's dying to meet you."

Something about Lala's delivery convinced me that there were no random situations in her life because she scripted each encounter. The only reason I didn't react to her manipulations with more anger was that I also suspected that fear prompted her careful planning and avoidance of chance.

Lala was peroxide and morning-bright, and Belle was inky darkness—black hair streaked with gray, and a still darker expression in her deep brown eyes. The yin and yang of cousinhood.

"Meet Belle, honey," Lala said.

"Pleased to meet you," Belle said. "What's Honey short for? Honora?"

"Amanda," I said.

She sat down and switched topics. "I just this minute got off the phone," she said. "I can hardly believe what I heard. Oh, boy, could I tell you things. . . ."

She was a Pushmi-Pullyu conversationalist. "Ah, please,

Belle," we were supposed to whine. "Tell us." Well I, for one, didn't.

"Do you know what she's talking about?" Lala asked me.

I shook my head.

"We don't mean to be rude."

"Who wouldn't know?" Belle asked.

"What if a person down here for a good time was too busy yesterday to pick up a local paper!" Lala snapped.

"I heard it on the car radio on Tuesday," Belle muttered. "Just that I'm not so good about names, but faces—"

"So there," Lala said. "So somebody might not know. The hotel is certainly keeping mum about it. Listen, darling, I don't want to upset you, but a man was killed in this hotel Monday, night before last. In one of the rooms. Murdered."

"Oh, that. Yes. I heard."

"Of course!" Lala slapped the side of her head. "My own Tommy told you yesterday. I was there!"

I raised my eyebrows and looked pleadingly at the waitress who hovered nearby.

"No place is safe anymore. You come to a nice hotel, meet somebody, expect . . ." Lala shuddered. "It makes me mighty happy to be out of the dating game. You never know."

"You take your life in your hands. Literally," Belle agreed.

"A bagel," I told the waitress. "Toasted."

"And a smear?" she asked.

I nodded. "And coffee."

Lala and Belle paused from their death and doom lip-smacking long enough to order French toast and a crew-sant with a side of prunes, respectively.

Then Lala leaned over and patted my wrist. "I hope you find somebody like my Tommy, too, but until then, I hope you're always very careful."

"And not only with your body," Belle said, intimations of disaster hanging off every word. "They talk about safe sex, but what about safe money, I want to know."

"They already have that," Lala said. "You ever hear of banks?"

"My condominium has a social club," Belle said. "But at first, I didn't connect that to his face."

"She means she wasn't sure of who had died until she saw the dead man's photograph in the paper," Lala explained. I felt like Alice, perhaps, in the company of Tweedledum and Tweedledee.

Belle nodded. "Then I made the connection. He spoke to our group a year ago. I remember the face, even though I didn't invest with him. I have my pension, my Social Security, and some C.D.'s, but I went to hear what he had to say. About *protecting* yourself. Especially single women. Widows. Besides, it was a night out. A little entertainment. So yesterday, I called Myrna Myers. I said did you see in the paper? Jesse Reese, that man who talked to the social club, was murdered. And she started spluttering and carrying on like I couldn't believe!"

Lala leaned over the table and wagged her finger in front of her cousin. "Do you remember how angry Grandma would get with you? 'Get to the point!' she'd shout."

"Huh?" Belle said.

"What about Myrna Myers, Belle?"

Belle sat up straighter and spent a moment pouting, then got on with it. "She hadn't seen the item. It was only a little notice, a little photo, on the second page of the *Inquirer*. I was surprised, frankly. I thought he was such an important man. Maybe that's just what they tell social clubs, so we'll feel like our speakers are top quality."

Second page. Small photo. Perhaps the whole story was so inconspicuous as to be passed over by most people. Perhaps it wouldn't include any mention of Sasha or me. Perhaps not a single relative would see it or worry over it or think to share the concern long-distance with my parents.

"Honestly, Belle!" Lala snapped. "Get to the point!"

Belle slowly pulled off a greasy corner of her croissant and stalled before speaking again, reestablishing control of her tempo, delivery, and news. "So I told her what happened, and Myrna gets all crazy, saying he wouldn't give her the time of day for such a long time, and now, finally, when she thought it was settled, she'll never get her money. Makes no sense to me, and before she can explain, she says she's got to tell the others, has to tell everybody. A couple hours later she calls me back. You know how she is, she went knocking door to door, all the club members, the ones she remembered had gone to hear him speak, especially one or two."

"This better be good," Lala grumbled.

"See, at least ten people had invested with him. Some gave him everything they had." She sipped delicately at her tea.

"So what? That's what he did. Invest money."

"Maybe yes, maybe no."

Lala raised a warning finger, then shook her head. "You're impossible. These people who invested with him, did they make out all right? Yes or no."

"Well, they got dividends right away, so everything seemed fine unless you had an emergency and wanted your real money back. The capital, as they say. That's the problem. What happened to the big money is a mystery."

Being with Belle was as good as a session at the gym upstairs. My pulse had reached near-aerobic speed and I could almost hear my heart pound. She was talking about a motive, one of the best—money. A motive Sasha Berg did not possess.

"It turns out that three months ago, when Myrna's son had that auto accident," Belle continued, "there were things the insurance didn't cover, like baby-sitters, because his wife had to go back to work and he was in no shape to—they have twins, you know—"

"Get to the point!"

Belle folded her hands and glared. We'd reached an impasse.

But it was an old game between them, and only after Belle had punished Lala a sufficiently annoying length of time did she clear her throat and continue. "So she asked for the capital. To liquidate her account. I think it's a bad idea to give your son everything, even if he had an accident, especially a son that hadn't exactly been the most self-sufficient type, but—" She looked at her cousin. "Okay, okay. Like I said, that was three months ago.

She still can't get her money back. They stalled, said she'd be losing money, said it was unwise, said that she'd wind up paying too many taxes. She kept saying she needed it. It's her right, you know. It's her money. But they did this and they did that—and in the meantime, another woman in the social club—she'd seen Myrna at the laundry—heard what was going on and she got nervous, too, and also asked for her money, and what do you think happened?"

"Nothing?" Lala whispered.

Belle nodded. "Exactly. One excuse after another about funds being tied up and Mr. Reese being unavailable. And Mr. Perrillo, too, he tried. His wife has the Alzheimer's now and he's not exactly too swift himself, and they convinced him that he had almost nothing in the account. He just gave up and said he must be confused. But even without him, by last week Myrna was boiling. Couldn't get a straight answer. Called the District Attorney's office and they said it would take time, did she have any evidence, Myrna's in Pennsylvania and Reese is in Jersey . . . you know the runaround. Let's be honest—who wants to help an old lady? Especially a poor one."

Lala nodded and twisted her new diamond ring. Her hand shook a bit as she did so, and I understood how tenuous her hold had been on security—at least until Tommy gave her some. I tried to be less judgmental about how she'd chosen to avert a poverty-stricken old age.

Meantime, Belle continued her agonizingly slow and convoluted trip through every trivial detail of the lives of everyone who'd come near her orbit. Her ideal audience would be an archeologist, used to patiently sifting through tons of detritus for one shard of value. I, however, practice a less patient profession.

I pulled a small piece off my bagel and dropped it on the plate, only to pull off another piece. What definite bits of information had I gotten from the woman's meandering conversational path? Mostly that Jesse Reese had taken old people's money and had possibly done something wrong with it, or at least wouldn't readily return it.

And during the months or weeks before he died, some people were aware of his shenanigans with the money, or were at least suspicious.

Belle had derailed and was now describing a gall-bladder operation, slowly reciting each symptom and stitch. For a moment there was some question of whether the patient had lived through it, then I realized we were still talking about Myrna. The operation had been a year ago.

How many people had been alerted to Jesse Reese's hanky-pank? I wondered. How effective were the condominium tomtoms? To how many people had Myrna directly expressed her confusion, irritation, and concern over the last three months—and to whom had those people spoken?

"The poor woman," Belle said. "She's finally over that, and now the whole business made her so upset, her angina started up. Almost every single cent she had saved in her whole life—twenty-four thousand six hundred and fifty dollars—was tied up with that man. As if she didn't have enough troubles with her son and his lazy wife and those twins, now. But then, finally, they tell her to come to the office on Wednesday. That there will be a check for all the money waiting, and Mr. Reese will explain everything. Sorry for the delay. Wednesday, so you understand why she was upset about his dying on Monday? I told her it will just take a little longer, that's all. She'll get her money. Maybe the check's already signed and waiting for her. It's like I always say. The squeaky wheel gets the worm."

I always said that, too. But right now I said, "I wonder if you'd be willing to make a few more phone calls, find out who Myrna talked to about Jesse Reese during the past few months, people at other condominiums, or people who go to churches that Jesse Reese addressed. Then try to reach those people and find out whether they talked to Jesse Reese themselves and what happened." I needed to know how much pressure had been on Jesse Reese these last few months.

"Why?" Lala asked. "Why do you care about old people?"

I tried to look indignant. "I'm hoping to be one someday. Besides, it's the right thing to do."

"A regular do-gooder," Belle said, but with admiration, not contempt.

"If we can find enough people with stories like Myrna's," I said, "then maybe they'd have a class action suit, get more respect from the D.A.'s office." I had no idea whether what I was saying made any sense postmortem. "Keep notes. I'll meet with you later today and we'll go over everything together."

Belle nodded. "So like I was saying, when Myrna's angina started, she called the doctor, and who does he turn out to be but Selma's son-in-law, you know—married to the daughter with the funny teeth?"

At this point I did not care for whom Belle told. I put my share of the breakfast costs on the table and stood up.

"Hon," Lala said as I said goodbye, "do you realize it's long-distance to Philadelphia? Tommy has a calling card, but—"

"Use it. You'll be reimbursed."

"Honey, it's peak hours, you understand?" Lala said.

"No matter." I nearly gagged getting that one out. One medical monologue of Belle's all on its own was beyond my financial capacity, but it was important to know what kinds of pressures, from where, had been on Jesse Reese in the last few weeks of his life.

"A lot of money," Lala murmured, but then she nodded, and seemed to trust me.

It was worth the risk. I'd find the money somewhere.

This was probably precisely the way the late Jesse Reese had thought, and look where it had gotten him.

147

Fourteen

I WALKED through the lobby ticking off the day's obligations and thinking as well about the data Lala and Belle had provided. There was a new and interesting light on everything.

I was consumed by the idea of a horde of angry and frightened senior citizens, worried, possibly with cause, that they'd been taken.

What had Reese really done, if anything, and what was facing him, and how much did it matter to him?

There was, of course, the possibility that Belle and her friends were on the wrong track. I didn't understand finance, let alone its nuances, so perhaps there were real reasons Reese couldn't or shouldn't liquidate the old people's accounts. Maybe he'd been in the right, protecting their funds.

On the other hand, was it possible that the small man seen by the witness was one of the elderly and enraged? And if so—who was his Sasha-look-alike cohort? An able-bodied child? A would-be heir avenging the evaporation of her inheritance?

But—in my hotel room? Why on earth?

It wasn't clear whether any legal action against him had been begun, either. It would be nice to think it had, that Reese was in immediate danger of exposure, but it would take Belle and Lala a while to find that out.

I sighed and thought about more tangible issues. Mackenzie's luggage still needed retrieving, and he and Sasha both needed revisiting. I'd never gotten to Reese's ex-partner Palford, and I wanted to talk with Poppy and/or Holly again, probe the inconsistencies in Poppy's story.

I did such a good job of ticking and thinking that I forgot to take the elevator down to the parking garage, and found myself, instead, standing at the boardwalk railing.

I breathed deeply of the beautiful June day surrounding me, and looked longingly toward the beach. It was not yet bikini weather, but it would have been a fine day to lie inert as a dead battery being recharged after a winter's worth of dimness.

If only it weren't for details like my best friend's being in prison and my whatchamacallit's being in the hospital. As the only ambulatory member of the trio, I had obligations. I stood at the railing, trying to savor and prolong the moment.

I looked out to sea while trying to organize my various errands geographically. Each of them would take me to a different part of the city. Picking up Mackenzie's suitcase at his hotel seemed a good first stop. Then down to the hospital, and back to the county jail and Sasha. Palford, then Poppy and Holly.

Maybe the police would give me more time with Sasha, even without Mackenzie's intervention. Maybe her cousin would be there. Maybe she'd even be released this morning.

I gasped, because just then, far down on the beach, I saw Sasha. She *had* been released and she was here, on the hard-packed sand near the water, the horrendously out-of-style brown hair that belonged on a country singer or a go-go girl an extravagant tangle, a tan cape swirling around her as she moved. I called her name, but the sounds floated away long before they reached her. I felt giddy with relief. Sasha was free! Case closed!

Unless, of course, I applied a modicum of logic, which against my will I began to do. It was June, and even if it wasn't setting heat records, it wasn't the frigid temperatures that called for Sasha's wool cape. Which wasn't tan, anyway. And which Sasha hadn't brought to the beach.

And which, therefore, she couldn't now be wearing.

The figure near the surf wasn't Sasha at all, but a creature of my wish-fulfillment. The woman on the sand turned toward the boardwalk and picked her way up. Not Sasha in the least, except for the hair. Another person with liberated locks, that was all.

Back to square one. I might as well get going to the dungeon to retrieve the car. I took one last sniff of salt air and turned.

"Hey! Where you going? I was coming up here to you, didn't you see?"

I swiveled back. The wild mass of curls had completely altered Georgette's appearance, subtracting years and creating a whole new persona.

"Didn't recognize you," I said as she approached. "You're looking very fancy."

Her missing teeth gave her laugh a melancholy note. "You like?" She patted her hair. "When I was a kid, I thought if I had curls, lots of thick hair, oh, then I'd be completely happy."

"Well, now you have them."

"A few problems left, though," she said with another smile. She seemed altogether buoyant today.

"Nonetheless, my compliments to your beautician."

"You mean the Dumpster on Pacific, behind Trump's. Got a pair of high heels there yesterday, can you imagine? Perfectly good shoes, and somebody throws them away." She patted her head again. "Just as good as the ones Zsa Zsa advertises. Or is it her sister? Where's the cute boyfriend?"

"He's—I never said he was my boyfriend."

"Well if he isn't, you're the dumb one." She giggled and looked almost coy. "Unless he's no good, that is. Some are. Maybe most. So be careful." And like that, the merriment was gone. Her eyes deadened, her mouth curled downward. I wondered whether she was on medication, or should be.

"Wish my son . . . if I had curly hair and a house somewhere for my son . . . only wanted to be *ordinary*." She looked at me. "If wishes were horses, right?" And then she sat down on the steps up from the sand and cried, rubbing a hand across her eyes.

I walked down to where she was and sat beside her, hoping my presence would provide comfort, since I had no idea what to say.

"Kurt Junior. He . . ." She shook her head with its heavy brown curls. "Drunk one night after his father died, and drove away and crashed and . . ." She exhaled and shook her head again.

"And Big Kurt." She waved her arms at the empty air. "Out of work, no insurance, then he gets sick. Dies, but the money, the money, it thinks I'm dead, too. Except for my sister."

I patted her hand, gloveless today. The cape, its former life as a well-used tablecloth recognizable up close, slipped off her shoulders. She wore a reindeer-patterned cardigan over a blouse with a round collar, and two skirts that I could see.

"I worked, you know, when he got so sick. Waited tables, but I couldn't always . . . after my son . . . headaches all the time. Couldn't sleep. My sister said not to worry, just get well, and as long as she had a roof over her head . . . And even after. Happily ever after, like in stories." She breathed in raggedly and looked at me. "Who is your boyfriend, then, if Mack isn't?"

"I'm sorry about your son and your husband and your sister. That's really hard." Everybody, I thought. Everybody gone and no safe harbor anywhere.

Her eyebrows arched in surprise, almost as if she'd forgotten that she'd just told me about her family. Then she looked down at her hands. "My sister worked so hard, her heart gave out.

She'd be sorry, too, if she could see me now. She thought our old age was taken care of. It's not her fault. Can't trust anybody. Do you have a job?"

I nodded.

"Not waitressing, right?"

"Right."

"Good." She leaned to whisper something. Once again a mild whiff of alcohol accompanied her closeness. "Shelters are no good. Too scary."

"Well, maybe not all of them. Maybe we could find one that wasn't—"

She shook her head vigorously, curls flying, and waved my suggestion off with both hands rapidly crisscrossing in front of her face. "No shelters for me."

"Can't you get welfare money, then? Get your own place?"

She shook the curls again. "Need an address to get benefit checks."

"You mean you have to get off the streets before you can get the check that would get you off the streets?"

She flashed the gap-toothed grin again. "Something like that. I saw him once, right over back there." She pointed over her shoulder, back toward the boardwalk and its buildings. "Dressed all fancy. He gave me a quarter. I said 'Where's the rest? Where's the part you kept?' He looked at me like I was scum. I'da had my sister's apartment if he hadn't robbed her."

The scattered elements of her stories began to pull together like pieces of a puzzle, and the picture that began to emerge frightened me on her behalf. The robbery, the sister's safety net—investments?—gone, the newspaper story she considered lucky, even the chambermaids who let her into vacant hotel rooms so she could shower. Access. Motive? "Georgette," I said, "who was it that gave you the quarter?" Would she still say it was Reese? Or would it now be J. Edgar Hoover, or Michael Jackson?

"I thought he was cute."

"The man who robbed you?"

"Mack. That's the problem, isn't it? They're so cute. And

where's Lucky? His mother watching him for once? People who have kids and don't even . . ." She looked at her hands again. One of her fingernails was black, as if something heavy had crashed onto it.

"The man who robbed your sister and you," I persisted. "What was his name?"

And with that, for her own unknowable reasons, I had crossed an invisible line, intruded, become a danger. She pulled away, emotionally and physically, moving to the edge of the stairs. "What's it to you?" she asked in a sullen tone.

I couldn't manage more than fish noises, semisilent bubbles of sound replacing words. "I—I didn't mean to pry," I finally stammered.

"Yes you did. You meant to."

"I—" My denial froze in my throat. What were the rules of etiquette to her? Why tell a polite lie to this woman while I was asking her for the truth? "Yes," I said. "I was prying and I meant to."

She rewarded me with a smile again. "Well, then it's okay." She sat forward and clasped her hands around her knees. "It's the lying that gets me. How about you?"

I nodded, somewhat shamefully, given my recent record.

"Does Mack lie?"

"He isn't like the man who robbed you and your sister." I hoped that put us back on course.

"He sure is a looker."

"Yes," I agreed. "More's the pity."

"My sister never married. Much older. Took care of me when our mother died. He told her the money was safe. Her life's earnings. Wigs itch, you know that? Ever wear one?"

I shook my head. "Did you try to get the money back? Did you see a lawyer about it?"

"Oh . . . all those papers to get together, and the landlord when I didn't have the rent made me leave before I finished, and where was I supposed to put everything then, so I lost stuff and in the first place, I don't know any lawyers, so . . ." She shrugged. "I don't know. . . ."

In Philadelphia there are always ads for people who, for a fee, promise to organize your life, from your kitchen cupboards to your time schedule. I wished there'd have been one for Georgette, for all the Georgettes. Somebody who'd have kept them from smothering in the minutiae of daily life and bureaucratic rigamarole, someone who'd have held them tight before they disconnected and drifted loose into the void.

"Wait here," she said, and with surprising speed and agility she was up and onto the sand and under the boardwalk to her private quarters.

I tried to estimate her height before she bent over to enter her lair. She was on the tall side, a rangy woman with big bones and wild hair. I, who surely knew more about the original than an old man with failing eyesight who was the only witness—I had mistaken her for Sasha.

A minute or so later she was back, holding yesterday's rumpled newspaper with Jesse Reese's face on the front. "Him," she said, putting the paper in my lap, photo up. "Serves him right. Why should he have a nice old age if my sister didn't?"

Her words were emphatic, but her voice was always low, a bit flat, as if by now she lacked the psychic energy to shout or rail. I wished I were as convinced that she lacked the energy required to murder. I did not want this woman to have been the killer of Jesse Reese. "When you read about it in the newspaper," I prompted, "you must have been surprised."

"I always knew it was going to happen. He was a bad man and he had to pay. *You* might have been surprised, but not me. I saw him. He liked that casino over there. I watched and I waited for this to happen."

"The wig," I said, trying a new tack. "It's really quite beautiful. Has it always itched? Or did that just happen when it got old—or is it old? It looks brand-new."

She looked completely fuddled. "New to me," she said after due consideration.

"How long have you had it?"

She continued to look confused. A sense of time was most likely not her strong suit. "Blink and me, we go out on Tuesdays," she said. "That's the best time, when the stuff is out there for pickup. Is that what you mean?"

I nodded. "Do you know which Tuesday it was? Yesterday was a Tuesday. Was it then?"

"You won't find one now," she said. "They took it all away this morning. They take everything away on Wednesdays." Her expression cleared. "But hey, you like the wig?" And she pulled it off and tossed it to me, like a dead animal. "You can have it." She overrode my protests. "Too itchy, anyway."

Now surely, if she'd committed the murder and read about it in the paper and noted mention of a brown-haired tall woman— surely not even Georgette would casually toss me criminal evidence. I didn't want to take away her thick brown hair, the source of her happiness, but I definitely wanted hard evidence. And I wanted the police lab to find out whether there was blood on it. Something. Perhaps evidence of someone else who had worn it. Someone who now had only one tiny pearl earring.

Georgette's head was slightly cocked, as if waiting for something.

"I'll borrow it," I said. "You'll get it back." I hoped that was true. If not, I'd find a way to buy her a thick-haired wig of her own.

"Aw," she said. "It's not like it's a pet you have to return to its owner. It's a wig, and I only had it for one day."

I remembered that yesterday she'd carried a roughly tied packet, the one with the high heels and the book. I'd thought she had a pelt in there, and I'd imagined dead animals, not a disguise chucked nearly at the scene of the murder. "So who cares about it, anyway?" she asked.

I grabbed one of her hands as I clutched the wig in the other. "I do," I said. "I really do!"

"Yeah?" She looked at me appraisingly, tightening her eyes like a merchant weighing produce. "How much?"

Georgette was no longer, if she'd ever been, a creature of sentiment. She couldn't afford to be one. "Let me rent it." I pulled out bills. "And you get yourself a room for the night, okay? Not in a shelter, a hotel."

She pushed the bills into the pocket of an underskirt, looking much more exposed and unprotected with her wispy hair, the skull showing through.

"You know, Georgette, you may have just saved somebody's life." I controlled the urge to dance, to shout, to carry on.

She showed no interest or curiosity. I couldn't blame her. When you're barely holding on yourself, you don't have hands left over for reaching out to save others.

But intentionally or not, she had provided the possible means to turn the searchlights off Sasha, and, waving the shank of hair like a talisman, giddy with hope, I descended into the bowels of the earth to find my trusty steed and charge off in defense of justice, truth, and horrific wigs.

When all of this was over, I was going to *insist* that Sasha get a decent haircut.

Fifteen

THE wig felt like an alien being, the spirit of the non-Sasha who had murdered Jesse Reese. Forget Mackenzie's luggage. It could surely wait to be retrieved. Nobody was going to be able to use it for a while now. I turned my itinerary around and went directly to jail. "Do not pass Go," I muttered to myself as I drove past the Monopoly board streets. The buildings were not nearly as well preserved or tidy as the little green houses and big red hotels I remembered struggling to acquire. Real-life properties in the real-life game had a shorter shelf life than their plastic equivalents.

I entered the station like a scalper, toting my trophy.

The desk sergeant seemed to endure rather than hear me as I explained the hows and whys of the wig. "Her? Hell, I know crazy Georgette," he said when I'd finished my presentation. "Everybody does. Always some bug up her—" He cleared his throat. "I used to patrol that area, and every time she'd see me, there'd be another complaint about being robbed. A real one-trick pony, except she wouldn't fill out forms or do anything except complain. Doesn't trust anybody. Can barely get her into a shelter when it's zero out."

"But this is different," I reminded him, all the while feeling sorrier than ever for Georgette, who had only half the idea and no ability to get her albatross off her back. "A separate issue. She found this in a trash can behind the casino, the day after Jesse Reese was murdered by somebody who had this kind of hair. When Georgette was wearing this wig, she almost looked like Sasha Berg, the woman you've arrested. Anybody tall would. This could be important evidence."

He poked a finger into his ear and shook his head, as if trying to scratch his brain.

If you want to push a woman toward hysteria, there is nothing quite as effective as confronting her with a truly impassive man, is there? My vocal cords twisted and strained, my decibel level rose to get through to the man—and I knew that if he dared to say "No need to get all upset about it," I'd kill him, right here, in the police station. "And there was a *pearl earring* yesterday," I said. "In my *shoe*! In the room *where it happened*! Do you know if they have the earring now? If they found out whose earring it was?"

"I'm not a homicide detective. Not on the case, ma'am." His face contorted as he attempted to swallow a yawn. Then he coughed and cleared his throat. "If you were told the earring would get to the proper authorities, it did. And so will the hairpiece." And before I could complete a request to see somebody who was directly involved in the case, the sergeant raised his hand like a traffic cop. "Person in charge isn't here."

"But you'll tell him where and how it—"

He nodded and tilted his head back, scratching his neck with his uniform collar. "You wanted to see your friend?" he asked.

"Sasha Berg. Yes."

"She's in there."

"Right, but you have my phone number in case he—"

"Better hurry, she doesn't have use of that room forever."

Dismissed. I gave the sergeant a vote of no confidence, and beseeched the gods of criminal justice to properly track the wig and the pearl earring.

Sasha needed to get out of this place, quickly. Even the small portion of the jail we now shared was the antithesis of welcoming, comfortable, or human. The walls looked painted with high-gloss fungus, the floor was dull black tile with an unsettling white squiggle, and the furnishings were equally inhospitable—a fake-wood Formica-topped table and chairs with slats that deliberately aimed for the aching small of my back.

And this was the nice part; the reception area. I could see a small reflection of what the cells must be like on Sasha. There is a thin and easily worn-away patina of confidence that separates winners from losers, and I already could see rusty patches in Sasha's armor. She shook her head at my suggestions of toiletries or fresh underwear or even a book, because she needed to believe she was getting out of here this afternoon. Her cousin the lawyer from New Jersey had said so.

"But in case it's not till tomorrow?" I quietly suggested. Her cousin had to file a motion. I had no idea whether that would move as quickly as filing his nails—or as slowly as filing her way out of the cell. Sasha grudgingly agreed to a short list.

"They probably won't let you take any of my things," she said in a flattened-out voice. "My underwear is evidence. I can't stand it." She put her head in her hands. I'd never seen her this way before.

"Then I'll buy something new, or you can have some of mine."

She looked up and raised her eyebrows. "Surely that exceeds the bounds of friendship, don't you think?" When I didn't answer, she sighed. "Okay, then. But if you bring a book, make it sleazy, all right?"

"I was going to loan you my personal copy of *War and Peace* along with the unmentionables."

She rolled her eyes. "If I thought I'd be here long enough to read it, I'd hang myself with my bra as a noose."

It wasn't easy making conversation. This was not exactly a forum designed to encourage the exchange of ideas. Besides, most ideas would have been impolite, insensitive. One avoided, for kindness' sake, the topic of what was currently going on—as in being locked up; what had been going on—as in having been locked up and accused of murder; and what presumably would continue to go on—as in being locked up forever. There are precious few topics left when the past, present, and future are eliminated.

"So Dunstan's really gone," she said after I'd brought her up to date. "Or Edgar, as it were. He's kind of intriguing, though, don't you think?" That's the kind of thinking that ensures that she'll get herself in trouble again, given the chance.

"You need monitoring," I said. "A caretaker. You make spectacular mistakes of judgment."

"Find me a woman who's still dating at age thirty and who hasn't made spectacular mistakes of judgment, then we'll talk. Meanwhile, let's stay with this mistake. The one about putting me in jail for something I never did and never could have done. They'll find Dunstan, won't they? Whoever he's becoming. He's the one who knows where I was."

"I'm sure they're giving it their all." That was a gross distortion of the truth. First of all, everything that pointed away from Sasha—Dunstan, the wig, the earring—was irrelevant if a person was completely satisfied pointing at Sasha. Second of all, unless *America's Missing Persons* decided to feature Dunstan this very week, he could be gone a long, long time. He was a man who knew how to establish a new identity, so where and for whom did one begin to look?

Still, this did not seem a time for the absolute truth. I couldn't bear the idea of turning the screws, then leaving her alone to dwell on the terrifying possibilities ahead, so I changed the sub-ject. "Mackenzie isn't going to find much except a bedpan for a while," I said. "He's in the hospital. He was shot."

Her eyes opened so wide, I could see white above the pupil. "Because of . . . did Dunstan do it?"

I shook my head. "Don't laugh, promise? I don't think I could handle it right now if you make fun of this."

She nodded.

"A kid did it. On the street. Mackenzie stopped him from mugging a little old lady."

"Shot," she said. "Jesus. What—shot where?"

"Atlantic Avenue, about—"

"For God's sake—I mean where is he wounded? What's hurt?"

"His leg and his ego. And he bumped his head, too."

She was quiet for a while. Her relationship with Mackenzie had been prickly for so long, I thought she might snicker, or cast aspersions on his expertise. Instead, she asked decent and appro-priate questions about his prognosis and current condition. She expressed sympathy. "When Mackenzie came here, Monday night—"

I was startled. She hadn't called him the flatfoot or the law or the narc or the pig or Eliot Ness or any of her other pet tags for him. She'd used his name—or the part of it we knew. That was a historic first.

"—I kind of started to realize he was probably . . . okay," she said.

All right, it wasn't an overwhelming endorsement, but it was close enough. I quietly rejoiced. Crime had accomplished what I never could. Sasha had mellowed toward C.K. "He *is* an okay sort," I agreed. "My life would be less complicated if he were not. But what made you change your mind about him?"

"I don't know. He came back again yesterday, before he went to look for Dunstan, and we talked. He said it was time for a truce so we could work together and get me out. Asked a lot about what I knew, which was pretty much nothing. And he showed me a photo of Jesse Reese. That was the first time I rec-ognized him. The person I saw dead was so . . . oh, it was horrible. But the photo—it was the man I talked to in the bar, before I went out with Dunstan. Anyway, Mackenzie promised to help any way he could, and to push on the police here, see who in Philly knew people on the force here. Things like that. I was impressed."

"Frankly," I said with a grin, "it worries me when you approve of somebody I'm seeing. You have such terrible taste in men."

She shrugged. "Didn't he tell you he was here again yesterday?"

He'd said something about talking with her, but I didn't remember discussion of a second visit. Maybe he hadn't had time to tell me, or maybe he'd forgotten, or maybe he truly believed charity should be anonymous. Or maybe he was such an okay sort, he took for granted such acts and didn't think they required explanation. I told her about the earring. "Did Jesse Reese by any chance wear small pearl buttons on his ears?" I asked. She nearly smiled. I told her about the glitzy and lame widow Reese and her sister-in-botany, Holly, about Georgette and the wig, and about Lala's cousin Belle and her friends. "There seem to be lots of people now who might have wanted the man gone."

"And probably every one of them knew who had that room." She sounded weary. "Frankie and his big mouth. He was proud of being able to comp me that room, so who knows who else he told? And whoever it was decided to become me by putting on a wig. That's all it takes. Can I tell you how awful that feels?" She twisted a somewhat spiritless tendril of hair around her index finger. "And I would *never* wear little pearl button earrings, so I'm doubly insulted."

"The witness was fairly senior. His eyes might not be the best for details. But even I, when I saw Georgette with the hair and the cape, for a minute, was sure it was you."

"What do you think it is, mass hysteria?" Sasha asked. "The miraculous vision of Sasha that opens locked doors? Can the room become a shrine?"

"Ah, but I know how the real killers got in." I explained about my experiment with the chambermaid. It was clever, Sasha agreed, but then her spirits sagged again. None of this answered the only important question, which was: Who was the make-believe Sasha? Until we found that out, the real Sasha remained framed.

"I didn't know anybody in the bar, except you and Frankie." Sasha played with a loose button on her cuff, tapping it with a fingernail until it rolled off onto the table. She put it in her shirt pocket with a satisfied smile, as if she'd completed a difficult job. "Did you frame me?" she asked. "The more I think about it, the more likely it seems. In fact, it's the only logical explanation. Admit it: you committed the murder. It all makes sense, then, except why you did it, of course."

"Thanks, but it works out even more perfectly if *you* committed the murder, and it saves time, too, since they've already fingerprinted you."

"Why would I murder somebody like Reese? I couldn't have gotten sufficiently involved to feel the urge. He was salt of the earth. Solid citizen. Man of the year. Not my type at all."

"There's a good chance he may have been a lying, cheating creep," I said.

"But I didn't know that soon enough. Had I but known he was a rat-bastard, I would of course have fallen for him and have been an actual, logical suspect. Instead, here I am, an actual, illogical suspect, and I didn't even get to have fun with the man first."

"You'll be out of here in no time." I hoped I sounded more convinced of that than I felt.

"Anybody could have done it, you know." She sounded morose. "A man, even, under the wig and a skirt."

"The kind of man you'd probably date," I said. It almost made her smile.

Still, by the time I left, not long after, I realized that the only impact my trip to the jailhouse was going to make was to ease Sasha's incarceration with clean undies and dirty reading material.

FROM THE IMMEDIATE LOOKS of it, my visit with Mackenzie was going to be as unproductive as the one with Sasha had been.

When I walked into his room, bearing his suitcase, he already had a visitor. So much for the quiet and private session I'd imagined.

"This is Pete," Mackenzie said. "He's on the force here, but he's got family in Louisiana an' he spent lots of time there. We're comparin' notes. Have a seat, let us bore you to tears."

The tears I shed were produced by yawns I couldn't prevent while the fellows reminisced about good times with their similarly enormous families on the bayou, and later, on the Atlantic City and Philadelphia forces respectively. Mackenzie's color was much better than it had been the day before, and his level of animation high. He was happy, having a great time.

This is who he is, I told myself. Adorable, fun, sexy, smart. But most of all, cop. You give yourself grief about it, dither over it, debate it, but the only thing you can really do about it is take it or leave it.

I left it, but only for a moment. I'm not proud of how I decided to improve the shining hour, but the truth is, I went to the nurse's station. "Could I see Mr. Mackenzie's medical record?" I asked.

"I'm not permitted to do that."

"I only want . . ."

She looked stern and intractable.

"Not the medical part."

"Yes?" She was not one of the more sensitive nurses on the floor. I hoped she specialized in comatose patients.

"His name. Could you just tell me what his name is on the chart?"

She looked at me as if perhaps she should wrap me tight in a white, sleeveless jacket.

"What harm could it do?" I asked in my sweetest, most subservient voice. That produced absolutely no response. "Then only his first name? Please?"

Her brow furrowed. "I don't think so." She shook her head.

"Why not?"

"Well . . ." She grudgingly pulled the file. "C," she hissed.

"Plain C." She smiled meanly, triumphantly. "*Now* are you satisfied?"

When Mackenzie was well enough to face charges, I would have him hauled in for failure to provide the hospital with full information about his name. Surely it was illegal, an insurance fraud or something.

Pete finally left, with promises to be back soon, and after the most cursory questions about health, comfort, plan of treatment, and the like, I continued the crime-oriented conversational theme, to keep up Mackenzie's level of enthusiasm.

We had catching up to do, all the way back to the flashy widow and her sister, then through the earring, the wig, the angry old folk, and, just because I was so proud of having figured it out, a reprise of the killer's method of entry into the hotel room.

Had even Scheherazade done a better job of producing engaging adventure stories? Mackenzie not only looked enchanted, he seemed impressed. For once, he didn't belittle my findings. "Interestin'," he kept murmuring. "All fits together."

I hated to end, but I had nothing left to pull out of my bag of clues. "That's about it so far," I said. "Except for a peculiar sense that the people here are too satisfied with the status quo and they aren't going to do a thing about changing it. I mean, are they searching for Dunstan, for example?"

He sighed, which I interpreted as a negative answer—nobody was overly interested in expending energy in a direction considered extraneous.

"How easy is it to get hold of a wig on a Monday night?" I asked.

"If, say, seized by a sudden inspiration to impersonate somebody else?" Mackenzie asked.

"Precisely. Is there a neighborhood Wigs Я Us? Would there be purchase records?"

Mackenzie was quiet for a while. "Lots of questions and directions," he finally said. "I will talk to Pete about them. Also was wonderin' where the man's car is. Thought maybe there'd be something in the trunk or the glove compartment that would shed light. It's an outside chance, but all the same—where is it? Pete says his car keys weren't on him and they haven't found a vehicle yet. Not at his house, either. Didn't seem the kind for a bus, and the train schedule was wrong for his timin'." Mackenzie shrugged. "Pete's a good guy, but I get the distinct sense they consider this thing solved and feel in need of no more than tidyin' up. So they maybe need help pointin' the way."

"Well, if you're going to be the helper, I hope you literally mean nothing more strenuous than pointing."

"That's precisely what I meant. But you're still mobile. Nobody took a potshot at you."

I pointed at my chest. Moi? He was suggesting that I sleuth? The one he called the overage Nancy Drew?

"There's a certain urgency in these things." He looked uncomfortable with the situation he had created. "Have to move quickly or ever'thin' goes cold. Think we could be a team?"

I nodded dumbly. A team. Following in the footsteps of Archie Goodwin and Nero Wolfe, Sherlock and the doc, Nick and Nora.

"I'll do the thinkin' here and you'll—"

"Yes?" I snapped. Maybe I even shrieked it. It was definitely not a hospital-smooth sound. "What is it you think I'll do as my part of the teamwork?"

"What do you think you'll do? What do you think I'd think you'd do? You'll have to be out there thinkin' an' walkin'." He grinned.

I wasn't sure if that's what he'd meant all along, or whether he'd reversed direction and bamboozled me.

"Down to business now," he said. "I think maybe we should know a little more about those investment plans and how they work."

"That's out of my league, you know. Anything that has to do with money."

"That partner of his. Ex-partner. He'd have an opinion on the man, don't you think? Could you free-lance another article? Or pretend to investigate on your parents' behalf? Whatever works."

"I was going there *anyway*," I said. "He was on my list before I even got here."

Mackenzie rolled his eyes. "I don't remember Nora telling Nick that she had the idea first. An' surely not snarlin' it."

I didn't say I was sorry, but I did smile.

"Ah hereby deputize you," Mackenzie said.

It felt more like being knighted.

We were off and running, or at least one of us was.

Sixteen

RAY Palford's offices were in a converted house in Margate. I climbed three broad wooden steps edged by blue-purple hydrangea bushes onto a wide white-painted porch filled with wicker furniture. For the first time, I felt at the shore. The real shore, as it should be.

Inside, the office was much closer to my fantasies of how a citadel of money should look than Jesse Reese's had been. Every furnishing had started out in the best circles and had since mellowed into understatement. Attractively aged Persian carpets, an inlaid wood coffee table, and buttery leather couches softened the reception area.

I wouldn't know from personal experience, but I assume that the harsh realities of profit and loss sound a lot better in this muted environment.

His receptionist was considerably younger than Miss Evans. A new generation, which was, perhaps, why I never once heard her echo the older woman's "I'm sorry." This time, when asked my business, I said something that was almost the truth. "I'm collecting information about the late Mr. Reese. Mr. Palford's former partner. My name is . . . Harriet. Harriet Vane." Well, part of it was the truth. Almost.

She nodded, rather curtly. Good thing so few people read these days, although I had heard that mysteries were enjoying a renaissance. Not Dorothy Sayers, perhaps? In any case, the general illiteracy makes it easier for the basically unimaginative to come up with an alias.

The receptionist checked her watch and double-checked his appointment book, then pressed a button on her phone and explained. I heard squawks and clipped questions. "Yes, Mr. Palford, I remember." She replaced the receiver and flashed me a wide, insincere smile. "He can see you for a few minutes. Then he has to leave for his scheduled meeting."

I thanked her and was ushered into larger, still more upholstered and waxed quarters. Surely investment counseling involved computer programs, numbers and guesstimates and projections on a little screen, but there was no hint of electronics. The office would have felt homey and familiar to Mary, Queen of Scots.

Computations were being made offstage, possibly in a galley belowstairs, filled with chained and half-naked economist slaves punching keypads.

Ray Palford stood behind a massive expanse of polished mahogany and slipped papers into a briefcase that looked made of glove leather. He himself appeared stitched of the same material. Tall, fit, smooth-skinned, younger than his dead ex-partner. "What is it this time?" he asked by way of greeting.

"Excuse me?"

"Brooke said you were investigating Jesse Reese, not me, so if you're here, there must be yet another snafu. I was afraid of this." He stopped filling his briefcase and gave me a stern look. "And I assume you have notified my lawyer that you were questioning me directly. Well," he said, "out with it. What now?"

"Listen, Mr. Palford, you've got me confused with somebody else. I don't have an 'it' to bring out. I just want to know about your former partner."

"What's happened with the suit?"

"You've mixed me up with your tailor?"

He settled into an amused relief. "Have a seat, have a seat." He waved me into a wing chair with a petit point design of the hunt. "Who are you, then? What's this about?"

"Grandmother Vane—she's housebound, but she's adamant about this, hysterical almost, and it does horrible things to her blood pressure and her heart—but she wants to call the police because she thinks Jesse Reese took her money. I'm not sure she's exactly . . . all there, you know? And now, of course, to make things worse, he's dead, poor man. I mean I don't think the police would be interested in a half-crazed old woman's . . . Anyway, I told her I'd consult another expert, and since you were once his partner, I thought maybe you could help explain things to her. We'd pay, of course, but I'm really at a loss. If we could make an appointment for you to talk with her, would you? I just had to find out—I promised her I'd find out today. She's panicking because of the news, you see."

He shook his head. "I'm sorry for your grandmother," he said. "If her suspicious are grounded in reality, of course. But as you may have inferred from my erroneous greeting to you, I am already embroiled in a lawsuit with the late Mr. Reese, and I feel that it would be improper for me to . . . well, I'm not exactly an impartial judge of Mr. Reese's fiduciary ethics."

"I don't know what to do," I said. "I tried talking to his assistant, but she—"

"Poor, pathetic Norma? You won't get anything except adoration from her. She'd faint if you suggested foul play. When they finally release Jesse's body, she'll probably commit suttee—immolate herself on his funeral pyre. She was Jesse's ideal woman, completely acquiescent. When I read the newspaper account of the manner of his death, about that big woman who killed him, I was surprised, in fact, that Jesse had taken up with a strong creature long enough for her to belt him. A fatal experiment, a very wrong change of pace for him. He likes people he can dominate, intimidate. Of course, even little flowers turn into man-eating plants. Look at his widow, an example in point. She was once Miss Sweetness and Light."

"Off-the-record," I said. "I really need some help. This is out of my league completely."

"What's off-the-record? What are we talking about?"

"Anything you say. Is it possible that Grandma's not crazy? That the man did worse than make bad investment judgments?"

Ray Palford raised his eyebrows and almost nodded. He looked at his watch, a wafer of gold, and scowled. "Let us say that Jesse Reese's and my philosophies of business—in fact our philosophies of life—were incompatible. I choose to believe that in both arenas, my preferences are the civilized ones. Mr. Reese, of course, would have and indeed did consider them timid or unimaginative. Had we both lived to be centenarians, we would have come no closer to agreement."

I picked my way through his weedy sentences. Was he angry? Enough to have killed Reese? I pictured him in a wild brown wig. It wasn't much of a stretch. A dab of lipstick. He had an androgynous face, fine-featured and smooth-skinned. "I've been told he was a gambler," I said. "Which is worrisome. Is that what you meant when you said he thought you were too timid?"

"Not necessarily or exclusively. We definitely don't—didn't— agree about ethics: business, professional, personal. We didn't even like the same music. Which is not to say that gambling wasn't a dangerous component of our incompatibility. Markers, like pipers, must be paid. But Jesse wasn't one to agonize over the future or contingencies. Agonizing over anything was one job Jesse had no trouble delegating."

I wondered if he could speak this way—full and flowery sentences and no hesitations—on any subject, or whether Jesse Reese in all his permutations had been discussed until the subject was as polished as the man's carved desk. I pondered this while looking at the photo on the console behind Ray Palford's desk. No pageant contestants here. His was a silver-framed portrait of three polished children, a woman straight out of *Town and Country*, and a man who looked like him, except for the mustache. He noticed what I was looking at. "A lovely family," I murmured.

"Thank you. It is a great comfort to have managed one partnership that worked out." He fingered his smooth upper lip. "I still feel naked. My dog didn't recognize me." He chuckled. "Now, where were we again?"

I looked at his smooth face. The better to impersonate a woman, my dear? "So, ah, given your differences," I said, "can I ask how the two of you ever became partners?"

"Much in the same way people who later divorce get married. We noticed the things that turned out not to matter and failed to notice the things that did matter. I thought the sum would be better than its parts. I have the analytic skills and I'm good at following things through, paying attention to details. Jesse had an excellent intuitive mind plus a quick wit and an easy way with people. An appealing combination, in theory."

"But the things you failed to notice?"

He stood up. I was afraid my time was up, but he instead paced the rug. "The greed, the gambling, the womanizing—oh, especially the choice of Miss Bloodsucker as his wife, which escalated and intensified all of the above but still, I thought, belonged to his personal life and was no business of mine, but I was woefully innocent and therefore incorrect about that. The man's only ethical doctrine is to always pay his debts, a definite virtue, to be sure, but less so if and when accounts have to be churned in order to do so, or values compromised in order to make the money to pay the debts."

Apparently, when started, the man did not need to breathe. He spoke like a Teletype machine.

"We shared overhead and research fees and the like but had separate lists of clients. Which is why it took being presented with a lawsuit before I realized what was going on. He had been borrowing from the general fund, from our own retirement fund. He had clients whose tiny life savings he risked or squandered—"

"Oh, no!" I said. "So it is, really and truly, possible!"

He raised his eyebrows again. "Off-the-record, remember? Because when one of those clients sued us, I also filed suit and severed the partnership of Reese and Palford. You know what they were calling us? Fleece and Pilfer. Can you imagine how it feels to have your name and reputation tarnished so unfairly?"

"And the lawsuit continues?" I asked.

He shook his head and made a half shrug. "Not that one. That woman died, and then nobody could prove anything coherent about what assets she may have had. Her heir was a disoriented relative—a sister, as I recall—who didn't pursue the logical course of action. I, of course, did not insist. Still, you can understand why I wanted no further association with the man."

I felt ill. She had been telling the truth, telling everyone, telling the policeman on the beat, telling passersby, telling it for years, but in the same disorganized fashion that had kept her from successfully suing Reese. All Jesse's victims now had a face—Georgette's—seared and defeated.

But the lawsuit I had meant was the one he had filed against his erstwhile partner. The lawsuit that was still pending after three years. Palford seemed capable of carrying a long-term hate. And I wondered, too, whether it was more expedient to sue the estate than the living man.

He glanced at his watch again.

I stood up. "You've been generous with your time," I said. "I guess it's best to know the truth, awful as it is. It feels even worse to speak so ill of the dead, after what happened to him. I really didn't want it to be true."

"Well, somebody certainly did."

"I don't think it was that woman they have in jail," I said. "She said she didn't even know him."

He raised both his eyebrows and looked diabolically amused. "If I were the police, I'd cherchez la femme, but la other femme. I'd cherchez la iron maiden. A very angry, insulted iron maiden with a bad, bad temper and enormous, deluded ambitions, la femme whose husband flagrantly cheats and—to add insult to injury—commits the *real* sin, which is to lose their money."

"His *wife*?" I said, with much too much forced naiveté. I silently apologized to Harriet Vane, who would never have taken on this role of dummy. Was this a real case of using a name in vane?

Ray Palford shrugged. "Who knows? Ultimately, who cares? Trust me, my dear, his loss is nothing to grieve over. What I mind is that his death has once again linked my name with his in news stories. And that is all I will say on the subject, which means, therefore, this is the end of the interview."

EN ROUTE to the jail, I stopped to buy Sasha prison panties. My affordable choices were divided between the garish, the pathetic, and the overly utilitarian. I picked through a pair with pitchfork-bearing devils stamped around the bikini line, a black and red pair with strategically placed hearts and flowers that didn't seem suited for solitary incarceration, and a cotton pair that might as well have had *Institutionalized* stamped on them. I finally decided that a pair saying *This is the day we wash our clothes* was the least likely to depress upon wearing or discarding. Even this purchase stretched my shaky budget. I had an ominous sense that I was heading for financial catastrophe. I was probably going to have to pay for my hotel room, plus Lala and Belle's telephone calls, plus the gas back and forth today, plus who knew what else ahead. I'd change my name to Mandy Pauper. I got so depressed about my perpetually pathetic finances that I returned to the hotel and snagged the shampoo and soap offerings, rather than buy large varieties of those items. "Little bottles are more optimistic," I told Sasha a few minutes later.

"They'll set bail tomorrow." Her expression was dark.

"Tomorrow!" I was surprised and delighted. Nothing on the faces of the officials I'd encountered had led me to believe they would release her in their lifetimes. "Tomorrow!" I repeated.

"Keep sounding like Orphan Annie," Sasha said, "and I will actually commit murder." She exhaled and looked a bit relieved.

"You know anything about bail?" she asked. "Do I have to pay interest for the loan? Oh, I must, or why would they give it to me? Geez, I was just getting ahead a little. Now I don't know if I'll get rehired by the saltwater taffy people and I'll have this miserable bail to pay for and how the hell did this happen? And you forgot my trashy book, too."

"Did not." I extracted the book. "From my own personal collection. Vacation reading from Philly Prep to you. Genuine, one hundred percent trash. Check it out. It has an all-verb blurb. Says it will make you shudder, throb, and pulsate."

"I've done enough of that for a while. It's expectations like those that got me in here in the first place. Tell me what I don't already know about."

I told her everything I knew—precious little, when I said it out loud—and what I didn't know for sure, but strongly suspected, which was that Reese's feeble ethics had disappeared altogether once Palford was out of the picture, until finally he was not only mismanaging, but manipulating the old folk's funds.

"I don't know about money," she said, "but I know about scams. Remember Riley?"

"I've never been sure whether that was his first or last name," I said.

"That was his both. Riley No Middle Name Riley. His parents weren't famous for having great imaginations."

I did remember Riley was the scam artist, successful and dangerous because of his astounding charm.

"Riley taught me a lot about the less than legal." Sasha sighed and apparently lost her train of thought. She looked dreamy-eyed.

"Reality check. Riley took your grandmother's cameo," I reminded her.

She snapped back. "And didn't even hock or sell it, there's the real pain. He gave it to another woman. So where were we?"

"The less than legal."

"It sounds to me like the late Mr. Reese was working what Riley called a Ponzi scheme. It's a pyramid scheme. Basically, you give me money to invest, but instead of really investing it,

I keep it. I pay you what seems like your interest, or dividends, or profits out of what the next person gives me, and so on and so forth. So you think everything's fine—but the real capital, the money you invested, is nowhere—except in my pockets."

"And Reese didn't expect a problem about paying back that money, ever, because most of his clients were old and would die. Their heirs would get the big surprise." The blatant cynicism of it made me furious.

"Listen, Mandy, that suite we were given, that one he usually was comped? They don't give that to little old ladies who play the nickel machines. Those perks are based on a percentage of how much they expect you to *lose*. A suite like the one we had? That's for a five-hundred to thousand-dollar-a-hand kind of player. Reese was a big, big loser, and that's probably where the money went."

The old folk would have been as well off putting their savings directly on the craps table. They wound up in the casino's vaults, anyway.

And how had the gambler's wife felt about the drain of her capital? Was she the greedy demon Ray Palford had painted? Was Jesse's murder her personal savings plan? And if that little lame creature had, indeed, murdered or arranged for it—who had been her accomplice?

I needed to talk to the former Miss Whatever, find out how much her Glitz store—or stores—needed an infusion of funds, and where they'd gotten their earlier supplies, find out whatever I could.

Immediately after leaving Sasha, I used the public phone in the courthouse, dialing information for her sister's number. Holly Booker. It was an easy last name to remember. Like the English literary award, like "book her."

The voice that answered belonged to neither of the sisters. "Mrs. Booker, she is at the work," I was told. "And her sister with her, too. Exercise, dinner. They not be back until many late."

What kind of a grieving widow was she, anyway? First she bleaches her hair, and now mourning becomes a facial?

"Many late" meant I didn't have to hurry. Besides, business didn't always have to come before pleasure, not if the business was busy in a casino spa. I'd go see Mackenzie first, give him an update. This time it'd be pleasure before business.

I thought I could be creative and reverse the cliché, but there's a reason it's so ingrained in our speech. So in order to teach me that, life provided the off-duty teacher with another damned learning experience.

Seventeen

A HOSPITALIZED man needed company. That was a given and reason enough for the visit. But I needed help as well. I had felt like a sea creature with aimlessly waving stalk eyes this morning.

I was sure that Mackenzie would have found USDA Prime clues in Ray Palford's office, surely something more than the fact that the man had shaved off his mustache. I wanted a cram course in Detecting 101. I needed to know how to notice the right things.

Besides, it wasn't ever the worst thing on earth to see Mackenzie. Particularly now. He was definitely on the mend.

His coloring had returned. Although it embarrasses him—he thinks it's something little boys are supposed to outgrow—the man's cheeks—except when the rest of him's been recently shot at—are always burnished, as if he's just breezed in from a wintry wonderland. With his rosy cheeks, blue-blue eyes, and partly silver curls, he's very much like a human version of our own red, white, and blue. Very patriotic man.

I settled next to the bed on a molded plastic chair so uncomfortable, I could no longer ignore my backache. I suspected the chairs had been purchased by an entrepreneurial orthopedic surgeon elsewhere in the building. "I think there are two definite possibilities," I began.

"As suspects? You're sayin' two, so it can't be an idea I had of a team of angry oldsters, workin' together like the seven dwarves did when they dragged Snow White to safety. So tell me about the two you suspect, startin' with his ex-partner."

"Damn, Mackenzie. Can't you let me have my moment?"

"I made some calls. Nothin' else to do except watch godforsaken talk shows. The topic on one was children who murder their siblings: Could your kids do it, too? Good lord—it makes the soap operas—yeah, thought I'd find out what they are, too—makes them look *pristine*."

"There's the wife, too," I said.

"There was always the wife. There *is* always the wife, in any case. So tell me about the ex-partner. I love story hour." He leaned back and smiled.

I realized how little I actually had to say. Ray Palford hadn't added much more than his own rancor and clean-shaved face. "What if," I said, "Ray Palford wore an enormous brown wig . . . ?"

Mackenzie looked dubious, so when I heard the knock, having no more to add, I welcomed an interruption. But only at first, and only for a very brief increment, because the nurse who bounced in looked as if her various parts were spring activated even though she was carrying a bouquet roughly the size of Vermont.

"Hello, hello, Mr. Mackenzie!" she said. "Look what just this

179

minute arrived! I said I'd bring it in since I was heading this way, anyway! So—how are we doing today?" She beamed at the fallen hero with much more intensity than his wounds warranted, and carefully placed the bouquet on the windowsill, after handing Mackenzie the card.

"The Weinstein family," he whispered. "Again."

"Yes, yes," Miss Pert said. "We're all so darn proud of you!" She clucked further admiration and sympathy and patted sheets and plumped pillows with unnecessary zeal. If you ask me.

"Need anything?" she asked him. "Anything at all?"

There is nothing more disgusting than enduring an adorable woman-child paying homage to a man with whom you are affiliated—particularly when you are not only older, nastier, and much less adorable and/or pneumatic than the aforesaid, but have failed in the only competition in which you had a chance—that of snagging significant information for the detective.

Nursie never once acknowledged my existence. I believe she mistook me for one of those life-sized replicas of people, something an earlier well-wisher had left behind as a prop for photo ops.

And despite our current crisis in health care, the city's finest did not object to his unfair share of hospital staff time, did not tell her to peddle the Florence Nightingale schtick to more needy patients who did not already have semisignificant others at their bedsides.

I ignored her as best as I could. I thought about the many questions still surrounding Jesse Reese's death. I pondered again why he was in Atlantic City with no intention of gambling. I wondered how much it had to do—if at all—with the old people at the condominiums. I wondered if anyone had found his car.

And meantime, although I was, of course, barely noticing Mackenzie's personal angel of mercy, it somehow came to my attention that she checked the room temperature, the condition of the water pitcher, the position of the window blinds, the chart at the foot of the bed, and the tilt of the quiet television set. Just when I thought she was going to offer to redecorate the room in any style he preferred and I was going to strangle her, she left.

"Where were we?" Mackenzie sounded dazed.

"You were lost in the swamp of hormones." It just ruins a man, treating him that way. "I, on the other hand, was figuring things out."

"Oh, yeah?" With Nursie no longer bobbling nearby, Mackenzie appeared to be regaining the ability to think. I didn't know whether to take that as good news or a personal insult.

"I don't think Reese was here for the salt air," I said. "He was a gambler. A man who didn't worry about contingencies or the future, according to his ex-partner."

"Not about other people's futures, maybe."

"Did they find his car?"

"No car, no car keys. Not here, not home, not anywhere near his office in Cherry Hill." Mackenzie sighed. "What if he was checkin' out?" he said mildly.

"Killing himself?"

"Not the type. I meant literally. Leavin'."

"Leaving what?"

"The whole shebang. The U.S. If we could subpoena his financial dealin's those last few days, I wonder how much cash left the country, or was converted into bearer bonds or—"

"Why? How are you managing this enormous leap?"

He blinked and looked slightly surprised, then spoke in a soft slur that should have to be declared a concealed weapon. "I'm basin' it on two things—one you noticed and one you heard."

"I hate when you do this."

"Yesterday, when you went to Reese's office? The photograph that wasn't on his desk. Why would it be missin'? The way you told me, Norma Evans didn't just shrug it off. She must have thought it was significant, too. If it'd have been of him, then I'd think she took it herself and was too embarrassed to say. But it was of Poppy. I think it was kind of a souvenir of his wife. She meant somethin' to him, or did when she was in the pageant."

"It could have been removed some other time."

"I think Norma Evans would have said so."

"And the other thing?" I asked. "The one I heard?"

"That he always paid his gamblin' debts. His one point of

honor. I think he came to Atlantic City to clear up what he owed—using, of course, other people's money."

"The Condominium Club."

"Other groups' funds, too, I'll bet. It's one thing to have powerless old people enraged with you. Very different thing to have a casino on your tail. And that's not maybe the kind of thing you'd tell your secretary unless you wanted her to be able to guess what was really goin' on, which you do not want to have happen. You do not want her knowin' you're about to skip an' put her out of a job to which she's dedicated her life. Ditto for the wife you aren't takin' along. An' you know what? I'll bet his wife—maybe in cahoots with the ex-partner—knew he was skippin'. Could you really keep a wife from spottin' clues here and there?"

"They say they're the last to know."

"That concerns a different kind of cheat."

"Anyway, Palford and Poppy as partners? He had nothing good to say about her."

"Maybe the gentleman doth protest too much this time." Mackenzie twisted his torso and awkwardly attempted to pour himself water, although with one leg trussed and plastered and hanging in a sling, body torque was not easy.

"Mind if I pour us both a drink?" I didn't want to suggest that he needed assistance. If the truth were told, dealing with the fragile male ego—unless you're wearing a nurse's uniform—is certainly the equivalent of coping with PMS, except that the male ego is needy every day of every month, forever. He shrugged. I poured.

And the detecto gods rewarded me for this small act of mercy with a gift of sudden insight. "Airport," I said.

"Huh?"

"He chartered a plane. That's why there's no car anywhere. It's near an airfield somewhere, or he gave it away. He flew in— and he was going to fly out. Fly away, isn't that what you said?"

"Checking out is what I said." Then he looked at me with all the approval he'd beamed onto Florence Nightingale earlier. Some of us just have to do it with our brains, I guess.

I beamed back. Felt pretty good, too. "Was there money in his briefcase?"

"No money. But a passport."

"His killer took it. The money, I mean." I pulled out my little map of Atlantic City and there it was, the private airport, Bader Field, not more than ten minutes away.

"Nice goin'," he said. No small print.

One small nonpneumatic step for womankind.

Eighteen

I LIKE having an agenda, a plan of action, a purpose, even if
I'm not at all sure how to implement it. But in this case,
snooping around an airfield, even a private and presumably
small one, was intimidatingly official. Even in my imagination, the web of regulations choked me. I felt silly saying words
as innocent as *flight logs*, let alone attempting plane-person
jargon.

The entrance to Bader Field was peculiar—tall redbrick pillars
that belonged more at the approach to Tara than an airfield, but
there they were. Once through them, the oddness continued
with an actual field—the kind used for football—to the left of the

gateway. The first airport with bleachers I'd ever heard of. I was sure there was a story there, but I certainly couldn't figure it out.

Beyond a nondescript building and an equally nondescript firehouse was a turkey-wire fence, and beyond it, finally, rows of small private planes parked on grass, near a runway that looked like a nice suburban street. I watched an elegantly attired middle-aged couple emerge from a red and white plane and stroll to a waiting limousine positioned in front of the firehouse.

Life was certainly sweet and easy for some.

I walked into the square, one-story office building, into a deserted front room dominated by a snack machine and an empty glass display counter. Luckily, the vending machine was full, its peanut-butter crackers looking good. I bought a package of them along with a soda. On the wall, a clock told military time. It was now 1326.

I munched and sipped and cleared my throat, but that didn't catch the attention of the male voices I heard in a back room.

I read a framed clipping on the wall and learned that this idiosyncratic little strip was the first place in the world to be called an AIR PORT, right around 1920. I've been saving factoids like that for years, in the event I'm someday invited to an actual cocktail party where people exchange bon mots and amusing bits of information.

Somebody went by the window in a hot-looking long orange coat. I quickly swallowed my peanut-butter cracker, but the man didn't come in. The plane people debated and laughed in deep male voices in the back room. I read the only remaining print material, which was laminated onto the display case. It was a newspaper photograph of blurry-faced early fliers hanging out here at the World's First Air Port. They looked to be having a good time. The figures were identified as Eddie Rickenbacker, Charles Lindbergh, and Amelia Earhart. "Wow," I muttered. "Wow," hoping this wasn't some archaic forerunner of the Elvis sightings in today's tabloids.

Although a small sign told me there was an attendant on duty, nobody appeared. The laughter grew more raucous from the back room. I walked over and knocked on the open door.

Unreadable maps hung on nearly all the wall space. I looked

at the one nearest to me, a map of air routes, climatological areas. Someone had been charting a path on it. A green chalkboard had pink airplane silhouettes in odd formations, with squiggly lines—maneuvers? spy information?—swirling around them. I felt as if I'd walked into the wizard's studio.

"Excuse me," I said, too softly. The three men remained huddled over a desk, intently studying something.

It was time for drastic action. Time for Ultra-Girl!

I silently apologized to Gloria Steinem, and walked toward the group in the style of Mackenzie's bubbly nurse, trying for her I'd-do-anything-to-please ambience. There must be something to it—some invisible rays it emits, amino acid production it stimulates—because without a word, the men slowly straightened up and turned toward me. "Hi!" I said with a Monroe wave, small and slightly incompetent. One man, quite tall and sunburned, wore a bowling shirt with BILL embroidered on its pocket flap. "Hi, Bill?" He smiled back at me. Actually, he looked delighted.

"I have this, um, business thing to discuss?" Nothing like making every sentence a question to establish yourself as a nonthreat. Or, of course, as a valley girl, but we were in New Jersey, after all.

"Business?" Bill looked sincerely disappointed. "Probably should talk to Jimmy, here," he said.

I would have voted Jimmy least likely to run an airport, unless by virtue of being too heavy to fly under any conditions, he handled the ground-based business by default.

"What for can I do you today, girlie?" He'd obviously had his head up a helicopter when advice was given about nonsexist behavior and vocabulary. However, I couldn't play Ultra-Girl and then protest being addressed as same.

"It's about, um, my uncle? He died?" I stalled, frantically searching for logical grounds on which to ask for information about flight records. The definition of foolish optimism was my stupid but persistent belief that last minute inspiration will save the day.

"Sorry to hear that." Jimmy did not offer grief-counseling. Instead, he looked wistfully down at the document they'd all been studying: *Sports Illustrated*'s swimwear issue. I had lost him to the ultimate ultra-girls.

"See, well, he rented a plane from you right before he, um, you know, died?"

"This isn't Avis, babe. We don't rent planes." He rolled a toothpick from one side of his mouth to the other.

So much for my brilliant theory. I felt crushed, and my back, in sympathy, had another, more serious spasm.

"Maybe he owned his own plane," Bill offered.

I hadn't thought of that. But since nobody had ever mentioned flying in connection with Jesse Reese's interest or activities, I shook my head. "I don't think so. Maybe you'd call it chartering, not renting?"

Jimmy rolled his eyes. I was a trial to him. "We don't charter, lady. People here own their planes."

I'd hit the wall and dead-ended. "Well, but," I began, hoping my mouth would lead me to a new perspective, because my brain wasn't. "Could . . . could he have chartered a plane somewhere else and had it take him here, then pick him up here?"

"Well yeah, sure," Jimmy said, as if I should have thought of that obvious, low-level concept before I started talking. "What about it?"

"Well, he did that, for this past Monday evening? And see, he couldn't use the second half because, well, like I said. Do you have the record? His name's—His name was Jesse Reese?"

"Hey!" Bill said, his eyebrows rising. "Isn't that—didn't I say that was the guy? Remember how I told you? On the news? The guy who got offed at the casino? In the bedroom, Jimmy, remember?" Bill spoke now to both of us, Jimmy and me, explaining. "Remember that guy was here from Pomona? Royally pissed because he wound up wasting half the night? Even though the guy—your uncle—had paid in advance. A lot of money, too, all the way to the Bahamas."

Gambling heaven. I should have guessed. To Nassau, to Nassau, with Grandma's money we go. And then, after that, who knew to where?

"I told you it was the guy on the news," Bill said. "When I

heard the name, I said how many men named Jesse could there be? Couldn't remember the last name, but aside from Jesse James, who else—"

"All right, all *right*! So I was wrong." Jimmy's eyes were now tight slits, but even so, I could see them flash with either interest or anger as they viewed me. He put both his hands up, palms out, making himself a breathing brick wall. No passage, no thoroughfare here. "No refunds," he said. "My condolences and all, but I can save you time and energy goin' after them. It's not like a round-trip ticket, it's a charter. That plane was rented for a certain amount of time, you know what I mean? And a rule's a rule."

I felt obliged to stay in character. "Not even for the gas that nobody used?"

"Wouldn't matter if your uncle was only going to Philly, doll. The price was the price. There's overhead, maintenance, rentals, and there's rules. You got your troubles and I got mine, and you can go all over the state, find the place where he chartered it— which sounds like it's Pomona—and for sure, that place'll have its own troubles."

"Well, then," I told the philosopher king, "at least make sure he's credited with his frequent flier miles." And I was out of there, but not before I heard Bill.

"Frequent flier miles?" he echoed with mild wonder before Jimmy brusquely shut him up.

SOMEDAY I'M BUYING ONE of those fake car phones so I won't feel so conspicuous when I have to say my thoughts out loud, particularly in a convertible on a June day. For the time being, however, I accepted looking like someone with serious problems as I nattered on, alternately arguing and agreeing with myself and my conclusions. Whenever I stopped for a light, I tried to speak more softly, but I nonetheless generated funny looks from people in adjoining lanes.

The emerging picture still had gaps, but if you fill in enough background, the foreground has nowhere to go but right in front of your eyes. So I muttered my story to the visor, hoping people thought I was talking to a speaker phone, wishing I didn't care what people thought.

For years, I told my windshield, at least back to Georgette's sister, probably before, Jesse Reese had been preying on old people with failing memories and increasing confusion, people who could be manipulated out of their life savings.

But recently, with particularly bad timing, he found himself squeezed between large gambling debts and the dawning wrath of some of his victims in the geriatric social clubs—all of whom had friends who were potential victims. The very connections that had supported his endeavors and his lifestyle now threatened to strangle him. His methods and practices were within hours of becoming public knowledge through a lawsuit, but he couldn't repay the old people and get them off his back, because he owed whatever he thought of as disposable cash to the casino. Add this squeeze to the problem of an expensive and enraged wife who had delusions of becoming the next Queen of Seventh Avenue, and a former partner who was determined to sue him to death even if it took forever, and Jesse Reese was in a serious pickle. So he decided to skip.

I stopped for a light. I loved how logically it all worked out. To a point. But what then? *"But,"* I said, angry with my own quibbles. "Why does there always have to be a *but*? Why is there always a very *big but*?

A chubby man in the next lane turned, his mouth a belligerent pout.

"The *conjunction*," I shouted. "Not the noun!" My explanation was lost in his exhaust fumes, but maybe he wasn't great with parts of speech.

But. What had happened then?

"Here's what I think." I looked around guiltily, but the pickup now in the next lane blared apocalyptic hip-hop and couldn't have heard a nuclear explosion, so I talked on. "I think the ungrieving widow figured out that her no-good, cheating hubby was going to split. Maybe his travel kit was missing or the checking account was suddenly gone, or the Pomona pilot called to verify his flight time—but something clued her in and

189

she decided to plug her leaking resources by terminating her husband."

Women and Money: The Saga Continues. Georgette lost and slept on the sand; Lala snared Tommy; Lucky's mother gambled; I taught summer school and Poppy murdered.

My vote for the tall accomplice was a man in drag, probably Dunstan, if he'd ever show up, although Ray Palford now seemed a potentially good bet.

Or else the cross-dressing part was last minute inspiration, along with the site. Pure serendipity because Reese's customary room had been given to Sasha and me. Or else they had always meant to use the room, his favorite room, but not to dress like Sasha. Or else . . . or else, or else.

WHEN I REPORTED BACK to Mackenzie, I was given another ego-boosting round of approval. However, my back was now clenched as tight as a fist, and I couldn't relax enough to gloat. I rubbed it while I was being complimented.

"By the way," he said, "I called the precinct here 'bout Poppy and Dunstan and Ray Palford, too. They were real interested, particularly in Poppy. Said they'd talk to her right away. An' my man says Sasha's cousin finally arrived. I think a strain of flakiness runs through the whole family."

"As long as it's just a personality defect and doesn't interfere with legal expertise," I murmured.

"I think this means you're retired, or at least on sabbatical for the rest of the day," Mackenzie said. "Whyn't you take care of that back? Doesn't your hotel have a spa?"

The thought of a massage shimmered just ahead like a mirage.

"Everybody's in place at the moment, so you're finally on vacation," Mackenzie said. "At least for an hour or so."

I MADE MY WAY across the lobby of the hotel, aiming my feet for the elevator bank.

"Sweetie pie! We were looking for you!" Lala and Belle advanced on me, talking all the while. "We made a million phone calls," they said in unison. "Going to cost a fortune!"

My back went crazy. "Don't worry about it, but right now, I am on my way up to the health—"

"Every apartment and church and synagogue and seniors' complex we could find in the book," Belle said with obvious pride.

"Incredible. Could we make a date for later? I have this thing in my back and I—"

"It's not really so incredible," Lala said. "We used a Philadelphia directory."

"We called Jesse Reese's office," Belle said.

It was easier to wait than keep protesting. Maybe they'd notice I looked like Quasimodo.

"I had such a good idea. I made up this whole speech. I'd say I was from the Greater Delaware Valley Seniors' Coalition—you like that? The GDVSC, I'd say, and then I'd explain. I said we wanted to put a notice in our bulletin about Jesse Reese's passing since so many of our people—I like that, don't you—our people—"

"Belle!"

"—and we thought it would be nice to mention some of his most recent appearances. So I found out his number and I dialed, but—"

"His office is closed," Lala said. "Permanently."

Belle sulked. "I was going to say that," she muttered.

"We have a few hundred names so far," Lala said. "People who gave him money. Some of them told us the amount. Twelve thousand, twenty-five, one gave him seventy-five thousand. Adds up."

"You're not kidding. I kept the tallies," Belle agreed. "I do it for our Thursday night consecutive rummy games. I'm good at it, I don't know why. It's kind of a gift."

Lala leaned near me. "Five and one-half million dollars we know of already."

I didn't have to pretend to be stunned. I thought their math must be wrong, despite Belle's expertise.

"After all," Belle said. "If two hundred and fifty people give him twelve thousand dollars each—and that is not exactly big money in this world, and most of the people gave him twice that, three times—that's three million dollars right there. The

191

amount he gave back as dividends—peanuts. Besides, there's more people—we didn't even *try* New Jersey, but I thought you don't have all the money in the world, do you? Phone bills aren't cheap, and even with a card, the hotel adds on its—"

"One woman who answered," Lala said, "had just come back from the hospital. She told us that while she was sick, and her son was going through her accounts, trying to take care of things, he'd gone to see Jesse Reese twice. Last week and this Monday."

"Monday? The day he . . ."

Both women nodded. "She said that Reese was very rude. Her son went to the office in Cherry Hill—he had an appointment—but Reese said something had come up, he had to leave. So this man followed him here."

I wondered if he was tall, if he knew Poppy.

"Another man said his son was a stockbroker who tried to transfer funds, to invest some differently. He said that he tried to check out some of the investments and he couldn't find anything about them. Thinks they were made-up companies. Fakes. He had a word for it, his son did. Something like that movie star, from *Casablanca*."

"Ingrid?" She shook her head. "Bergman? Humphrey? Bogart? Sam?"

"That's it—Bogart."

"That's the name of a company?"

"No, no, all those investments were Bogarts."

I didn't correct her and say *bogus*. The image of tough investments with cigarettes hanging off their lips was too appealing.

"So the son, he got real worried and called his lawyer."

"When?" How much pressure was hitting Reese all at once? Belle shook her head.

Lala seemed to stretch, to grow taller. "And my Tommy heard that Miglio's mother had turned over a nice amount to Reese last year, and about a month ago decided she wanted to surprise her children with a trip for everybody back to Italy, but Jesse Reese didn't know who he was messing with. Miglio has a very bad temper, particularly when mothers or money are concerned."

The woods were suddenly crawling with would-be Reese lawsuits or assassins, or at least serious irritants. No wonder the man was leaving the country. "You're incredible detectives," I said. "I salute you. If we could get that list together, I think the police might be interested."

"You're standing funny," Lala said.

"Yes. My back. I pulled something yesterday."

"So why aren't you upstairs with the masseuse? Honestly, young people don't know how to take care of themselves. You act as if there's no tomorrow. You have to take care of your body. When you're older, you'll understand. Go!"

I went. Next to the spa entrance was a glass-walled room in which Holly Booker led an aerobics class. Actually, it was more of a tutorial, with one apple-shaped and unenthusiastic participant. I have to hand it to Holly. She wasn't daunted by her class size or by vigorous exercise. She shouted encouragement and popped on and off the step and clapped her hands as if she were guiding the entire world through its paces. And she had been doing so in her glass cage for forty-five minutes already, according to the schedule on the wall.

"Quite amazing, is she not?" the statuesque blond woman behind the desk said. "She does that a few times every day."

I tried to squelch my guilt at still not getting around to a regular exercise program. Each day, I devise another plan. I'll walk to school and back, I'll jog there extra early and shower in the girl's gym, I'll go to the Y three times a week, and so forth. And each day, the plan that wins consists of sleeping that extra hour and promising to begin the next day.

Anyway, today my back hurt too much to climb that imaginary staircase. I expressed my need for a massage. Anytime at all, I said, but soon. "My back is killing me."

"Have you been under any tension lately?" she asked sympathetically. I nearly laughed, but it hurt my back. I thought about the last three days, and my ligaments twisted and double-knotted themselves. "I'm a schoolteacher," I said, instead of even trying to explain. "Finished the term last Friday."

"Ah." She stood up. "That explains everything. And you're in luck. I've been sitting out here for twenty minutes, waiting for my four o'clock. At this point, I consider her a cancellation, wouldn't you?"

It wasn't really a question, but I nodded agreement anyway, and probably, in my mean-spirited and selfish way, would have considered it a cancellation one minute after the hour.

"If you'll accept forty minutes instead of a full hour, I'll reduce the rate."

Her name was Greta, she told me as we walked down a door-lined hall. We passed several women having tune-ups—one in red stripes on the treadmill, one in a tropical print leotard on the StairMaster, one in gray sweats doing leg lifts. The wardrobe demands of exercising are an additional hurdle. Do I really need one more area in which to be poorly dressed?

We passed a cubicle in which a woman was having a pedicure. Then we were at the door that said MASSAGE. And all would be well, all would be well.

And all was, until we opened the door. Because the table was already occupied by someone—something—its head covered by a bloody towel. A free weight—not particularly large, probably ten pounds at most—was on the floor, along with a dark puddle.

Greta's four o'clock.

Greta screamed and screamed. She was so solid-looking, her hysteria came as a shock. The women in the other section stopped their machines and came over and then they, too, screamed. The pedicure woman walked in like a duck with cotton wads between her splayed toes. She screamed, too.

The body on the table was silent. Its small, bare feet poked out of the sheet covering the rest of its torso.

A large white hook on the wall held the clothing that had been discarded in anticipation of a massage. A pink sweat suit—unremarkable except for the square brass rivets that accented each leg and arm. A brass-topped pink cane lay on the floor.

Poppy's last fashion statement.

I, too, would definitely consider this a cancellation.

Nineteen

MY thoughts piled one on top of the other, clashing and competing. I needed an auxiliary head to hold the overflow.

Women crowded at the doorway, their numbers ever-increasing. I watched with remote horror as a green mudpack cracked and fissured with its wearer's screams. We surged and withdrew. The massage room was tiny to begin with, and we were all huddled as close to and as far from the table as possible, trying to be near, but to avoid even proximity with the corpse.

For what felt a very long while, I let my thoughts accumulate without trying to sort them. *But she ...* echoed between my ears. *But she's the murderer.* I shook my head. She was the victim. *But that doesn't make any sense.* I couldn't fault that one.

Why was she dead? Who killed her? Her partner? How would he have gotten into or out of this all-female enclave?

Wigs. Sweats.

But the police had the wig.

Anybody can get a wig!

In that case . . . who?

For a second I felt too tired to even consider possibilities. I nearly wept. My back hurt. I wanted to lie down and have somebody press out the pain. I looked at the figure on the massage table almost enviously.

"Should I call an ambulance?" somebody behind me asked. "Has anybody called?" After a lot of consultation, it appeared we were all better at gaping than at doing something. The questioner was delegated to phone.

"The police!" I roused myself long enough to call after her. "Call them, too!" I stared at the remains of Poppy Reese again and tried to connect a few synapses.

Ray Palford's smooth, newly shaved face intruded.

Yes, I decided. He was the one. The accomplice who decided to use her and lose her. Or maybe Poppy had never been his accomplice. Maybe Ray Palford and a small buddy had killed one and then the other of the detested Reeses. With both of them gone and no children to challenge his claims against the estate, he'd most likely get what he wanted.

It made sense, if murder can ever be said to make sense.

Outside the room, across the hall, thumping music still pounded, encouraging imaginary women to work those muscles. It reminded me of the aerobics class near the entryway. Somebody had to tell Holly.

Greta suddenly advanced to the table and reached out, lifting a corner of the towel.

"No!" I said. "Don't touch anything until the police get here."

Greta's hand opened and the stained terry cloth once again camouflaged the victim. "How is this possible?" she screamed. "In *my* room! I was here with my last—minutes ago! I was just *here!* And I never saw her! The police, are they going to think that I did this?"

"No, of course not," I said, but I did notice that the rest of the group remained silent and became even wider of eye.

"I think I know who that is. . . ." The manicurist, small and curly-haired, had edged to the side of the clump of women. "I could be sure if I could see her fingers." She walked up to the table, bent over and studied one of the dangling hands. Then she straightened up, smoothed her pink smock and nodded. "Royal Raspberry. Acrylic refills. Just like I thought. My three o'clock."

"Holy God," another pink-smocked employee said. "I gave her a cleansing facial at two. She said she was having her nails done and then a massage." She backed up, her hand to her mouth.

Another pink smock spoke. "Her? The red crew cut?"

Crew cut? Red?

The manicurist nodded. "No wig today. I think—I thought the crew cut was kinda kicky. She liked short hair with workout clothes. Always matched hair color and style to her ensemble, she told me. Part of her fashion philosophy." She blew her nose.

A crew cut. Then both her hairdos and colors had been wigs. The big dark hair Sasha described in the bar Monday night and the brassy 'do I'd thought a bleach job the next day. The big dark wig in the hotel room on Monday . . . But she was so short, never to be confused with Sasha.

"Ohmigod." One of the bright leotards had now made it to the front of the little crowd. "I thought maybe somebody had a heart attack, and I know CPR, but . . . ohmigod! What's that towel . . . ohmigod! It's all stained, and that dumbbell, there, it looks smeared with . . . *ohmigod!*"

The free weight's brushed aluminum surface was gory. It was relatively small and would normally be innocuous-looking, not that difficult to lift and very easy to swing. We didn't have to search for a Schwarzenegger.

I heard her from out in the hall. "That's crazy," Holly insisted in her deep voice. "I just saw her an hour ago." She sounded like a very untough child convincing herself that nothing lurked in

197

the night closet. "Had her nails done and wanted me to see the color. She was perfectly—" Then Holly Booker pushed her way through the women and gasped.

"Are you sure?" I whispered. "Don't rush to any conclusions. It might not be . . ." After all, we only had a similar body size and wardrobe in front of us. Until the police arrived, the face and definite identity of the dead woman would remain speculation. Maybe Poppy's rivets were popular in these parts.

"Poppy!" Holly cried out when she spied the pink sweats on the wall. She walked over and turned them around. "Oh, Poppy! She just showed me this new design. Watermelon Workout, she called it." And, indeed, on this side there was a big green-edged slice of fruit with brass sequin studs for seeds. "It's a prototype," Holly whispered. "One of a kind." She ran out of steam and stared at her sister, then back at the floor. She pointed down and sobbed.

For the first time, I noticed a pair of pink gym shoes halfway under the table.

"See those socks? They match the sweats. She was a genius!" Holly's voice softened, became almost reverent and definitely heartbroken. "And there's a gym bag option that—that"—her voice cracked as she sobbed out—"looks like a gigantic watermelon slice!"

"Everybody stay where you are!" The voice was male and gruff. "Hotel security," he said. "Police on the way, meanwhile, what's the problem?"

Silently, everyone except Greta, who stood mourning the sanctity of her room and her table, stepped back and out, allowing security a free view of precisely what was wrong. I watched his head pivot from the inert form on the table to the bloody free weight, then back up. The gray-brown fabric of his shirt strained across his back as he took a deep breath. He was the man who'd been stationed outside the ill-fated Eastern Suite when I came to retrieve my clothing. I hoped his short-term memory was bleared and that he didn't remember me.

He cleared his throat and turned to face the gaggle of women.

"Everybody here who was here?" he asked. "I mean, nobody left, correct?"

My eyes roved over the one who knew about the hair, then the manicurist and her client, toes still splayed around cotton. The duo in leotards, the candy cane and the jungle print. The green face and she who applied the gunk to her client. Holly and her aerobics student, both of whom appeared to be in shock. Greta the masseuse.

"Where's the one, you remember?" The candy-stripe leotard elbowed the other. "The one doing stretches."

"Stretches. Geez, I'll never get to that now, and I'm so tight. Geez." She patted her nonexistent stomach.

"Wasn't there somebody on the mat?"

"I was," a slightly rounded woman said. She wore gray sweats and I remembered having watched her lift her legs.

The second one nodded rather dubiously. "Yeah, but before you. Somebody else. I remember because I wanted to use it after her, so I was watching how long she took, but my time wasn't up on the treadmill, so you started. I think she left just before we heard the ruckus."

"What did she look like?" I asked.

Both leotard women's mouths opened slightly. "Look like?" the one in the red and white repeated, as if it were an incredible question.

I nodded. I knew they'd get the concept eventually.

"She needed work. More than leg lifts. I mean she wasn't gross, but still . . ."

"She had dark sweats, plain. Like guys wear, you know?" her friend said.

"How about age, or hair color, or height?" I suggested.

They looked surprised and challenged by the questions. "Faded blond, maybe?" candy-striped said. "Maybe not, though. I don't know. She wasn't eye-catching. Not *feminine*. Nothing special."

Nothing special and gone. A depressing combination.

THE POLICE CAME, looking perturbed. They herded us into the exercise room so that the forensics team could work on the crime scene. It was surprising how chilly the room felt in the absence of vigorous movement. Getting someone to raise the temperature was our first big challenge.

Controlling postmurder politics was another problem. Both Greta and Holly claimed stage front. "*I* found her. *My* room," and the like from the former, and, sadly, "*My* sister," from the latter. The manicurist and skin care specialist had their moments as well.

Since the crime appeared to be no more than twenty minutes old, we were all questioned, whether or not we had something to say. I waited my turn with the others. We all seemed to have a postdisaster need to discuss what little we knew of recent events.

"She was right on the brink of fame," Holly said. "So excited about the store. Signed the lease yesterday. Just this morning, she said, 'Everything's going to be all right from now on, Sis.' "

Since nobody else seemed to know that the deceased had been a recent widow—so recent that her husband had not yet been buried—nobody else appeared to find her optimistic outlook and time of lease-signing as inappropriate and suspicious as I did.

"Brave," Holly added. "Good things were going to happen to her, and she deserved it. She worked her whole life to get somewhere, and had so much bad luck. Her first husband was such a . . . and this second one . . ." She shook her head. Mere words could not convey what Jesse had been. "And the accident, too, of course. But now, everything was going to be different. She had a dream and it wouldn't quit. I ask you, how many people have a vision? A whole look that is theirs? This is given to very few."

The women murmured. Our group was taking on the tenor of a camp meeting, but before we canonized St. Poppy of the Rivets, her sister was summoned for her session with the detectives.

I wondered whether Sis had much to gain from the recent deaths. Somebody should check whether she was heir to the Reese money. I was warming to that when I suddenly stopped dead. There was no way to commit murder while leading an aerobics class in a fishbowl of a room.

I worried about my turn with the police, gnawed at what might happen, and thereby missed what was actually going on until the leotard twins cleared their throats. "—count you in?" the jungle-printed one asked me.

"For what?"

"For Holly's sister. I mean, we can't have been here and not do something, act like we don't know."

"Flowers?" her companion said. "From all of us?"

They looked eager and enthusiastic, so I obviously was the only one who found it somewhat bizarre. Greetings and consolation from the strangers who found your sister's corpse. "Sure," I said. Probably, in the face of such random cruelty, we all needed to do something, anything, to feel a bit more in control. Besides, perhaps any comfort, however bizarre, would be welcome.

"Holly's a gem," Greta said. "A treasure. And very close to her sister."

"A *large* bouquet," the candy-striped leotard said.

I extracted my share from my ever-thinning wallet. And then it was my turn to be questioned.

I need not have worried. The police were only interested in one murder, even after I reminded them that the corpse's husband had been similarly bludgeoned two days earlier.

"Not with a dumbbell!" one who looked straight out of *Night of the Living Dead* exclaimed.

"All the same," I said, "they're connected, don't you think?"

"Whatever we think, we'll think. How about you let us do it—the thinking—and you help us do it by answering our questions. Where exactly were you?"

I kept trying and they kept putting me down, shushing and patronizing me.

So, finally they knew only what they wanted to know, which was pretty much nothing. "Don't leave the area yet," the older one said. "We might need more information."

What a laugh. I decided that the indoor plumbing was part of the area, and I made my way to the john. The security guard I'd seen earlier was stationed by the exit near the combination changing room, shower, and bathroom.

"I just figured out who you are," he said. "What's with you and your friend? Some kind of grudge against the Reeses? The police are going to be very interested. You'd better be careful, young woman. Watch your step."

"Thanks for your concern. I really appreciate it, but right now, I'd appreciate the ladies' room even more." Having further offended him, I left.

I was tossing the paper towel into the wire basket when I became fully aware of how large and excessively empty the tiled space was. It wasn't surprising, given the situation, but still, it felt unnatural and chilling, as if the absence of sound could also echo off the white tile walls. The facility was probably never crowded, even when the police hadn't rounded up the few attendees. People did not come to Atlantic City for a healthy getaway. The spas were entertainment centers for wives bored with their husbands' gambling. Still, the changing room wasn't meant to be a ghost hall. The showers were empty, the blow dryers still, the benches unoccupied, and the lockers closed.

It had the drained and unnatural silence of a school at night. And the trash, too. The only sign that life had ever been in here was in the wicker container brimming over with used bath towels. It looked like the wastepaper baskets at Philly Prep each night, another phenomenon that confused me. Our students write so little and yet produce so much trash.

Maybe those kids grew up to be the people who don't exercise, but produce countless used towels.

I am not fond of things that do not make sense, mostly because when investigated, they do make sense, only not the way you wanted.

I poked a finger into the towels and stirred. A bit of black fabric appeared. I pulled off the top few towels, and then the overlarge pile made sense. It was boosted by a discarded and empty workout bag, plus a warm-up suit. Black, so the dirt didn't show.

Basic sweats—was it what the exercise sisters outside had considered a masculine workout ensemble? Worn by the person who was not *feminine*?

I held up the pants. I could have worn them. Ditto for the top.

Not that I was thinking of taking them, you understand. Particularly not after I noticed the wet splat on the front, or after I'd touched it, to find out what it was, and found out that it was blood.

Fresh blood that I bet would test out to be Poppy's type. I dropped the sweats and took several deep breaths. I looked around, double-checking that my impression of emptiness was accurate. I tiptoed toward the bathroom stalls and checked the open portions at the bottom of each. And then stood sideways and looked through the slats for shadows crouching on toilets.

There were none. There was nobody in the showers. I was alone. I breathed slightly more easily.

A shower and dressing room is not often provided at the scene of a murder. How convenient this one was. And it was standard operating procedure to arrive with a change of clothes as well. He must have been in the exercise room, on the mat, the leotards had said, then gone into the massage room for murder, then into here until everyone was in a group elsewhere—until the police came in, passing the ladies' locker room—until it was safe to strip, wash, change, and leave. Which brought us up to just about now.

I knew I could rush in to the police and tell them about my find—and face a forever of questioning and then a jail cell for two.

I was too easy a suspect—in collusion, I was positive they'd say, with Sasha. I could be, with a stretch of the imagination and a shrink of my torso and hair, the still-missing shorter partner. Case closed.

I took deep breaths to quell a flurry of panic—and knew I wasn't going to offer myself to the police like an unsanctified sacrifice.

Besides, the unfeminine, sweat-suit-shucking, freshly washed Ray Palford was very possibly still in this building, but not for as long as it would take the police to question me.

I opted to run now, talk later, to hit his trail before he disappeared. Catch the culprit before the police caught me.

I opened the locker room door and looked right and left. The security guard was off telling the cops of my guilt by association. Very soon the law would be aimed my way, in search of half of a murderous duo. It was a theory they'd love. High-concept. All the makings of a movie of the week or an Oprah special. Girlfriends who kill. Could yours?

I was getting out of here not a second too soon.

Twenty

I REALLY missed Sasha. I pushed the lobby button, breathing hard. I needed her nearby, saying, "Are you out of your mind? Get back in there and tell the police about the sweatpants. It's their job to find the person who wore them."

Sasha and I are a good balance because our forms of insanity differ. She's berserk when it comes to men, but is otherwise fairly rational. I tend to veer off track in matters civil, and at such times I need a monitor.

Speaking of which, I missed Mackenzie, too, even though when he monitored me, I found it oppressive and annoying. In any case, I had neither of my brakes on hand, and about when

I realized that, I arrived at the lobby and there was too much to do to waste time wondering if I should do it.

The one thing I was sure the leotard women would have noticed—even on an otherwise completely forgettable person—was an ensemble that didn't fit properly. So despite the little man's description of the tall woman who'd killed Jesse Reese, if she'd actually been as tall as Sasha, those sweats would have looked like knickers and note would have been made. Unless, of course, we had a tall but anorexically thin murderer, on whose frame fabric drooped, but that, too, the leotards would have noticed.

I didn't realize how much I wanted to discover Ray Palford trying to blend into the crowd, wending his no-fuss, non-noticeable way to the exit with the kind of cool deliberation it had taken to murder, shower, and change—until I absolutely couldn't find him. Every time I saw a brown-haired man his size, I speeded up as much as my still-aching back allowed and scanned, but Palford must have been a common variety of man, because there were dozens of almosts, but no Ray.

I peered into the casino, where the light was dark and bright at the same time. Tricky. A great place to disappear, and I certainly couldn't find Ray Palford. Instead, I gaped at what appeared to be a seven-foot man with a tiny head bobbing above a row of slot machines.

"Don't stare," my mother had taught me. "It's rude." I tried not to—besides, I didn't have time for staring—but the man was so very odd. And then, he really appeared—all of him this time, and I realized the figure, or at least its topping, was Lucky, my tough-talking, self-sufficient five-year-old former companion. At the moment, he'd dropped precocity and reverted to his rightful childhood. His face was puckered and fuchsia, and he was sobbing, "Mommy!" My former homeroom student, Eric, had the boy riding on his shoulders. I could see a rip in Lucky's jeans and what looked like a bad bruise.

How had they gotten in there? The casino was absolutely off-limits, and Eric was already skirting the law with his job permit.

"Lucky!" I called. "Eric!" But Eric was playing hero at the moment, carrying the wounded to safety, his step sure and forward-moving and not about to be deterred.

He moved with such confident stride that nobody stopped him. There was a message there for all of us.

Another message, just for me, was that I had lost my killer.

"Precious! Stop!"

I half turned and saw Lala and Belle, both waving broadly. "More news!" they cried out.

"No time!" I called. There was, alas, all the time in the world now, but it wasn't socially acceptable to say, "No patience!"

"It's important!" Lala had changed into a new ensemble, turquoise this time. Old Tommy had better have deep pockets, because Lala was diving into that pot of gold headfirst.

Belle, still in this morning's outfit, had relacquered against the humidity. Her hair sat on her head like a fibrous hat. "You wouldn't believe," she said.

"The *wig!*" I suddenly remembered. "What happened to the wig?"

Belle raised her hand to the top layer of her hair. "This is not a—I never wore a—Lala's the one who wears wigs."

Lala colored deeply. "You could have had the decency to say it looked funny." She blinked hard and for a moment dropped all the effort and muscular skill that kept her face in place, and turned into a seriously old woman.

"I didn't mean either of you," I said. "Your hair always looks beautiful. I meant . . . the killer's wig."

"Killer? Weren't we talking about a lawsuit?" Belle asked. "The missing money?"

If Ray Palford had been the one in the black workout suit, then surely he'd worn a wig—and where was it? Would he dump the suit and bag and carry incriminating evidence along with him in his briefcase? And what about the earring? Poppy wasn't the sort for pearl earrings—they didn't go with brass—but Palford was even less likely to have been wearing a pearl stud in the ear while killing. What was wrong with my brain?

"We have five more names," Belle said, "and one of them has

a nephew who's a lawyer, and he's absolutely going to start a class action suit, to get the money from the estate."

"Great going," I said. "There's a woman named Georgette. She lives under the boardwalk. Add her name to the list."

"Under the boardwalk?" Lala's mouth hung slightly open. "Georgette?" All her worst nightmares were reflected on her face. All mine, too. Except for the ones about a killer in pearl earrings.

Pearl earrings. There was only one pearl-earring type out of all the characters I'd met lately. Her. Norma Evans, the barely visible woman. Perfect in pearls. Perfect all around, except for any apparent motive.

I'd worry about that later. Right now, I was thinking of Norma Evans in partnership with Poppy Reese. Tiny, wig-and-slacks-wearing, cane-toting Poppy. Capable—when she took off her luxuriant brown wig and put it on Norma's head, and when she was seen by a passing elderly gentleman—of being mistaken for a small man herself. As was Norma capable of being mistaken for Sasha.

It was all perfect, except that by now Norma would have dissolved into the wallpaper and the floorboards, never to be found if she didn't want to be.

I couldn't imagine her running out of the hotel, so I tried to imagine, instead, where and how she would have proceeded once she left the spa.

Where would I go if I could go anywhere, because nobody ever noticed me?

I'd go anywhere I damned well pleased, I thought. And I also thought that if I'd just killed my second victim, my former partner in crime, and I'd done it with the cool aplomb that had me showering and changing at the scene of the crime—I'd want a drink. I'd maybe need a drink. And I'd have it. Why not? I certainly wouldn't rush outside, where, as far as she knew, the police might already be, waiting for someone who might fit the black and bloody workouts.

Belle was still talking. I heard her voice as if coming from a passing car, distant and unrelated to me. I walked toward the bar and looked in.

She was sitting almost where Jesse Reese had been two nights earlier. I wouldn't have recognized her, and I was sure Frankie didn't.

Norma Evans had cut her gray-brown hair and she was wearing dark red lipstick and tortoiseshell eyeglass frames. It was enough to give her an entirely new, albeit equally forgettable, persona.

She saw me and stood up, pushing so hard that her drink fell on the floor.

"You!" I said. I moved toward her. "It's you!"

"Hey!" Frankie shouted. "Mandy, isn't it? Have you heard any—"

And during the split-second automatic head turn at his *hey!* Norma Evans shot around and past me with amazing speed. I turned and ran after her through the lobby, limping and lurching with the hot spears of pain in my back.

"Baby doll!" Lala called out. "What are you—"

"Stop her!" I shouted. I looked for a guard, even as I realized how futile my request was, how much time and explanation it would require. Grab that incredibly respectable-looking woman? She was everyone's third grade teacher, favorite lingerie clerk. The aunt the family felt sorry for.

But she had done it, I was positive. Finally, all the jarring details quieted down and fit. She was the one who'd driven Poppy down here. The two of them had known Reese's escape plans and were following him—probably with murder in mind. And then they saw Sasha and heard, via Frankie's joke, what room she was in, and the coincidence of hair and place altered the details of their plans. It didn't take much.

And it didn't matter much because Norma Evans was gone. Sucked into the casino, a gray invisibility in the chronic glare.

I searched for her inconspicuous, well-tailored shoulders, her demure skirt, her low-heeled pumps.

"Have you gone crazy?" Lala screeched from behind me. "You'll give us heart attacks."

That angry voice on the answering machine in Jesse Reese's outer office—the voice that sounded like metal grating. Poppy had every right to call her husband's office—but so angrily? And Norma, who'd ignored an earlier caller, had leaped to silence that one.

One thing didn't yet make sense. Poppy's motives were easy enough—she'd be financially better off with a dead husband than one who fled the country with his fund, but I didn't understand what drove Norma Evans.

"Miss Pepper! Tell him I'm okay." Eric, with Lucky still on his shoulders, was being propelled toward the exit by a security guard, his hand on the young man's elbow. "This guy's like accusing me of kidnapping!"

"I never said kidnap," the guard insisted. "I said—"

"Abducted," Eric said. "Geez!"

"The little boy's mother's in here." I kept moving, searching for a sign of Norma. "Eric's trying to help." Norma Evans was gone, lost in the maze of money machines. Soon she'd be out the door and gone for real and forever.

And then I spotted her. I thought. "See that woman?" I said to the guard. "Get her. She murdered somebody."

"Miss Pepper!" Eric nearly dropped his grip on Lucky's legs.

The guard, on the other hand, didn't even pretend to look. "That's a cheap way of getting these kids off the hook," he said. "I'm a little too savvy for the old look-over-there game, anyway."

"What's going on?" Lala and Belle arrived together, puffing between words. "Honey," Lala panted, "if it's about the phone bill—if you're afraid we're dunning you, don't worry. We only—"

"Either of you these kids' mother?" the guard asked the two women. His eyes weren't all that functional, unless he was flirting.

Lala shrieked with laughter. "My *grandchildren* are twice his age!"

"Poor tyke has a boo-boo." Belle's voice had gone high and singsongy. "Do you have an itsy boo-boo, little boy?"

Lucky stopped snuffling. "Who you calling a little boy?" he demanded.

Once again I thought I saw gray dim the neon-brights of a slot machine. I took a step away. "Help him find the little boy's mother, please," I said to Belle. "She's gambling in here somewhere. I can't. I have to—" Their voices faded as I moved toward where I thought I'd seen Norma, past the center row of poker and craps tables. The robotic voices of machines encouraged the players on. The background music softly pulsed out of the walls, and always, from everywhere, was the sound of silver going in and coming out of machines. Above the bank of tall slots an electronic machine tabulated total winnings, a number that escalated even as I glanced up at it.

But I wasn't a winner. I had lost Norma and the game was over. Doom was setting in with cement hardness. The very worst scenario—Sasha permanently accused—was becoming inevitable. I needed Norma Evans right now. I needed to be able to show her to the leotard girls and the masseuse and Holly while whatever memory they had was fresh. If she left, she would blend into her surroundings somewhere else. She could imitate her former boss's aborted plans and take the money and run. Take it right now.

In fact, she probably was doing just that.

I had to find her and keep her right now.

And even then I'd have no real proof. A pocketbook that kept reappearing, an overheard voice on an answering machine, and maybe a pearl earring. If I was unbelievably lucky, and she was much dumber than I thought, she'd have kept the earring's mate, hoping to find the lost one. Great.

If I was even luckier than that, her pocketbook would be full of incriminating money in one form or another.

I rounded one corner, scanned the row, saw only three ancient stone-faced women offering up coins to their machines, and a young girl with orange hair sipping a drink and giggling while her boyfriend—his hair butter-yellow and frizzy and even bigger than hers—popped coins.

I turned and scanned another row, then moved on toward the craps tables, chasing shadows. There were too many corners and possibilities. She could appear where she had not been the second after I left and this could go on forever, until she reached the exit.

I moved toward the door that led to the boardwalk, then backtracked—what if she exited via the casino lobby, instead?

I looked longingly up toward the ceiling where, I knew, everybody—or at least everybody's money—was being observed nonstop. I wondered what level of commotion it would create if I tried to get up there, to enlist their assistance, to signal from below.

I didn't have to wonder long, because at that moment I spotted Norma nearing the exit.

"Hey!" I shouted, running in her direction. "*Stop!* Somebody stop her!"

She stopped herself, looking completely innocuous. When I reached her, therefore, she was ready. Her right arm grabbed my shoulder in what must have looked the friendliest of poses, but which hurt. "Shut up, now. Don't move. There's a sharp cutting object between your third and fourth ribs," she said.

I was wearing a green linen blazer, white T-shirt, and tan slacks, none of which offered the protection of, say, a bulletproof vest, so I was immediately able to verify that she was telling the truth. Something pointed was about to do painful acupuncture on internal organs about which I'm sentimental and possessive.

"You're in big trouble," Miss Evans whispered.

I'm mortified to admit that my first response was more suitable for Scarlett O'Hara. My knees buckled, my head grew light. But Philadelphia never was a part of the Old South, so I shook myself back to consciousness. It was too late for a swoon.

It was, I feared, too late for everything.

Twenty-One

"**S**URPRISED?" Norma Evans said, propelling me along. "Blinded by preconceptions about women of a certain age? By your own stereotypes? Call yourself a feminist, I bet. Sisterhood is all—but you still underrate middle-aged sisters. My hair turns a little gray and I become invisible, a nonperson, ready to be victimized, right? I'm certainly not an actor, a doer, a person to notice. Who'da thought the old dame packed a knife? Can you pack a knife or only a gun?" She interrupted herself to giggle, which didn't seem much improvement or much endorsement of her mental health.

"Help!" I squawked.

"Stop sniveling! Act like a *woman!*" She managed to simultaneously clutch my arm tighter and press the knife in closer. I gasped—shallowly. A normal inhale would result in a puncture wound. I tried to contract all my muscles—but the one in my back that was already in a slipknot made any movement tricky.

" 'S killing me!" I croaked, conserving my air and rib cage.

A man at a computerized poker game looked my way. "This one's killing me, too." He returned to his game.

"No joke!" I pushed out words with the exhale, feeling my sides shrink in. "This woman's—" I was out of air.

Norma pushed the knife along my newly tightened sides. My skin gave way with the sharp hot rip of shredding nerve ends. My eyes teared.

"People in here don't *care* about us," Norma said. "They're too busy with their own good times. You know that a man once had a heart attack and died, right on the floor—literally, down on the floor, dead. And people walked over him to get to the machines? That I once saw the doctor administering CPR under the craps table—but the game went right on above them? The way those sick people felt is exactly how it feels to be *me*, all the time now. To be no longer valuable, over-the-hill."

Was this really the time for polemics? Still, I wondered whether I'd live long enough to experience mid-life devaluation firsthand.

And while I mused and winced and worried, she steered me toward the outer wall of the casino. Her grip on my upper arm was amazingly tight. I tried to shake loose but couldn't. I used my free hand to claw at hers—but she immediately scraped me with the knife in response. My side was on fire. Surface wound, I reminded myself. Surface.

"Another myth shot to hell," she said. "I'm strong. I work out. I lift weights. A woman alone has to be able to take care of herself. You aren't much of a reporter, are you, Hildy? Came to find out about me and you didn't learn the first thing."

"I didn't—I was trying to find out about *him*. Jesse. I never connected you with—"

"Nonsense," she said.

"Help!" I shouted.

"Testing me?" She gave the knife another jab. Once again I told myself that if she were wounding me seriously I wouldn't feel it this much, that superficial cuts hurt worse than deep ones because with the latter, the nerve was severed. Therefore, even as I felt the wet warmth of my own blood—therefore, I had to stifle my panic and understand that I had no more than a paper cut on my side. Several paper cuts. That's why I hurt like hell.

I glanced down, just to check that no vital organs were now on the outside. What I saw was a small but growing rusty stain wending its way between the green linen fibers of my blazer. My jacket's ruined, I thought inappropriately.

I controlled the urge to bawl.

I was less able to stifle a ridiculous flood of household hints that flashed onto my mental screen. Ought to get this into cold water. Pour baking soda on it—or was it club soda?

I was obviously losing my mind, worrying about laundry problems when I was being knifed.

And nobody turned to look, to wonder, to speculate on what my words—or the stain—meant.

Norma chuckled, a sound that made me shudder. But then, over the mildly insane laughter, I heard an Ethel Merman boom of a voice from somewhere behind me.

"How'm I supposed to find his mother, a woman I never saw?"

"Lala!" I shouted. "Help!" I could almost see my words absorbed by the noise of the machines, the clothing of the players, the distance.

But I had caught someone's attention. A man actually looked up from something called a Triple-Play. "Need help?" he asked. His eyes, however, were on Norma.

Nonetheless, I nodded, vigorously. "She has a kni—"

Norma pressed and spoke right over me. "It's all right." Her voice was soothing, telegraphing not to worry, all was well, as long as all was in her hands. "She's had these attacks since she was fifteen," she said. "Chronic hysteria. Takes time and fresh air."

The man looked from the great gray and solid woman to me. "What kind of a mother leaves her little boy alone, anyway?" It was Lala again, somewhere close.

"Lala!" I screamed.

"Lala? Jesus." The man twirled his finger in a small circle next to his head, using the universal sign for insanity. He whistled softly, then nodded sympathetically at Norma. "I don't envy you," he said. Of course. Who was he going to believe? Stability itself or incoherent, screaming, tear-streaked, and disheveled me? Lala's parents chose a bizarre moniker—and it would cost me my life.

Norma jabbed me again. I was going to look like a scored piece of meat. I was going to *be* a scored piece of meat. "Absolutely no more screams." Norma's mouth was close to my ear. "Cut it out, or I will. Get it?" She laughed at her grisly pun. "You're not even smiling," she said. "But I, myself, find my wordplay *side-splitting*. Get it?" I felt mildly ill, couldn't bear thinking about my split side, my injuries, my bleeding, and what they might mean. Not to mention my back, which at this point, all on its own, was enough to paralyze me with pain. I nodded woozily. We must have looked like mildly drunk women, steering ourselves toward the exit.

"I was really surprised to see you—little Hildy Johnson, from McKeesport, Pennsylvania, and formerly of *His Girl Friday*—showing up in a bar in Atlantic City? What an incredible coincidence, and what a stroke of luck. I never thought I'd find you again, although I wanted to."

"I get around, so what? And why would you want to see me again?"

She pulled the outside door open and shoved me through it. "You stole a *tape*," she added, as if that act were the very heart of the problem.

I instinctively pulled back, to express amazement, but she had me in her grip too tightly. "It wasn't like it had state secrets on it," I said. "The whole world was supposed to see it."

We were outside now, on the boardwalk. I eyed the crowds.

Nobody eyed me back with any real interest. I felt again how alone a person could be no matter the numbers around her. I knew that if I screamed and Norma remained calm, looking like somebody caring for me, passersby, who didn't want to be involved in the first place, would happily accept the idea that they weren't needed and would move on. And then Norma would kill me with her stiletto. It seemed wiser to stay alert and see what she had planned next. Surely she didn't intend to do away with me while this many witnesses were around. Since they weren't gambling at the moment, they'd pay attention to a capital crime happening in front of their eyes, wouldn't they?

She turned and stood in front of me now, as if in intense conversation, and the knife was rerouted to just below where I put my hand when I pledge allegiance to the flag. I tried to decide whether I could pull her off me with my one good arm and my very bad back faster than she could slice my heart.

"Let me go," I said in a reasonable voice. "You're outside now. You can leave."

"Did you make a copy of that tape?" she asked. "Tell me the truth."

"Are you telling me this is about pirating laws? I don't get it. I'm sorry, but it was boring. Why on earth would I copy . . . ?" But given that she was, as they say, in my face, almost literally, I thought about hers. That ignorable, forgettable face had been on the tape.

Somebody with the tape could identify her. Give the police five minutes of talking heads—her talking head. Otherwise, she was a woman no one would clearly remember, a woman who could disappear in a moment, and undoubtedly had planned to do just that. Maybe still did.

Her breath on my face was minty. "Jesse thought I'd be perfect. People would identify with me, he said. He was right. I was perfect. A pathetically perfect target for him. So yes. That was me playing me, telling the entire world that I was a single, self-supporting fool who invested her savings—*all* her savings—in Jesse Reese's no-fail fund. That was his form of pension plan. He

217

added to the amount twice a year, too. But who cares? He was leaving, skipping out, taking it all. Of course, when we filmed that, I had no idea he planned to rob me of everything."

Of course. It wasn't about pirating or love or power. How had I not realized that the same terror I felt and Lala felt and Lucky's mother probably felt was driving Norma Evans as well? None of us wanted to wind up penniless and alone. And of the two options, alone was by far the preferable one. That's all it was, and it was everything and all around me, like a message being shouted in Sensurround for days now—and I had missed it. I didn't exactly feel sorry for her, but I did *see* her for the first time, and understand at least a bit of her. "How did you find out about what Jesse was doing?" I asked her.

She looked in pain herself. "That was the worst part. He didn't even try to be subtle about it—as if he didn't *remember* that I'm the one who took care of his life. That I knew every one of his secrets—his other secrets. Suddenly, he acted like I was an idiot—*me!* Like I was the same as everybody else. As if I wouldn't notice that he was keeping his passport in his briefcase, or that he'd packed up his wife's photograph, or—this was the giveaway—that he agreed to appointments with threatening lawyers and a bunch of really angry old people who were suing. For seventeen years he'd made me tell people he was out of town or already busy or otherwise unavailable if it was going to be a sticky situation. I always had to force him to deal with reality. He made sure it was next to impossible to see him when he didn't want to be seen. Then suddenly, we had real problems—disaster looming—and he'd say sure, schedule them for next Tuesday, for June the tenth. Everything he wanted to avoid was scheduled—no problem—on June tenth or after, until I knew that he was going to disappear on June ninth."

She had one hand on my shoulder and the other, the knife hand, to my diaphragm, and she leaned in close, her face twisted with rage. To anyone passing by—to all the people passing us by in wide arcs—we looked like a local nuisance to be avoided.

I kept scanning them, however, looking for an expression of human concern. Human curiosity. Who is that woman being chewed out on the boardwalk, Mom? I thought I saw Eric Stotsle and a small dancing figure that could be Lucky up ahead. They'd been freed.

"But did Jesse Reese ever once say you must know what's going on, Norma, but don't worry—I've taken care of you, protected you? Did he say you won't wind up without a job, without a cent, living out of a shopping cart? Did he *care*! Like I was *invisible*—or didn't matter—he was going to rip me off along with everybody else! Or else he thought I was as dumb as his wife."

"So you called her. Became partners, a team."

"Why not? We had similar concerns. You don't have to be a rocket scientist to know that if your no-good husband skips the country with all the money anybody ever gave him—less the part he lost at the tables, of course—you're never going to have your precious store."

Those Reeses were really bad at picking partners.

"Besides," she said, "together we could take him. She was the one could doctor his drink, invite him up for a quickie, as he called it. I surely couldn't. But I'm strong. I could finish it. I made up some stupid pretext. Papers he forgot to sign. He didn't pay enough attention to me to care. She was fine, until after, until she changed her mind about the fifty-fifty and wanted it all. She was the *wife*, she said. She was going to frame me and keep everything except for a *pittance*."

It was amazing how wonderfully this two-time murderer distinguished between transgressions. Taking lives was a necessity, but taking money was serious.

"Since her accident, Poppy had painkillers that could stun a mule. We were going to make it look like a mugging—until we saw your friend. The hair, the room—it was perfect. Destiny."

"You went in while the maid was turning down the beds, didn't you? And stayed till she left, and wedged the door so it wouldn't lock." Why did I have to ask that? Why did I care, unless I wanted a tombstone that said, "She figured some of it out."

Norma shrugged acknowledgment. Her mind was on the future, not the past. "Now," she said, "we're going around the corner."

I felt the knife point at what I thought was my breast bone, and I froze in place. I really, truly, didn't want to test out how penetrable or not that portion of my anatomy might be.

"Why?" I knew the answer. With great frugality, she was going to recycle her original mugging plan. Once off the boardwalk, Atlantic City's untended streets are great places to get rid of somebody, and this time Norma could handle the job all on her own. And no Mackenzie to the rescue.

I knew I should have paid more attention in geometry. If only theorems would have mentioned times like this—times when the issue of whether a knee raised to a forty-five-degree angle is on the proper trajectory, and whether the impact of said knee would push the hand of the kicked forward or backward—seemed of vital importance. Or was that physics?

Too late to find out, except by experiment. I took a deep breath, looked her in the eye, and raised my knee as hard as I could, as fast as I could.

It didn't have the same dramatic effect as it would have with a man. All the same, it surprised her and threw her off balance, which was enough. Her grip on me loosened, and I pushed and kicked. Even better, her grip on the knife also loosened. It clattered to the boards as she staggered back.

"Lookit!" A ten-year-old boy in a T-shirt that reached his knees stared at the knife covetously.

"Get over here, Tyler!" a woman in yellow screamed. "Right now!"

I raced to the knife. No pain, no gain, I told my back as it screamed in protest. No pain, no life. I put my foot on the knife. The boy galloped away.

Now, people were paying a little more attention. They stood back warily and kept their distance. "Somebody call the police!" I shouted. "Stop that woman!"

The two women nearest me looked puzzled by my remark. "Stop who?" one of them finally said.

The other shook her head. "She's crazy," she said. "Leave her alone."

"Lucky?" A high-pitched voice called his name. "Lucky, where are you? It's Mommy!"

"You better find him," a familiar voice warned her. "It's not right for a mother to leave her kid—I should tell the cops about you— Look over there! It's her! Darling, it's you, oh, my God!"

"Lala—" I realized that the spectator's gallery thought I'd been the knife wielder, the one who'd dropped it. "And you," I said to Lucky's mother, "take care of your son or we'll have to—" But this wasn't the time. What I had to do was pay attention to Norma, who was backing her way into invisibility. *"Her!"* I shouted.

"Oh, hey!" Georgette had entered the circle. "Mandy. Where you been all day?"

People backed off from Georgette. I seized the moment and the knife and ran after Norma. The sight of me, knife in hand, triggered screaming, seething pandemonium. For the first time, somebody actually shouted for the police.

Meantime, I got to Norma, or at least to the gray collar of her blouse, and I tugged with my unarmed hand.

"It's Miss *Pepper*," I heard. "Miss Pepper in a catfight!"

"She has a *knife!*" somebody screamed.

That was true. I did. But I wasn't planning to cut anyone with it, not even Norma. I didn't even think to use it. My desires were simple—I wanted to make her stop killing people, including me.

We failed, however, to discuss our various agendas, and I'm afraid we couldn't have made them mesh in any case. As it was, while people screamed and Eric enthused and Lucky's mother called his name and Lala said, "Darling, you aren't that kind of a girl, you have to stop," and Georgette burst into tears, Norma twisted inside her blouse, just enough to give her a decent trajectory.

The patchwork pocketbook hit my head with much more force than I'd have predicted. It must be that geometry thing again. I don't know what all she carried inside that bag. Not cosmetics, surely. Perhaps all of Reese's money was in coins. Or she'd stolen Poppy's stash of brass rivets along with Reese's money. Most likely it was just another example of her skill and expertise at bonking—after all, she'd slammed Jesse with a lamp, and Poppy with a free weight. She was good at this.

But something hurt enough to make the clunk of impact the next sound I heard as I collapsed onto the boardwalk. It isn't true that you see stars. I didn't, at least. It was more like those damned casino lights—trails of them blinking and wound around with neon.

The last thing I heard was somebody saying, "Look at that drunk. Dead to the world."

I knew he wasn't right about the drunk part. I hoped he wasn't right about the rest.

Twenty-Two

SOMETIMES it takes a lot—like a semiconscious woman sprawled on the boardwalk—to demonstrate the basic humanity and decency of people, even at America's favorite vacation destination. The point is, they cared.

"You all right? Hey, lady, are you okay? She didn't hurt you too much, did she? Need a doctor? Need help?"

Don't tell me people have gotten callous, I thought. Despite the wind tunnel howling between my ears, I heard those lovely, considerate sentiments. They gave me heart, gave me reason to struggle to keep afloat, to fight the swirling dark that wanted to swamp me.

It took a half-dozen more solicitous questions for me to realize that not a one of them was directed down at me. All, all were for sweet graying, genteel Norma.

"Don't worry. I got her knife," a man said. "She can't hurt you anymore."

From then on, rage and indignation kept me from passing out. I wanted to tell them they were wrong, but I was in something like that paralytic nightmare state when danger is at your heels but you can't lift a foot to run, can't move.

And while I struggled for breath and an end to the black dizziness gulping me down, I heard Norma play right back into their hands. She murmured something about "crazy young people and drugs," and I heard a knee-jerk ready assent, as if I were the very image of a junkie.

"If you'll keep her here, I'll call the police," Norma said.

"N-N—" I managed. The resourceful Miss Evans had just given herself an exit line. The odds against ever sighting her again escalated. My protests, however, became mush on my thick and cottony lips, and I could almost feel the boardwalk planks shake gently as she strode off with the crowd's blessings.

Their attention turned to me, their captive. Some had never seen a junkie mugger before, and several felt obliged to share the nuances of their astonishment at the sight of me. But they didn't quite know what to do next. The baddie was flat on her back. The goodie was off to get the sheriff. Wasn't this the happy ending? Or was there some important, possibly dangerous element they hadn't quite grasped?

There was a lot of speculation about what to do till the law arrived—tie me up, perhaps? One woman, for reasons that escaped me, gave me a long look, then screamed "Help! Help!" in a fake voice, like a bad movie extra. It certainly couldn't have been because she feared me. There I lay, as threatening and active as road kill. Maybe I offended her aesthetically.

I began to understand that I was neither dead, unconscious, nor likely to become either. I had just been seriously stunned. I was becoming unstunned.

"Miss Pepper's *down*! You see that, Lucky?" That was Eric,

somewhere out of my line of vision—a line that for the moment only went straight up—behaving as if this were a sporting event. If I ever got him in my class, I was going to flunk him, based on today's performance.

"You know her?" a spectator asked.

"She's a *teacher*!" Eric said. "At Philly Prep, my school."

In fact, I would flunk him in subjects I didn't even teach.

"A teacher! My God, no wonder schools are in trouble. A teacher with a knife, did you ever hear such a thing?"

"Why do you think they have metal detectors in them nowadays?"

"Metal detectors in teachers?"

"You read that things have gotten tough in the schools, but really, this is—"

"You're hurt!" A familiar voice amidst the idiot din. Belle, telling me what I already knew. "That woman you were with is no good! She looked like such a nice person, but—"

"Stop 'er—" I began. "She—"

Lala bent over me.

"Don't get near her!" The speaker looked ready to stomp me.

"She's not contagious," Lala said. The skin of her concerned face sagged and pooched forward like a basset hound's. I forgave her all her manipulative sins and decided I was, in fact, in love with her. "We'll get her, cookie," she whispered for my ears only. "Tommy's here, too." And with a sigh and a creak of bones, she stood back up and the world's oldest posse was off and if not quite running, then at least huffing and puffing as quickly as it could.

"Lucky, you come down from that boy's shoulders," his mother said.

"You'd better keep an eye on him," I said to the sky above my face. But I had a real sense that the grandma patrol had successfully intimidated her.

"Isn't anybody going to do anything?" It was Eric again. I could see a long, tall two-headed body. Lucky was still riding Eric's shoulders. "The old lady bashed Miss Pepper!"

"No . . ." someone in the crowd said.

"She did! The old lady's crazy! And look—Miss Pepper's bleeding!"

"Young man . . ." But the objections were less emphatic, enough so that I thought perhaps Eric had actually planted a seed of doubt. Maybe I'd reconsider that grade.

"Somebody ought to stop her," Eric said. "I don't care if she's old."

"Eric, please—" I began, but he couldn't hear me. I was having a very bad day, and my back was having an even worse one. A splat on the boards is not a therapeutic alternative to a massage. I was probably paralyzed for life. And julienned. A very, very bad day.

"Where's that cop she called?" somebody asked.

"You know how they are when you need them."

They could await Norma's cop along with world peace, and both would arrive at about the same time. I therefore had a chance, a window of opportunity, if only I could open it. My energy pumped back in, fueled by the vision of Norma Evans in pursuit of her imaginary telephone, melting into the traffic, ignored and invisible.

This was no time to be on my back. I rolled over, slowly, and worked my way into an undignified crawl position. Halfway there, I saw a tidy flash of gray about a block away. "There!" I shouted. "She's—"

"She's trying to stand up," a woman explained to the others, as if I were some alien species. "Is that all right?"

Nobody bothered to answer. The little crowd was rapidly losing interest. We had lasted longer than a sound bite.

I closed my eyes, took a deep breath, and pushed myself up onto elbows and knees. Norma Evans had disappeared into the horizon. What was visible was Georgette, staring at me and sobbing, her skirts shaking with misery.

"No," I said. "I'm okay. Nothing bad happened." I wasn't sure which layer of her woeful history she was revisiting through the sight of me. "I'll be fine." I said it emphatically, and decided that perhaps it was actually so. Or maybe it was the four-footed position. This was how humans were meant to get around, and we'd screwed everything up trying to balance the whole shebang on two legs. Maybe I'd stay this way, start a trend.

"That woman," I said to Georgette and anyone who'd listen, "that woman in the gray blouse—you can't let her get away. She isn't calling the police—she's escaping. She killed two people."

"Oh, really," the scowling woman near me said. "I've heard crazy things in my time, but this . . ."

"Who?" Georgette sniffled, looked around. "What woman?"

Where was Norma Evans? I pushed on my hands and unscrunched into a standing position. My back throbbed out an S.O.S., demanded bed rest and peace, remembered that this was supposed to be my vacation. My bloody side seconded the motion.

I thought of people with broken backs who lifted cars off their injured children, or ran for help on shattered tibias.

But my new Spartan bite-the-bullet determination didn't help me spot Norma. What I saw instead was a cluster of uncentered turbulence—Lala's turquoise suit, Belle's blue back, Tommy in spiffy whites, Eric with Lucky on his shoulders, and Georgette loping in their general direction, although she had a tendency to stop and talk en route.

They were all still moving, which meant Norma Evans was still uncaught but in their sight. I took an experimental step, winced, and clenching my teeth, made a second, slightly less painful move. I could do it. I would do it. I would get her.

"Here he is!" someone shouted. "The cop!"

Norma had actually called the police? I was stunned into immobility, and afraid, suddenly, that I'd made up everything about her. Good lord—maybe what she said was true and I *was* the criminal. I felt another attack of dizziness.

"Okay, who's been shouting for help here?" The policeman did not look pleased by the commotion. He was beefy and slow, moving as if his bunions ached. "What's the ruckus about? What's going on?" His eyes squinted in suspicion.

"It's like she told you when she called," a woman said.

"Who you talking about?"

"That *lady*," the woman insisted. "She was with this other

lady, a younger one, who had a knife. I think she was mugged. The lady who called you."

The straggly crowd's attention had shifted to the patrolman, who had every right to be mystified about what was going on, since it was obvious to anyone who wasn't fixed on Norma's eternal innocence that she hadn't called him. I felt some relief.

A burly man who, if he had a single operational brain cell, could have been helping to catch a murderer, instead pointed at me. "It's her! She had a knife!" he shouted. "But I disarmed her."

Disarmed me? Picked the thing up off the boardwalk was more like it.

"You still talking about the lady who supposedly called me?" the cop asked.

I backed up, step by step.

The burly man held out the knife. "See? I took it from her." In a few days he'd probably receive the Mayor's Award for heroism and believe he'd earned it.

He deserved the booby prize. He brandished the knife, obliterating whatever fingerprints might have been left. Didn't he know anything? Watch TV or read books?

"Hey," the policeman said. "If that's evidence of some crime . . ."

I backed up more as the crowd moved in to see more clearly, to watch the handing over of the knife to the patrolman.

It was my exit cue. While the patrolman took out a notepad and asked him to explain everything again, I headed for the wings and ran. Or, more accurately, hobbled and staggered, hunched over.

"Hey!" a woman said. "She's—Wasn't she out cold? I thought—"

"Stop her!" the knife man called. "She's the one!"

"The one what?" the policeman asked in his methodical voice.

"The one! The knife girl!"

It had a certain ring, that. Mandy the knife girl. As in, perhaps, knife girls finish last?

"She went after the old lady with a knife."

"Oh," the policeman said. "Stop!" He'd finally gotten it. "Stop!" he shouted, loudly enough for me to hear it a half block away. "Stop or I'll—"

But he couldn't shoot into a crowd of people. And meanwhile I was nearly at the second commotion, in front of a store with a green-and-white-striped awning.

"She was right here!" Lala said.

"Where?" I could see only my little band of stalwarts and a cluttered souvenir storefront window. And, of course, a lot of red streaks of pain.

"Stop!" the patrolman shouted.

"Maybe she went down the ramp," Belle said. "Toward Pacific Avenue." She and Lala and Tommy took off again. Georgette looked the wrong way, surveying the watery horizon. We were not the world's best posse.

"No! She's *there!*" Lucky shouted from atop Eric's shoulders. He was barely noticed by the rest of what I'd begun to think of as our gang. Being five and ignorable was the story of his life. I followed the trajectory of his index finger. It led behind us, through the window filled with pennants and plastic Miss America and Bert Parks dolls and miniature rolling chairs and inflatable money and shell-encrusted picture frames and a red and yellow plastic globe that said I HAD A BALL IN A.C.—and into the store. I wasn't seven feet up in the air the way Lucky was, so I couldn't see beyond the display, but the high wall of clutter made the store a perfect place to disappear. And it probably had a back door.

The patrolman approached. Talk about flatfoots. This man was not built for the chase. He waddled, side to side, in obvious foot pain. No wonder he was in such a testy mood. "Avoiding arrest is a serious offense, lady!" he shouted.

Being arrested seemed even more seriously offensive. I was too easy a scapegoat. Another bad girl from out of town, Sasha's sidekick, trying for a third kill.

"Nobody ever listens to me," Lucky whined.

"Lucky! Get down from there!" his mother shouted. "You could get hurt!"

"In a minute." He was beginning to sound like a normal kid, and she like a normal mother.

I reached for the store's door. It felt too heavy to move. My back pulsated.

"Stop!" It was the knife man taking vigilantism too seriously. "Gotcha!" But he hadn't got me. Not quite.

I pulled the door half open.

This time the man's hand made contact. Actually, two did. They felt thick and damp and final, one on each of my shoulders.

"Not *me*!" I shouted. "I didn't—" No use, no use. I could see through the half-open door that there, at the back of the store, was Norma in huddled conference with a salesperson. I guessed what she was asking, what safe exit she was requesting. And here we were, making a chaotic ruckus and justifying whatever paranoid story she'd tell.

Goodbye, Norma Evans. Hello, lockup.

Except that at precisely that instant there was the bellowing, cracked-voice, adolescent shout of "Go!"

And, almost simultaneously, a fearsome shriek—the long, banshee type that only young, young vocal cords can manage or find intriguing—and through the air, like a trapeze artist without any equipment, like Tarzan without vines, like a wild avenging bird or a cannonball with a five-year-old's features, flew Lucky.

People screamed and rushed forward to grab him, but he arced down, landing smack on the man grabbing me.

The man bellowed and let go. Lucky, his face radiantly triumphant, clung to his back, pulling on his hair like a baby monkey.

I had never seen anything like it in my life. I applauded.

"Run, Miss Pepper!" Eric shouted. "Get her!"

An A, Eric. An A plus. The kid was a genius. Reckless, maybe, but definitely a creative thinker. My running was not quite as graceful as Lucky's dive, but I raced into the store, inspired by both boys. If Lucky could ignore the laws of thermodynamics and fly, then I could move fast, ignore my twisted muscles and cuts.

"Stop!" I screamed because the saleswoman, a wrinkled and frightened creature, was pointing through a stack of cartons. That way to freedom, I was sure. The saleswoman relocated her pointing hand to her chest, crossed herself and mouthed a silent, urgent prayer.

Outside, there was a lot of audible scrambling. I could hear Lucky's piping voice and the deep grumble of the patrolman. I knew what was next. The law would amble in, grab me, and let Norma become history.

The saleswoman could pray all she liked. Norma, a foot or two beyond my reach, was no dummy. She bolted in the direction the finger had pointed.

I had no choice but to do a Lucky.

It gets harder all the time to have the imagination and heart to fly, particularly from a standing position and with a seriously hurting back and side, but I did my best. I visualized myself in the NFL, a quarterback or a tight end, or whoever it was that used his body as a javelin and hurtled. I imagined myself a five-year-old boy with a daredevil's heart. I even screeched, à la my mentor, and it indeed had a momentary opiate effect.

Just long enough for it to work. Not, perhaps, with grace and elegance. I managed more of a splat than a soar, but the thing is . . . I grounded her.

I grounded her and then, because I'd had a very long day and it definitely seemed time to relax, I sat on her. She was as comfortable as an ergonomic chair, and my back didn't feel half bad.

The saleswoman sobbed, even though at this point crying seemed redundant and unnecessary. Even the dunderhead policeman would surely be swayed when he saw the contents of Norma's pocketbook. I was sure she had been en route to her disappearance, and whatever she'd taken must be close to her person.

"Look, look!" the saleswoman cried. I had brought down more than Norma. We now sat and lay, respectively, amongst the porcelain shards of playing-card salt and pepper shakers and a music box, which had become excited by its plunge and played

"By the Sea, By the Sea" in a tinny up-tempo while miniature bathers in 1890 suits twirled under a beach umbrella.

"MY HERO," Mackenzie said later that evening, when I was allowed to violate visiting hours partially by virtue of having become an emergency room patient myself. "Notice my nonsexist language," he added.

Half my side was bandaged and the other half was black and blue; my back felt as if it contained a large, electrically charged metal plate; my green blazer was ruined; and the saltwater people were not rehiring Sasha, which meant the two of us were stuck with the hotel bill.

"I have to be honest," I said. "You make a pretty shabby Nero Wolfe. I was supposed to do a little footwork, that was all, then we were supposed to gather all the suspects around this bed. And then, you'd tell them who the guilty one was, and that guilty one would crumple."

"I must have forgotten." He looked almost sympathetic. His color was completely back, and his smile once again unfairly dazzling. "I would have helped you tomorrow, if you'd waited. They're releasing me."

"Sasha's getting out, too," I said. "It all worked quite tidily, don't you think? You're shot, she's imprisoned, and I'm embarking on a life of chronic pain. This qualifies as the world's worst vacation ever."

"If, that is, I can establish that I have somebody to, well, kind of . . ." It wasn't like Mackenzie to be coy or evasive. "Well, see," he said, "I can't move the leg for a while now, so I'm going to have some trouble takin' care of . . . of ever'thin'. Of me."

His eyes were back to their neon-blue and laugh lines—or perhaps slightly anxious lines—fanned out from them while he waited.

I spoke very softly. We were on thin and uncertain ground. "I assume that your medical coverage would handle a visiting nurse, wouldn't it?"

He nodded.

"So this isn't about saving money, as in C for cheap?"

He shook his head. "No, on both counts."

"Or about having an in-house slavey?"

He shook his head so vigorously his salt and pepper curls bounced. "You're a regionist. Unfair to the South and its people."

His accent escalated even though he appeared semiconscious on the surface. "As an experiment?" he asked softly.

I privately acknowledged that I had come to the beach to rest and to think the two of us through, and it was Mackenzie who'd wound up with both the time and the ability to do so. And he obviously had. Despite being a poetry lover, Mackenzie wasn't exactly quoting the Passionate Shepherd and saying "Come live with me and be my love"—but he was nonetheless saying "Let's get this moving forward."

And scaring me more than anything else had this week—or year.

Was it possible that *I* was the one who wasn't ready? That *I* counted on our never having the Big Talk or reaching crucial junctures? That I needed distance while Mackenzie needed partnership—the way the arcade computer had said?

"Well, hey," he said. "Don't panic. Since we both have time off now, I was thinkin' we could try this somewhere else, you know?"

He sounded like pure mush, farina with a few consonants, but he was giving me an out, a compromise solution.

"Mandy," he said. "I don' really need nursin' a-tall. Been trainin' on crutches and I did fine." The words drizzled out, consonants vaporized. His speech was in meltdown.

The man cared.

"You deserve a vacation," he said.

I laughed, even though it hurt. "Nobody deserves another vacation like the one I just had. Or, in fact, the one you just tried to have. Could we call it something else?"

"Agreed," he said softly. "So how 'bout we call it a start?"

ABOUT THE AUTHOR

GILLIAN ROBERTS is the *nom de mystère* of novelist Judith Greber. Under her mystery alias she has written four other Amanda Pepper adventures: *Caught Dead in Philadelphia,* winner of the Anthony Award for Best First Mystery; *Philly Stakes; I'd Rather Be in Philadelphia;* and *With Friends Like These . . .* A former English teacher in Philadelphia, she now lives in Tiburon, California.